CALLING

MOLLY HARPER

Calling

Ebook ISBN: 9781641971812
KDP Print ISBN: 9798784667823
IS Print ISBN: 9781641971942
Interior illustrations by Polina Hrytskova @PollyKul

NYLA Publishing
121 W 27th St., Suite 1201, New York, NY 10001
http://www.nyliterary.com

1

There was raspberry jam on the ceiling.

How did raspberry jam even reach a fifteen-foot ceiling?

Was it some sort of jam-specific spell? Was this the end-result of physics combined with the energy of a dozen rambunctious youngsters at breakfast? Or was I finally facing the fruit-based consequences of what had proven to be a series of ill-fated decisions I hadn't been prepared to make?

I stood in the dining room at Hazelcliffe Manor, staring at the ceiling, pondering these questions, when my closest friends, Ivy Cowell and Alicia McCray, approached, slipping their arms through mine.

"Strawberry?" Alicia guessed.

I shook my head. "Raspberry, actually."

"Hmm, that's new." Ivy pursed her lips. In unison, we tilted our heads as we gazed up at the jam constellation.

It had been a difficult few months here at Mrs. Winter's country estate in South Wickeshire. It sounded like such a simple idea at first. Step one, disrupt our holiday at Alicia's home in Coventry to search for a secret training facility we'd heard might be located in the nearby mountains where Changelings like myself were being trained to serve as bodyguards to the magical elite. Step two, use a flying airship, also owned by Alicia's family, to move those children across the country, somewhere safe, where they wouldn't be treated like tiny soldiers. Step three...

We never got around to figuring out step three.

Also, step two had been interrupted when my nemesis, Miss Morton, confronted us, burning the Mother Book and consuming the ashes to cement her place in a dead politician named Sebastian Crenshaw – while announcing her plans to use necromancy to attack magical society with an army of the re-animated dead.

Step two had gotten rather complicated.

And despite months of searching, we hadn't found a way to bring the Mother Book back from the ashes. It seemed vital to our success, having that knowledge back, and we'd thrown ourselves into the search whole-heartedly. But there simply wasn't a title in the Winters' library called, *How to Undo Your Massive Magical Foul-Up, Which Might Doom the Whole World*.

In anticipation of our arrival, Mrs. Winter had sent her staff away from Hazelcliffe Manor, which was perfect for our needs, but a far cry from her palatial mansion in the capitol city of Lightbourne. The estate was a working herb farm owned by Mrs. Winter's branch of the Brandywine family. The bucolic stone house was quite luxurious, all things considered. The rooms were spacious, painted in calming blues and filled with sunlight. It was exactly what the children needed, after being kept on a wind-plagued mountain for who knows how long. We were only meant to be there for a few weeks, but our residency had lasted through the winter months. Mrs. Winter had assigned the staff and farm tenders elsewhere, explaining that a floral blight had halted operations temporarily.

At first, the children's collective relief that they escaped the school was enough. They slept. They ate rich, filling meals, provided by the one adult they could trust from the mountain facility – their cook-slash-housemother, Mrs. Lumpkin. But they stayed in their rooms, unsure of what to do. And while Mrs. Lumpkin was handling a good deal of the cooking and cleaning, *someone* had to gather food from the kitchen garden. *Someone* had to gather eggs and milk the cows. *Someone* had to keep the house from becoming a pit of chaos and dirty socks.

More often than not, Alicia, Ivy, or I were that someone. While I had grown up as a servant in Mrs. Winter's house and could probably clean most of Hazelcliffe in a matter of hours, my friends were not accustomed to this sort of labor and sometimes left more serious messes in their wakes. Mrs. Lumpkin found their efforts endlessly entertaining, while also letting me know I didn't make beds up to her standards, either.

Eventually, the Changelings' uncertainty faded and they became… children. They ran. They played games in the gardens. They gathered in the kitchens for late-night biscuit raids. They staged massive food fights at the breakfast table.

I suspected this was how we ended up with jam on the ceiling.

While she was a housekeeping wonder, Mrs. Lumpkin was very little help when it came to bringing order to the household. She'd seen firsthand how callously the children, including her own son, Robert, had been treated at the "Crenshaw School for Gifted Youth." And she was just so thrilled to see them enjoying themselves and living comfortably, Mrs. Lumpkin couldn't bear to tell them "no." And yes, it was lovely to see smiles blooming on their faces, but I was the one who was going to have to explain to our hostess how we got jam on her ceiling.

"Mrs. Winter is not going to be happy about this," Alicia said. "Or the state of the library. Or the upstairs water closet."

"Alicia," Ivy interjected.

"Or the parlor," Alicia added.

"You're not helping," Ivy told her.

Alicia added, "Or the second-best parlor."

Ivy sighed and drew her ritual blade, Prudence, from her sleeve holster and drew the symbol for "cleanse" on the air. The light green shape floated gently toward the ceiling, like a stain on the air, where it effortlessly scraped the jam from the plaster. Unfortunately, we had not considered that the jam would have to land somewhere – and it landed on Alicia's face.

"I should have expected that," Alicia admitted, wiping the splotch of smashed fruit from her eyelids.

"I'm so sorry!" Ivy exclaimed, though it was from her attempts to hold in her cackles rather than the mortification she might have felt years ago. "It's not funny."

"No, it's very serious," I agreed, flattening my lips together and nodding. For the first time all week, laughter bubbled up from my throat. I coughed, making a sound like a constipated bagpipe. I glanced up at Ivy, at the sight of her face, a perfect cameo of brown skin, contorting as she tried to hold her giggles in – I covered my mouth with my hand. My shoulders quaked and I took deep gulping breaths.

"If you're going to laugh, you might as well do it now," Alicia muttered.

I burst out laughing, nearly collapsing into a dining chair. Ivy doubled over, howling, her dark curls bouncing wildly.

"You know, sometimes, I think we magicals forget about little things like gravity and need to be reminded," Alicia sighed as she drew the "cleanse" symbol on the air with her own blade, Resolve. The turquoise symbol floated upwards and the jam dropped harmlessly into a bowl I held.

I grinned at her. We'd managed to advance to wordless magic, simply drawing the symbols on the air with one's blade, over the years. And I was proud to have mastered a few advanced bladeless spells, even if they sometimes turned out badly. But for Alicia? Doing any spell well and without negative consequences was a major accomplishment. Just the previous year, she wouldn't have been able to aim a spell at her own person without risk of serious injury. From birth, Alicia had suffered from reverberation. When any practitioner used magic, the body suffered gradual damage from the energy drain of creating spells. Most practitioners were able to heal from this damage quickly. In reverb patients, the magic echoed inward and instead of healing, the damage festered and eventually killed them.

Alicia survived much longer than most reverb patients, because her mother's influence limited her to small spells. The disconnection from her magic, her very life force, kept Alicia undersized and sickly. Somehow, after combining magic between the three of us to defeat Miss Morton at Miss Castwell's, Alicia's magic had come back full-force and couldn't be contained. She was growing up before our eyes, physically and metaphysically. Once small and sickly, she was just as tall as I was now, leaping right over the awkward adolescent phase into creamy skin and a refined, elfin bone structure that emphasized her large green eyes.

"I would rather the reminders didn't land on my forehead," Alicia grumbled as Ivy wiped at her eyes.

"I would tell you I'm sorry, but that would be a lie," I giggled. "I really needed that."

"Being the de facto leader of a dozen or so children is rather stressful," Alicia agreed.

"I keep waiting for the other shoe to drop. For Mr. Crenshaw's re-animated corpse to show up at the front door," Ivy sighed. "Or worse, my grandmother."

I shuddered. I didn't want to think of Mr. Crenshaw's body, and how it trembled and collapsed when we cast Miss Morton out of it. But we had every reason to believe Miss Morton was still using that body as her "vehicle," considering that Mr. Crenshaw had been seen in Lightbourne, behaving in a distinctly not-dead fashion. Miss Morton had managed to impersonate him for months – long before we realized she was curling inside him, controlling him like a puppet, which was more than a little embarrassing. From what we heard, she was using Mr. Crenshaw's political authority to further her cause – revenge on Guild Guardian society at large for wiping her family off the map.

When I'd first arrived at Miss Castwell's, Miss Morton had approached me as a mentor, as a friend. I trusted her, only to find out that for her entire life, she'd hidden the fact that she was descended from the (not quite) extinct family of necromancers. I thought she'd recognized in me that element that didn't believe I belonged there. Instead, she was just trying to get access to the Mother Book, to drain us both of magical energy to launch her on this road to megalomania.

"Your grandmother isn't so bad," Alicia objected. "She only wants to rule your family, not the world as we know it."

"That *you're* aware of," Ivy muttered.

"Sarah!" a high, girlish voice shrieked upstairs.

I bolted for the staircase. It had been strange, returning to my real name, the name under which I'd served the Winter family. The other Changelings had been confused, me introducing myself as one of them, Sarah Smith, while I was known to my school friends as Cassandra Reed. So we'd all simply agreed that I return to myself, to Sarah. And while it was an adjustment at first for Alicia and Ivy, they made the effort, which only proved that they were worthy friends.

"You mentioned another shoe?" Alicia asked as we scrambled up the sweeping staircase to the guest wing. We ran past portraits of apple-cheeked, laughing Brandywines of generations gone-by – not exactly the memory I had of my sternly elegant former employer. Great Houses like the Brandywines and the Winters specialized in certain areas of magical research. The Brandywines were master gardeners, supplying herbs for potion markets around the world. They presented themselves as jolly farmers, but they were just as ambitious as the Winters, healers who balanced the art of curing the sick with their need to run the world. Mrs. Winter was the perfect blend of the two families' skill sets.

I ran to the guest bedroom where I was sleeping and found Lizzie, a little girl of around nine, pointing at my vanity mirror. After years of living in spartan facilities where little about her life was soft or pretty, Lizzie relished living with older girls. She would spend hours in our rooms, playing with our things, trying on our clothes, using our hairpins to arrange her lustrous black hair. She would bounce between our rooms, spending hours going through our trunks, gazing at herself in the mirror, imagining herself at a ball, practicing her fan-fluttering skills. She was just so earnest about it, we couldn't tell her no – which I supposed, made us no better than Mrs. Lumpkin. Besides, she never damaged what she played with. If anything, she would scold us for not being careful enough with *our* things.

Lizzie was hopping up and down, my lace shawl bouncing off her shoulders as she waved wildly. I paused, wondering how she was able to jump gracefully in high-heeled boots when I could barely walk in them. Lizzie took my face in her little hands and turned my head towards the glass. Bright red lines were forming on the mirror, shaping into letters.

Someone was sending me a scrying message. While formal invitations and society correspondence were sent by proper messengers on pressed linen paper, quick notes to close friends and family were written on mirrors with the tips of our blades. The words appeared instantaneously on the mirror nearest the intended recipient, no matter where they were. It was a rather ingenious method of communication, which Mrs. Winter and I had not made use of since our arrival at Hazelcliffe. Mrs. Winter worried our adversaries might find some magical means to intercept our private messages, so we'd taken several measures to obscure our location and identities – including addressing me as her fictional friend, Mrs. Agatha Pennythorn.

"Dearest Agatha,

I'm so pleased you and your companions are enjoying the countryside. While I was saddened to receive news that you couldn't travel to Lightbourne, please don't trouble yourself to return from your holiday. It would be a shame for you to cut your enjoyment short on my account, especially with the busy season upon us. Things are so tedious and hectic in town right now." Behind me, Ivy and Alicia clamored into the room, smacking into my back as more words appeared on the mirror. *Allow me to extend my invitation indefinitely, so you might enjoy the restful quiet of the country. Also, I am sending a parcel of much-needed essentials from our fair city. Country life should be a bit more agreeable with them. No need to thank me. Cordially, Annie."*

I chewed my lip, considering. "That's Mrs. Winter's handwriting, but that doesn't sound like Mrs. Winter."

"Mrs. Winter allows you to call her 'Annie'?" Alicia asked, frowning.

"Aneira Winter would never allow anyone to call her 'Annie'." I snorted. "Mrs. Winter once used the cut direct on an acquaintance, Wilhemina Pond, who had the nerve to call out her proper first name, without permission, on the sidewalk *in public*. Mrs. Winter pretended not to know her and climbed into her carriage. Mrs. Pond was removed from her research guild. Madame DuPont would no longer take dress commissions from her family. Mrs. Pond had to move to America where nobody knew her."

Alicia and Ivy winced in unison. Perhaps it had been a mistake, to use open, though vague, communication instead of complicated ciphers and codes that were so popular among the Guardian set these days. But it seemed to me the best way to show anyone who might be watching that we weren't trying to hide anything, and therefore, not worthy of monitoring, was to be as boring as possible. It took work to be this unremarkable.

"You have to look through the filter of passive aggression and figure out what she's really trying to say," I noted, pointing at the words. "Lizzie, could you go get Robert, Cathy, and Mrs. Lumpkin, please?"

Lizzie nodded, carefully folding my shawl and leaving it in a neat pile on the bed.

"Well, unlikely pet names aside, this isn't the *busy* season," Ivy scoffed. "Nothing happens in Lightbourne this early in the spring. My mother always complains how *bored* she is sitting around the house, waiting for invitations that will never come."

"Mrs. Winter wouldn't make a mistake like that unless she was trying to tell us something," I muttered. "Everything is so *tedious* and *hectic,* right now. That communicates a certain amount of annoyance and dread. Mrs. Winter hates anything tedious. She wouldn't give two figs for my *enjoyment*, but she wants me to stay in the *quiet* of the country where no one can find us."

"Something must be happening in town," Alicia reasoned. "She doesn't want us to move from our current location."

"And she doesn't want you to thank her," Ivy added.

"Which is also incredibly unlike her," I said. "Mrs. Winter is a stickler for observing the social graces. You respond to a thoughtful message with another thoughtful message. So, she doesn't want me to respond. I suppose she's still worried that someone is watching our communications."

"What's happening?" Robert asked as he, Cathy, and Mrs. Lumpkin filed into the room, with Lizzie trailing behind them. As the oldest people in the house, we'd formed a sort of council of elders to make decisions for our group. The next oldest Changelings, Joseph and May, were only twelve and it seemed cruel to force them back out of the childhood they were enjoying for the first time.

Alicia blushed a hilarious shade of magenta at the sight of Robert. In the weeks since we'd arrived at Hazelcliffe, the two of them hadn't formally defined their relationship, which was really none of our business. She was happy and that was all that mattered. However, watching her cheeks go bright colors whenever he entered a room was one of the highlights of my day. But I had no time to enjoy it now. I would have to file it away for later consideration.

"Mrs. Winter seems to think it wouldn't be safe for us to try to move at the end of the month as planned," I said. "Something must be happening in Lightbourne."

"Would it be worth going to the nearest town? Looking for a newspaper?" Robert suggested.

Alicia clutched at his hand. "No, you couldn't. It's too risky."

"We've stayed here too long as it is," Cathy insisted. "You know what that Miss Morton wants to do. We need to stop her or get out of England and find some place that's safe from her."

"There's no place that will be safe from her, if she gets what she wants," I countered.

"All the more reason to move," Cathy told me.

Cathy was a lithe, quick-witted girl around our age, who had been called "honey" by Mrs. Lumpkin when she'd been living at the mountain school. Of all the people at Hazelcliffe, Cathy worried me the most. The last time I'd made friends with a Changeling my own age – the first fellow Changeling I'd ever met – she'd stolen the Mother Book and gave it to Miss Morton. My former ladies' maid, Jenny, hadn't wanted magic. She just wanted to go back to her life the way she knew it. That hadn't happened, of course. I presumed Jenny was still with Miss Morton somewhere. I hoped she was all right. Unlike my own sister, Mary, who had sided with Miss Morton against me – out of pure spite, rather than desperation – I couldn't be angry with Jenny. She'd only wanted normalcy.

I just didn't want to repeat that experience with Cathy. She was unhappy, as Jenny had been, and unhappiness could make people do desperate things. So, we'd given Cathy what we hoped was the space to be herself and find some peace. When she found a few old-fashioned riding habits in the attic, at least twenty years out of date but much more comfortable to run about the farm in, we offered to hem them and make them more comfortable for her. When she cut her dark hair off at the nape of her neck, sending Mrs. Lumpkin into an all-out tizzy, we offered her our hair pins to make styling it a bit easier. Cathy ignored our offers, but at least she was less verbal about doubting every single move we made.

For the most part.

At least, to our faces.

"There's too many of us to just run into the night, without a plan, Cathy," Ivy said gently. "We can't put the smaller children at risk."

Appealing to Cathy's love for her unofficial siblings might have seemed like a low blow, but it was an effective one. She would never put the other Changelings in danger, so she simply pursed her lips into an unhappy line and grumbled, "Fine."

"So, we're staying here for now?" Mrs. Lumpkin asked, stepping between her son and Alicia. Mrs. Lumpkin didn't really like that Robert was interested in Alicia. She didn't think that anyone was good enough for her "sweetling." The fact that Alicia was an heiress to one of the largest fortunes in magical England made very little difference to her – which was also very entertaining… for Ivy and myself, not Alicia. She didn't find it amusing in the least.

"It would appear so," Ivy said.

"Well, that's a relief," Mrs. Lumpkin said, shrugging. "My rhubarb isn't due to come in for another few weeks."

"Yes, rhubarb was the key to the girls' strategy, Mum," Robert said. Mrs. Lumpkin swatted at him lightly, even as she smiled. Like me, Robert had shown signs of magic when he was just a baby – which was supposed to be impossible for us, and all of the other Changeling children, because we were born into non-magical "Snipe" families.

Generations before our births, magical people had been quite alarmed at the scientific progress that non-magicals had managed to make during something called "the Industrial Revolution." While Guardians might have enjoyed the luxuries of steam engines and gas energy, magical practitioners from across the world agreed that non-magicals would eventually create weapons beyond magic's strength or ability to protect magical society. Magical families hadn't agreed on any issue for generations, but they agreed to form an international "Coven Guild" to approach non-magical governments all over the world. Those governments were informed that the Coven Guild would be running things from now on. It was their job to protect us from the escalating threat of our own technological innovations, they claimed, before we did real damage to the planet and ourselves.

Over the years, the world's course was reversed to a system where non-magicals were a paid servant class with no political power. We worked in Guardian households. We learned trades. We earned a fair wage. That was the best we could hope for. Guardians made decisions that shaped society, the economy, and magic itself. As long as they were accepted into the right research guilds after graduation from their various schools, they could study any number of magical occupations.

My family did not have magic, nor did any of our friends and neighbors. I was told so every day of my life. I believed it, right until the moment I levitated one of Mrs. Winter's favorites vases out of sheer panic. My parents, who worked as the Winters' housekeeper and gardener, had given me magical suppressants as a toddler to hide these talents. Like Alicia, it kept me under-sized and sickly, until the day my magic decided it wouldn't be contained any longer.

Afraid that her family would suffer social and political ruin, Mrs. Winter gave me a false identity and placed me at Miss Castwell's Institute for the Magical Instruction of Young Ladies as her heretofore unknown distant cousin from the expansive Brandywine side of her family. And for a few months, my life had been a bit of a fairy tale – the Changeling child born with magic she wasn't supposed to have, who learned to live among the rich and powerful... until I made the mistake of befriending the school librarian, Miss Morton.

I thought I'd been alone in the world, the only Snipe born with magic in history. After revealing her true character, Miss Morton had laughed at my ego – rightfully so. I wasn't the Chosen One. I wasn't even the chosen one in a dozen. Certain powerful Guild Guardians had known about Changelings' existence for years, but had kept it to themselves. They made a resource out of children like me, training Changelings to serve as magical, expendable bodyguards. That's what was happening at the mountain school. Robert and Cathy were supposed to be the next graduates.

"I still don't like this," Cathy told me, giving her usual disapproving grimace. "We can't sit around forever, waiting and planning. Your Miss Morton isn't just planning. That madwoman is on the *move*."

"I won't say that you're wrong, Cathy, but the goal is the same as it always has been, to keep us all safe," I said. "Anything else – like preventing Miss Morton from taking over magical society as we know it – is merely icing on the cake."

"That answer is vague and unhelpful, as most of your answers so far have been," Cathy sneered. "I suppose I should congratulate you on your consistency."

"If you have a better plan, Cathy, we're more than willing to hear it," Ivy replied.

As Cathy did not have a better plan, she huffed out of the room without another word – which I supposed was better than a direct insult. It was at times like this, I really missed the Mother Book. The book was the one special thing about me in this group. As the Translator, I was the only person who could read its magical cuneiform, spells, and information left behind by previous generations, and discover its secrets. Every time I'd needed answers over the previous year, the book would guide me. I would approach it with a question on my mind and it would flop open to some page that would eventually lead me in the general direction of the information I needed. It was never a direct route, because that would be too easy, and the book wanted me to learn.

To be fair, Cathy was right to be frustrated with me. I was simply moving too slowly. I couldn't seem to make a decision or consider an idea without seeing all the things that could go wrong. I'd never been responsible for so much before, beholden to so many – and not just in terms of the people in this house, but everyone. No matter what I did, there was a huge chance that many people could get hurt. Innocent people. People I loved. And at night, when I was alone, staring up at the canopy over my bed, a tiny, shameful part of me wanted to give up, go home, go back to my normal life, where I didn't know anything about magic or secret evils or how the world really worked. I wanted to go back to my parents and their lovely mundane, not-potentially-world-ending problems. But I couldn't. I'd seen too much. Most of it, I saw through the ever-shifting pages of the Mother Book.

And I supposed, that never knowing magic would have meant never meeting Ivy or Alicia, never knowing real friendship. It would have meant never meeting Alicia's brother, Gavin, who I was almost certainly in love with – though I hadn't had time to fully explore what that meant, either.

I paused, stroking the charm bracelet on my wrist with tiny books attached to the chain. It was a library I could carry on my arm. Gavin had given it to me as a courting gift. It was one of the few personal things I'd kept with me on our "travels," besides my ritual blade, Wit.

I turned to Alicia and Ivy. We were having growing pains of our own since coming to the farm. We were accustomed to having every moment of our day scheduled and managed for us. Gone were the Castwell green gowns laid out for us each morning. We had to decide how we would spend our days, what we would wear, what we would eat and when. It was terrifying to suddenly have so much control of our daily lives… and that was when we didn't take into account the magical and social revolution we had inadvertently started.

I was becoming a young adult and I didn't much care for it.

As usual, my familiar, an imperious blue-green songbird named Phillip, sensed my distress and landed on my shoulder with a peep, nuzzling against my neck. I got the strange feeling that maybe Phillip missed the book as well. He'd spent a lot of time in my room, on his little driftwood perch near the bookstand, well, sulking, in a bird-ish manner.

"Missing the Mother Book again?" Ivy asked, while Mrs. Lumpkin frowned. Phillip was the only familiar at Hazelcliffe and she did not approve of animals roaming unfettered in the house.

I nodded. "I can't help but think that if I had the book, I would have some idea of where to start."

"Again, with that silly book. No use crying over spilled milk, Sarah. Better to make use of what you have," Mrs. Lumpkin grumbled. "And *I* have pies in the oven. Let me know if there are any more dramatic announcements. Keep the bird out of my kitchen."

"Mum doesn't really know what it's like to have a familiar," Robert told me gently. "Or what it's like to lose a centuries-old artifact that contained all the magical knowledge of generations past."

"Thank you, Robert," I said, nodding.

"You could always try to make a new book, you know?" Lizzie told me from my vanity seat, where she was carefully braiding my Castwell green ribbons into her hair.

I stopped suddenly, turning towards her. "What do you mean?"

"Geoffrey's father was a book binder, before he came to the mountain school. He knows all about making books. He would tell us very boring stories about it at mealtimes," Lizzie said, flipping her braids over her shoulders. "You should ask him."

"Lizzie, you know we've been looking for a way to bring back the Mother Book for months. Why didn't you say anything before now?" I asked.

Before flouncing out the door, she said, "You didn't ask."

"Do you think that could work?" Ivy asked as I stared after Lizzie, speechless. All of our attentions were focused on retrieving the book from its destroyed state. It hadn't occurred to me that we had the will or the right to create a new one.

"I don't see why not," Alicia said. "You said the book was more aware than most objects, that it had a mind of its own. Maybe we just try to invite that mind into another book?"

"Or we could create a new monster that we have to fight off

instead of concentrating on the Miss Morton problem," Ivy sighed.

"That is also a valid point," Robert agreed.

"Please stop agreeing with us," I told him.

He smirked. "All right, then."

"Robert!" I snapped at him, but with little heat, because I was laughing.

Alicia gave him a fond look. "As much as I enjoy you vexing my friends, now may not be the right time."

"It's always the right time for that," he replied. "The faces they make are hilarious."

IT TURNED out that all we needed to do was to give the children a joint project and they became a creative force to be reckoned with – a truly terrifying creative force.

Geoffrey, a small boy around eleven years old, whom Mrs. Lumpkin had called "sugar lump," was more than happy to tell me anything I wanted to know about assembling books from paper, canvas, and linen. His father didn't make magical books, of course, but he assured us that assembling one would be simple enough if we were willing to dismantle other books for spare blank pages. Every book seemed to have a few blanks, but to get to them, we would have to tear the books apart. Mrs. Winter's library books. I tried not to think of that part as I stacked potential titles on the library table.

Meanwhile, Robert went outside to find a birch tree stump, which he planed into thin rectangles to serve as covers. He spent hours in the garden shed, sanding the planks smooth, but I suspected he was just staying out there longer than necessary, just for the sake of peace and quiet. Meggie, a ten-year-old with pale, freckled cheeks and flaming ginger curls, crawled through the attic to find a bolt of undyed linen in an old hope chest. Lizzie offered up her favorite hair ribbons to use as binding cords. Her giving them up for "the cause" was oddly touching, even though they were technically my hair ribbons.

As the children descended on the library to find more suitable titles to deconstruct, we realized there were other problems to consider besides Mrs. Winter's bibliographical wrath. For one thing, we didn't have a book press or printer's ink. And there was also Ivy's notion that we would accidentally create an evil version of the Mother Book, which sometimes woke me up in the middle of the night in a cold sweat.

"How are you going to remake a priceless font of ancient wisdom from pieces you're scavenging from other books?" Cathy demanded from the second-level balcony, which housed histories of England's magical families. She glared down at me, hands on her hips.

The library was my favorite room in Hazelcliffe Manor. Shelves, bursting with books, lined the room from floor-to-ceiling, which might have made the room feel claustrophobic, if not for the large windows on the second level. On the (frequent) evenings when I couldn't sleep, I curled in one of the deep leather wingback chairs, flanking the large fireplace, staring into the flames. Over the white marble mantle, the Winter's sigil of a raven plunging at an apple, had replaced the Brandywine blossoms. It reminded me of my first day of Miss Castwell's, when the book had broken through its glass display case to mark me as Translator.

"I just… have a feeling," I told Cathy, rubbing at the dragonfly mark on my palms, a gift from the Mother Book on the day it chose me. "I know it doesn't make much sense, but so much of my work with the book was based on feeling magic, instead of knowing it."

"You're right, that doesn't make any sense," Cathy told me.

I shrugged. "This just feels like the right thing to do. And if you don't want to help, you don't have to."

"She's going to help," Meggie shouted, shooting a hostile look at Cathy. "She's just being contrary. It's all she's done since we got here."

Cathy pulled a rude face at Meggie, whom Mrs. Lumpkin had called "little bairn" at the school. Mrs. Lumpkin would not have appreciated Cathy making faces at her darling. Part of me wondered whether this hostility was Cathy's true personality or if it was simply a response to being kept in that harsh place for years, raised by so-called adults who didn't encourage her to feel human emotions. Maybe she was only displaying negative emotions like disdain and distrust because she hadn't been allowed to express them at the school. I hoped it meant she felt safe with us. Or at the very least, she would eventually display something else.

"We appreciate your support, Cathy," Ivy told her.

Cathy grumbled and tossed aside a copy of *The Rise and Fall of House Grimstelle.* I caught it and tucked the book into my "late night reading" pile, because it could eventually prove useful. Grimstelle had been Miss Morton's family house, a once-powerful group of necromancers that had been pruned from magical society after their experiments and in-fighting were deemed too dangerous to the public good. Miss Morton was a fringe descendent, deeply resentful of losing her place in society, the family money, the legacy she believed was hers.

There were moments where I ever-so-briefly sympathized with Miss Morton. Every House had its magical gifts – for House Cavill, it was mystical metallurgy; for Brandywine, it was horticulture – why should Miss Morton suffer, simply because her family's gift could be dangerous? But then I remembered that Miss Morton had actively used that gift to put me and my own in peril and my sympathies dried up.

Shaking my head, I turned back to the books in my hands. Harvesting them made sense. The blank pages had been stored in those books for decades, and they'd been absorbing all the magic over the years. But destroying Mrs. Winter's books? Flinging jam at her ceiling was one thing – willfully destroying her precious cache of botany books was another.

I thumbed through a copy of *Vibrations of Crystals from Amethyst to Zektzerite.* Between the title page and the opening text, there were two entirely blank sheets of paper. Taking a deep breath, I closed my eyes and pulled the paper from the book's spine.

"So we have enough books to pull pages from? Excellent." Alicia noted gleefully, joining me at the table. I nodded, putting the paper aside.

"You look like you might throw up," Ivy told me.

"It's very likely," I said, as the others took up their own books and began ripping out papers. We spent hours in that fashion, paring blank pages from the books and clearing away damaged editions once we were done. The scavenged books were placed in a pile that we would probably bury in the backyard and never speak of again. Eventually, I had a stack of two hundred pages roughly the same size.

I took Wit out of my sleeve holster as the dragonfly mark hummed. Just like I'd told Cathy, sometimes magic was about following instinct instead of a plan, and assembling the book now *felt* right.

"Wait, we're going to try this now?" Ivy exclaimed.

"No time like the present. I think we've waited long enough, don't you?" I asked them. Both Alicia and Ivy gave me apprehensive looks, but joined me, nonetheless.

Meggie ran for the linen and wood we'd collected while Lizzie threw the ribbons at me. I didn't even know what spell to use, but my hand was moved by some invisible force to make an eight-shaped sigil. It felt like "bind" and left a bright gold stain upon the air. I was acting on instinct, and some of the best magic I'd work came from instinct. It felt *right.*

The others gathered around me, hands joined, watching as the papers flew into the air, swirling in a strange, bird-like flight pattern over our heads. Magic crackled between them, in a rainbow of lightning against the ceiling. The wood planks and linen floated upward and for just a second, it looked like the lot of them were going to form a bookish shape. Lizzie hopped up and down, clapping, as the ribbons snaked upwards to the paper. "Look!"

Alicia and Ivy joined hands. All of us seemed to hold our breath as the whole arrangement seemed "this" close to a finished book. I could almost feel that connection to the Mother Book, reaching out, nudging against my magic like an old friend bumping my ribs with her elbow. But then the connection broke and I felt it slip away.

And suddenly, chaos.

2

The papers exploded out of formation into a snowfall of burning bits. The wooden covers spun across the room and shattered on either side of the Winter raven sigil over the mantle. The ribbons dropped to the table, a pair of smoldering snakes. The pile of discarded, damaged book bits in the corner burst into flames. The other children scattered out of the library, yelling. Even Robert stumbled back, dragging Alicia with him, as the flames reached towards the ceiling. Cathy had abandoned the library – and us – without a single look back.

"How is there a fire?" Alicia yelled from Robert's arms.

"I don't know!" I shouted back, while flailing my hands in a most undignified manner.Ivy rolled her eyes and pulled her blade from her sleeve. She drew some symbol I didn't recognize on the air and sent it flying towards the fire. The bright purple shape hovered over the blaze, forming a sort of sparkling bubble around it. It shrank, weakening until it snuffed out with a hiss of smoke.

"Tell me honestly. You both forget that you have magic sometimes, don't you?" she sighed, clearly disappointed in the both of us.

"To be fair, I just got magic recently," I protested.

Now, we only had to contend with the dark gray smoke roiling through the air, making it difficult to breathe. Well, that and the screaming children. We coughed, waving the smoke away from our faces. The library was in absolute shambles.

"We need to vent the smoke!" Alicia insisted as I magically gathered our materials. They were – much to my surprise – mostly undamaged. Alicia and Robert strode to the windows, opening those that would budge.

"What in the world are you lot doing in there?" Mrs. Lumpkin yelled from the kitchen.

"Nothing!" we cried as a unit, glancing guiltily at each other.

"What was that?" I asked Ivy as she used that handy "cleanse" spell to gather the ashes from the carpet.

"Well, the nicest way to describe it is a sphere of suffocation," she said. "It's supposed to be an offensive spell, sucks the oxygen out of the air in a defined space, which would slow someone down fairly effectively in a fight. But it's also useful when it comes to unexpected blazes."

"That's rather sinister," Alicia noted from the open window as she sucked in great lungfuls of air.

Ivy shrugged as we walked to the front door, hoping to create a cross-breeze to let more of the smoke filter out. "It's not as if Miss Morton is going to throw confetti at us."

"She makes a valid point," Alicia said.

"Don't show that spell to Cathy," Robert called from the library.

I opened the front door and immediately yelped at the sight of an adult, backlit by the late afternoon sun. Reflexively, I threw up my arm and a wave of magical energy *flexed* around me. And then I realized very quickly, I'd made a mistake.

Dora Lockwood, Castwell's very proper headmistress, stood outside Hazelcliffe Manor's door. She was wearing a sensible brown tweed traveling gown with a matching wide-brimmed hat, pinned to her iron gray hair. She was pallid and travel-weary and slightly annoyed and I'd just thrown a magical shield at her. Her sensibly clad feet actually scooted back a few inches before she squared her shoulders and halted immediately.

Tilting her head, she looked past me and watched as the children scrambled around the house, screaming about the fire. Geoffrey and Robert carried the book ashes towards the kitchen, pausing at the sight of a newcomer, before continuing on their way.

Headmistress Lockwood coughed, and somehow it sounded judgmental. She waved her hand in front of her face. "Well, ladies, I see that you continue to sow confusion and disarray wherever you go."

ALICIA, Ivy, and I sat under a barely green arbor behind Hazelcliffe, pretending that Headmistress Lockwood wasn't glowering at us like we'd been summoned to her office at Castwell's for crimes against magical academia.

Alicia, who spent a good portion of her time lying to her overbearing mother's face about her whereabouts and activities, was the best at appearing completely unaffected. Between sips of tea, she stared up at the lilacs growing overhead as if they were the most interesting thing she'd seen in her entire life. Ivy and I were less successful. It was difficult to remember that this woman wasn't our headmistress anymore, as we, technically, weren't enrolled at any school, much less hers. Also, she had a very effective glare.

We'd barely managed to compose ourselves from the shock of Headmistress Lockwood's arrival when Mrs. Lumpkin had ushered us all out into the garden. Mrs. Lumpkin didn't even blink at the sight of a strange adult in the house after so long in seclusion. Since we weren't screaming or declaring this intruder to be dangerous, Mrs. Lumpkin just assured us she would have the house to rights in a blink while none-too-gently shoving us out of the door. And then it occurred to me that as the de facto hostess at Hazelcliffe – or at least, the only person present who had a connection with Mrs. Winter – it was up to me to start the conversation. I'd never hosted anything in my life. In fact, the very idea made me a little ill. I hadn't even prepared refreshments for our visitor. Mrs. Winter always presented visitors with a lovely tea tray piled high with little sandwiches and iced cakes. I was failing utterly.

Fortunately, Mrs. Lumpkin had far more social skills than I did and bustled out with shiny silver service laden with goodies. I had no idea how she even managed to bake the little cakes with all the other tasks she took on in the kitchen. She was like my own mother – a wonder of quiet, long-suffering competence.

Mrs. Lumpkin carefully set the tray on the table and put a reassuring hand on my shoulder before rushing back into the house – presumably before the children could find her hidden cache of secret cakes. This led me to another hurdle. I never served anyone tea in my life. I merely delivered the trays and left the social niceties to those qualified for them. Fortunately, Ivy sensed my distress and immediately began assembling the hot water and leaves. That left me to attend to the conversation.

I cleared my throat. "So, Headmistress Lockwood, what brings you to Hazelcliffe Manor? Shouldn't you be at Miss Castwell's… running Miss Castwell's?"

I was proud that I managed to keep my voice so steady when I had so many other questions. How did Miss Lockwood find us? Why was she here? Had something happened to our families? But as Miss Lockwood didn't seem distressed beyond her usual level of annoyance, I assumed that nothing catastrophic had happened.

"I have resigned from my position at Miss Castwell's." Miss Lockwood sniffed, before sipping her tea. "To be honest, I wanted to leave before I was dismissed. I bribed every watchmaker in Lightbourne to alert me if any gold watches were ordered from their shops, any watches inscribed with my name and any message of thanks for my service. When I received word, I resigned immediately. I refused to be tossed aside into 'retirement' like so much rubbish."

"Who would have the power to dismiss you?" Ivy asked.

"I'm being replaced by some young nitwit whose father is on the Senate's committee for education. She's never taught a day in her *life*. She's not even a graduate of Castwell's. She went to a ladies' finishing school in *Switzerland*."

Though it occurred to me that Swiss magical boarding schools had an excellent reputation, it would not do to point that out. Besides, all three of us were struck silent. It had never occurred to me that Headmistress Lockwood's position at the school wasn't permanent. Miss Castwell's and Headmistress Lockwood had always seemed like a combined symbiotic organism. And she never struck me as someone who cared about impressing her superiors. If you'd asked me at school, I probably would have told you I wasn't sure she was aware she had superiors.

Headmistress Lockwood told me, "Do close your mouth, my dear. You look like a dying salmon."

My jaw snapped upward with a click of my teeth.

"I'm sorry, Headmistress Lockwood. We know how much the school means to you," Ivy said, covering my inability to produce words.

"I suppose, under the circumstances, you should simply call me, 'Miss Lockwood'," she conceded.

I shuddered. It seemed unnatural and *wrong* somehow, to call her 'Miss Lockwood.' It seemed worse than calling Mrs. Winter by 'Annie.' Suddenly, I remembered Mrs. Winter referring to a "parcel" of essentials that would make life in the country easier. It seemed obvious now that she'd meant Miss Lockwood. It was all I could do not to bury my face in my hands. Could she have possibly given me a less helpful hint?

Also, I would *never* tell Miss Lockwood that Mrs. Winter had referred to her as a "parcel." Never.

"How did you find us?" I asked. "Does anyone else know that you're here?"

Miss Lockwood accepted the prepared cup from Ivy with a wan smile. "Thank you, Miss Cowell. Well, your families have not been very adept at designing a believable excuse for your continued absence from society. One hears all sorts of outlandish stories. It's been said that all three of you contracted a fever while staying in Scotland and you're taking the waters at Baden-Baden. Another tale spread by the girls at school insists that you, Miss McCray, are being courted by the Duke of Nova Scotia, and Misses Reed and Cowell are serving as your chaperones."

"There are no dukedoms in Nova Scotia," I noted.

"Yes, I found that rumor to be the most distressing as it revealed how little some of my students understood geography," Miss Lockwood groused. "Before I left, I redesigned the school curriculum to include more world studies than dance lessons this fall."

"I doubt the students will thank us for that," I murmured.

Alicia snickered and cleared her throat to cover it. Mrs. Winter had made some attempts to cover for our sudden departure from Coventry. She'd assured the Cowells that we were simply taking our time, enjoying the sights of the countryside and would return home in time for school to begin. Despite the rumors flying about, the Cowells were so convinced that their daughter was a perfect, faultless being who would never lie to them, that they believed Mrs. Winter completely. Mrs. McCray, on the other hand, had hired multiple men-of-business to track us. Mrs. Winter had written that the queries were becoming quite annoying.

"But the most preposterous rumor of all was that you'd been allowed on an unescorted tour of the Continent, gallivanting about museums and historic sites," Miss Lockwood drawled. "As if you could do that without leaving the entire continent in smoking ruins."

"I would say that's unfair, but..." I glanced towards the house, where a gray haze was still drifting out of the library windows.

"And you decided to seek us out for yourself?" Alicia asked. "How, exactly?"

For the first time since she arrived, Miss Lockwood seemed pleased. "It's an ingenious little bit of spell work on my part, even if I do say so myself. Miss McCray, your mother was very concerned that your condition would worsen without warning and you could be left alone somehow, somewhere on campus without anyone realizing that you'd taken ill. So, at the beginning of each school year, including this one, I would ask Nurse Lacewing to add a vitamin solution to your medication schedule. The potion allowed me to track your location at any time, to ease your mother's anxieties."

Ivy and I were shocked speechless, gaping at her, while Alicia managed to squeak out. "You've been tracking me?"

"Not actively," Miss Lockwood assured her. "In fact, I've never had to use it because you never took ill. Not seriously ill, at least. But when I began to hear all these strange rumors about your whereabouts, I became curious. I activated the spell, looked on a map and imagine my surprise that you were in South Wickeshire. Specifically, on one of Mrs. Winter's family estates, after she insisted that you were still enjoying the charms of Coventry."

"And how long does the effect of the potion last?" Alicia demanded.

Miss Lockwood waved her hand dismissively. "It wears off every fall, just in time for us to give you another dose at the beginning of the year. So, it's fortunate that I decided to look for you now."

Alicia's face went even paler. "I am very unhappy about that."

"Why hasn't Alicia's mother used the spell to track her here?" Ivy asked, her hand on Alicia's shoulder.

"Knowing your mother as I do, I never gave her the means to use the spell for her own purposes," Miss Lockwood told her.

"Well, I suppose that's something," Alicia huffed. "And should we worry about the teachers from the Crenshaw school putting similar spells on them?"

"I'm certain that if they did, they would have shown up at Hazelcliffe's door by now," Ivy muttered. "They don't seem like the type to give the children a long holiday."

"Most likely, they were over-confident in their ability to keep the children contained," Miss Lockwood said, sounding almost proud as she added, "They hadn't counted on the three of you."

My eyes narrowed at my former headmistress. Clearly, she hadn't told Alicia or Ivy's parents that she'd found our location, because Mrs. McCray hadn't kicked the door down to drag Alicia back home. So why was she here?

"I suppose, given the suspicious frown you are making no effort to conceal, Miss Smith, that you're wondering what brought me here," she said, making me sit back in the chair. Though I knew she couldn't read minds – at least, I was ninety percent sure – our former teacher's ability to read our facial expressions was always unnerving.

"Mrs. Winter told me everything," she added.

I was sure my expression shifted from curious to aghast.

How had that happened? Mrs. Winter and Miss Lockwood had been bitter enemies since their schooldays, something about Mrs. Winter teasing Miss Lockwood for being shallow and vain… which was honestly, hard to imagine. Their enmity had almost kept me from being allowed to enroll at Miss Castwell's. I still wasn't sure how the day would have ended, had I not been chosen by the Mother Book.

"Yes, I doubt she would have done so, with any other option available to her when I confronted her, but here we are. So, yes, I know how you three came to be hiding here. I know, that somehow, you managed to lose the Mother Book to Miss Morton's machinations, while somehow also making her more powerful. And I know that you are a Changeling, Miss Smith."

I swallowed heavily. "Oh, dear."

"I should be annoyed, I suppose, that you were able to move about the school undetected, but I find that I'm impressed," she said airily. "A bit mystified, actually, how you adjusted so well. I've suspected for years that such things were possible, but of course, I never met a Changeling myself, until now. It will be interesting to observe your techniques now that I know."

"What's happening? Back in Lightbourne?" I asked suddenly. "There's no love lost between you and my former employer. She wouldn't have sent you here unless the situation was dire."

Miss Lockwood's dark eyebrows winged up, so I added, "I thought we were speaking truths. Mrs. Winter wouldn't have told you about me or sent you here without reason. Has something changed in the capitol? Are you the reason she just told us not to leave Hazelcliffe?"

Sensing my distress, Ivy and Alicia instinctively reached for my arms, laying hands on my wrists. More than ever, I could feel their magic nudging against mine as surely as I could feel the warmth of their skin through my cotton sleeves. This was a recent development, likely related to the spell we'd used against Miss Morton to unmake her into the strange ghostly being she was now. I didn't know why this sensitivity to each other was only developing now at Hazelcliffe. Maybe because I'd spent so much time dreading Alicia's vision of Lightbourne in ruins, overrun by fog and the undead, that I couldn't open myself up to that connection? Maybe because I'd spent so much time in Scotland trying to protect Ivy and Alicia from being hurt by keeping them at a distance? I could only hope it was a positive development that would help us prevent what we feared. I'd spent far too much time being afraid.

"It would be better to be honest with us, ma'am," Alicia noted quietly. "Why would Mrs. Winter not tell us you were coming here?"

I would also have to remind Alicia and Ivy never to tell Miss Lockwood about the "parcel" reference.

"Because we didn't want anyone to follow me if your communications were monitored." Miss Lockwood sighed. "The attempt to force me into retirement is part of a larger scheme, I'm afraid, though I can't see its full design. Mrs. Winter wanted someone she could, well, I won't use the word 'trust,' but she wanted to know that you and the children were safe and supervised. And as I am an unmarried woman, I can disappear far easier than Aneira Winter. Especially when Mr. Winter is so firmly within Mr. Crenshaw's sites."

I gaped at her and she gave me another pointed look. I closed my mouth quickly.

"Mr. Winter has been appointed to multiple committees in the last few months, legislative responsibilities he has spent a lifetime vigorously avoiding. He can't refuse without appearing to be quite suspicious," she said. "And while it might appear to be a promotion, particularly as Mr. Winter is now practically living in the Senate headquarters, Mrs. Winter assumes that this is a warning to her, that if the Winter family doesn't quietly abide Mr. Crenshaw's agenda, they will suffer. Mr. Crenshaw, or should I say, Miss Morton, can hurt Mr. Winter much more effectively as he's close at hand. Any number of options, from physical injury to political scandal, are at her disposal."

Ivy's brows rose. "Mrs. Winter told you about Mr. Crenshaw?"

"Yes, if for no other reason than to remind me that Miss Morton managed to work under my nose for years without my realizing her nefarious intentions," Miss Lockwood muttered. "It's still hard to believe that Morton has taken over Crenshaw's body. It's even more disturbing that you can't see a difference in his behavior. She's an adept mimic. I'll give her that."

Guilt and alarm seemed to be fighting for control of my

nervous system. Cathy had been right – here we were, hiding in the countryside while Miss Morton was proceeding with her plans. Mr. Winter was in danger. Magical society was in danger. And we were endangering the library with misplaced spells.

"Well, ladies, I do not mind telling you that I am disappointed." Miss Lockwood set her cup aside with a clearly disappointed *clink*. "I taught you far better than this – dignity, discipline, responsibility."

"Well, this was our first fire, magical or otherwise," I protested.

"Though I commend you for attempting to reclaim the Mother Book, we'll discuss that ill-fated attempt at spell work later," she replied dryly. "But I am referring to the sad state of affairs in which I find you. The three of you are merely attempting to survive, instead of thrive. These children aren't receiving any sort of instruction, so of course, they're out of sorts and rowdy. They have no structure to their day. The housekeeper has shown herself to be a capable woman, but it's patently unfair to put her in charge of so many, particularly, when she has the responsibility of keeping this household from collapsing on itself. And was that strawberry jam on the dining room ceiling?

"It was raspberry," we replied together.

"I've asked Mrs. Lumpkin to prepare a room for me in the guest wing and I will require space in the library. I will devise a schedule to keep the children occupied and the house standing," she said, rising from her chair. "The new regimen begins tomorrow morning."

"Miss Lockwood, what of the situation in Lightbourne?" I asked, as she began walking toward the house. "Don't you have any suggestions?"

"Of course not, I'm not the Translator," she retorted. "If I were you, I would focus on a much more thoughtful approach to resurrecting the Mother Book. We will discuss your losing the most important artifact in magical history at another time."

My head bowed, to hide my embarrassed expression. With that, she turned on her heel and walked away.

"Did she just assign us homework?" Alicia asked, staring after her.

I nodded. "Yes, she did."

"Is she allowed to do that?" Ivy wondered.

"Are you going to tell her 'no'?" I countered.

As Miss Lockwood disappeared into the garden in a swish of skirts, I stared after her, feeling oddly bereft.

"I don't think she can give us demerits any longer," Ivy told me gently. "There's no reason to look so distressed."

"I know," I said, shaking my head. "But it had almost been a relief, to have another adult present who might advise us, to take a little of the weight from our shoulders. And it appears that Miss Lockwood has no plans to do that."

Alicia scoffed. "We've been doing just fine on our own."

"When we were on our own, we came up with a plan to spirit a bunch of children off a mountainside in a flying boat and hide out in the country with no supervision," Ivy reminded her.

"And it was a plan that worked!" Alicia exclaimed.

"I think we need to review your understanding of the word 'work'," I replied.

3

As Miss Lockwood promised, the children were on a schedule again by the next morning, and they did *not* appreciate it. When she woke them by ringing a bell that magically echoed through each of their rooms, they stumbled in their pajamas into the foyer, rubbing at their eyes. They stared at the new adult in the household, curiosity barely tamped by their irritation at being awake hours before their previous "whenever they felt like eating breakfast" routine.

The headmistress had taken her dinner in her rooms the previous night, though I wasn't sure whether that was to protect her travel-frazzled nerves or to make her introduction to them as authoritative as possible. It was probably the latter.

"Hello, children," she called, using a tone I recognized from school… a tone that sent a little shiver down my spine. "My name is Miss Lockwood and I will be supervising your lessons from here out. Misses Ivy, Alicia, and Sarah are familiar with me and my methods, so I'm sure they can answer any questions you may have. Mrs. Lumpkin has a wholesome, nutritious breakfast prepared for you in the dining room. I expect you dressed and fed and waiting at the library table within the hour."

With that, she disappeared into the library and the children turned to us with an expression of utter betrayal on their faces. Most of their questions were centered around "do we have to?" and "can she really make us do lessons?" Eventually, we persuaded them that yes, they did, and yes, she could, and they would be better off spending this time getting ready.

Over the next few days, the children complained mightily – particularly about the lack of cakes at breakfast. A few of them cried. Jam was flung with much more vehemence. But eventually, they were up and fed and waiting for Miss Lockwood at the library before she arrived each morning.

I feared that Miss Lockwood's approach to magical education would be too harsh for this group. She was entirely pragmatic. At Miss Castwell's, she'd insisted that magic was not some wellspring of whimsy and mystical power inside of a practitioner – but the ability to manipulate the universe through the laws of mathematics, chemistry, and physics. And yet, over the last few months, I'd learned that while magic was based on science, on our ability to reach between molecules and bend the physical world to our will, it was also about instinct, emotion. Magic was a living thing, a current in the universe that had attached itself to our very beings. And I was getting a strong impression that magic didn't approve of the way it had been used over the last century or so.

I wondered how Miss Lockwood's worldview had changed now that she knew a lot of people had magic – without the Guardians' approval or permission. But I didn't have a chance to ask her because she never had a minute alone. One of the children was always clamoring for her attention. And she did try to help with household chores, but after a particularly disastrous – though entertaining – attempt to peel vegetables, we all agreed it was better for Miss Lockwood to focus on the curriculum for the children.

Mrs. Lumpkin seemed relieved that Miss Lockwood had some flaws, even if it was being inept at household management.

As the oldest, Robert and Cathy were excused from lessons and appointed to help the three of us strategize and research the resurrection of the Mother Book. And while Miss Lockwood refused to take those tasks off our hands, or the chores that we did to help Mrs. Lumpkin, having the younger children occupied gave us more free time to focus and just *think* without interruptions… or explosions.

We established a sort of office in the second library, researching a more thoughtful method for recreating the Mother Book. It was refreshing, returning to calmer days filled with study and quiet, time spent with people my own age. Mrs. Winter didn't write again, which I took as a good sign. Gavin didn't either, but that simply meant he was following our carefully dictated rules to keep us all safe. So, we threw ourselves into what work we had.

Robert turned out to be quite the research fiend. Having never been allowed access to a library, he'd never grasped exactly how much he loved books. He could recall the location of every book he'd ever touched, and was adept at moving through the house quietly, without being spotted by the younger children. While helpful, Cathy had little enthusiasm for the project, but I thought perhaps she was helping us because she was bored and there was little else to do.

But still, we made progress. Cathy, Alicia, and I went to work soaking the old blank book pages and milling them into new. It was exhausting and messy work, but we thought perhaps fresh paper would be more accepting of new magic. Also, the upper body work seemed to exercise some of the aggressions out of Cathy. Ivy found a title on magical objects with their own life forces. Robert found another tome on how to make a "template book" – a magical book that offered up whatever text the reader wished for with just a tap of the blade on the page. It reminded me of how the Mother Book worked. Whenever I had a question, I just had to meditate on the book and it would find a way to answer it… indirectly and without a lot of specifics, but it would still answer.

Truly, I missed the Mother Book.

Within two weeks, we were ready to try again. We had a carefully designed spell resembling the "template book" spell plus a meticulous plan listed on paper in Ivy's exquisite handwriting. We reviewed the spell about a dozen times, went over the symbols involved and the crystals and herbs we needed. We were prepared, or at least, far more prepared than last time. But with memories of smoke billowing out of the windows fresh in my mind, I found myself standing outside the door to Miss Lockwood's rooms, papers in hand. It was hours after the others had gone to bed. I didn't tell Ivy or Alicia that I wanted our teacher's opinion on our work. I didn't want to undermine their confidence, but it felt inadvisable to try on our own without guidance. We could only set the library on fire so many times before we did permanent damage.

"Come in!" Miss Lockwood called. I stepped into the guestroom to find her sitting in a comfortable wingback chair in front of her fireplace. Her gray hair was braided and thrown over her shoulder. She was wearing a soft dressing gown of dark green velvet. A cup of chamomile tea steamed on the side table with a plate of Mrs. Lumpkin's crisp vanilla biscuits.

There was a certain distance Miss Lockwood had maintained from the girls at the school – most likely to protect her sanity. She didn't eat meals among us or let us see her in anything but a perfectly starched, time-of-day-appropriate gown. Seeing her out of context like this – in her robe, eating biscuits – it was incredibly disconcerting.

I wondered how Miss Lockwood felt, being a guest in Mrs. Winter's home.

The distraction of these thoughts left me standing at Miss Lockwood's door, staring at her, which she seemed to find equally disconcerting.

"Miss Smith, is there some reason you're interrupting my rare moment of privacy?" she asked.

I cleared my throat. "We're ready to try again with the book."

"Are you?" she asked pointedly.

Ignoring her point, I replied, "Would you mind reviewing our plan?"

"I believe I told you – I'm not the Translator," Miss Lockwood reminded me.

"No, but you are the person who will have to help me evacuate the children from this house, should we set it alight again," I replied. "And do you really want to have to explain to Mrs. Winter how that happened?"

Rolling her eyes, Miss Lockwood swept her arm to welcome me into her room. She gestured again at the chair across from her resting spot, which I sank into, awkwardly. I was still wearing my dinner dress, because the idea of appearing before her in my nightgown felt far too vulnerable. I felt exposed enough, sitting in this room while she perched her reading glasses on the end of her nose and scanned my papers. From nowhere, she produced a fountain pen and made notes in the margins. And those marks were made in red, which was somehow, all the more disheartening.

What if this didn't work? What if nothing we did mattered and my separation from the Mother Book was permanent? Had I remotely accepted the possibility? I knew it was unwise, to rely on it so much. Depending on the book was what landed me in this predicament in the first place. But it couldn't hurt, to have an inexhaustible font of ancient magical knowledge at one's disposal, right?

It was at moments like this that I was reminded how young I was, how much was resting on my shoulders, and how much I was making up as I went along. Miss Lockwood set the papers aside, peering at me over her reading glasses. "I can't guarantee this will work," she warned me. "But it has a better chance than the last half-hearted attempt you made."

I cleared my throat. "Thank you, ma'am."

"Consider these changes to your calculations," she told me, handing me her corrections. "The smoke damage should be minimal."

"That's the best we can hope for." I nodded, taking the papers from her. She seemed to want to say something else, which kept me from rising and rushing back to my room. "Is everything all right, Miss Lockwood?"

"Decidedly not," she sighed. "But not because of anything you or any person in this house has done. Oh, don't look so frightened, Miss Smith. I'm only suffering from a shift in perspective."

Not quite sure how to respond, I backed toward the door. But she looked up, pinning me to the floor with the power of her gaze. "How did you bear it?"

"Bear what?"

"Having everything you knew about the world turned on its head," she said. "Living in a sphere so different from your experience? I see now that I didn't spot the weaknesses in your story, not because you made such a convincing young Guardian lady, but because it simply never occurred to me that such a thing was possible. And it's galling, that my mind was so narrow. I once prided myself on my intellectual curiosity and openness."

"I'm... sorry?"

"Yes, well." She sniffed, then offered me a rare half-smile. "Teaching these children, even over the past few days, has been rewarding in a way I didn't anticipate. I have been locked away in the hallowed halls of Miss Castwell's for so long, I forgot what it was like to teach people who *thirst* for magic, who want to learn because not knowing would give them pain. These children reminded me of how much joy there could be in teaching. They gave that back to me. And you played a small part in that, so I thank you."

"So maybe it was a good thing that I took a place at Miss Castwell's and deceived you?" I suggested.

She scoffed. "Well, let's not talk nonsense."

~

THE SECOND ATTEMPT at raising the Mother Book died not with a scream but with a whimper. But then, after the whimper, there was a scream.

We waited until the other children were occupied with Miss Lockwood's lessons and went out into the yard. The planets were nicely aligned for new work. This wasn't some whimsical and spontaneous attempt. So why did I have this strange feeling of foreboding hanging over me?

"I still think this is a terrible idea," Cathy told me, lounging under a huge old oak near the clearing where we were working the spell.

"Yes, thank you, I'm aware," I replied.

"Come on, Cathy, we're all pitching in here. If Sarah says the book's important, it's important," Robert chided her as he placed the book-making materials in the center of a circle we'd created from inscribed crystals and stones. "We'll need it, in what's to come."

"This better be worth it," she grumbled, standing and brushing her pants.

We ladies arranged ourselves in the best magical alignment, north, south, east, and west, with items at our feet representing the four elements. Robert stood outside of the circle, with a bucket of water, a thick blanket, and a medical kit, just in case. We needed someone untouched by the magic we were about to work, to supervise.

Each of us had our blades in our hands and carefully inscribed our pre-planned symbols on the air. Almost immediately, the birchwood covers Robert had carefully wrapped in linen rose into the air between us. The pages whirled in the same bird-like pattern as before, as if the book was trying to knit itself together mid-air. A bright blue energy swirled around the mass of papers and hope actually rose in my chest.

A gentle warmth spread through my chest. It felt like receiving an embrace, and that hope rose even higher. Maybe my feeling of foreboding had just been nerves? Maybe this was going to work?

"I feel it," Cathy whispered and for the first time, I saw her smile. Her whole face was transformed and she looked like the young person she was. "Can you feel it? Bumping against the inside of my head, like a memory."

"Me, too," Alicia marveled. "Is this what it felt like to you?"

I smiled as I nodded, too moved to speak. And for just a second, I thought the book had come back to me, like an old friend. And I was about to introduce that friend to others just like me, to share that love and magic. Instantly, I felt better than I had in months.

Each of the other girls hissed in pain and clutched their hands close to their chests, as if they burned. I could see outlines of insect shapes imprinting themselves into the girls' skin. It was a familiar sight to me, who had received a metal dragonfly mark on my palms when the book had chosen me. Did that mean my friends would also be Translators? Would I be able to share this burden? Somehow, that was even more exciting than finding other Changelings, knowing that I wouldn't be alone in this responsibility.

But then, just as the book seemed to be knitting itself together, that connection I felt forming inside snapped. I slumped forward, all the tension in my body draining away. The paper, linen and ribbon collapsed to the ground in a heap. Ivy and I groaned in unison while Cathy's expression went back to its usual sullen irritation. "I told you this was a terrible idea."

"Is that it?" Robert asked as Alicia nudged at the pile with her foot. "All preparation and nothing? I can't believe it!"

"Well, I wouldn't call it 'nothing,'" Ivy said, holding up her palm to show me the reddened outline of a dragonfly. While I was sure it had been very unpleasant, it hadn't quite formed the metal mark I'd received, and I was sorry for it. Ivy and Alicia deserved their own marks, their own magical tattoos, drawing the very minerals from their own bodies to show that they had worked magic of great skill and importance – and since it would match mine, I supposed it would mean that they worked the same magic I did?

And Cathy? Well, I wasn't sure she would be happy about it. But she deserved her part of the credit as well.

"At least nothing caught on fire?" I suggested, trying to find a silver lining to this failure.

Somewhere in the house, we heard a shriek that curdled my blood. We froze, staring at each other for a moment and then bolting towards the house. I'd never seen Alicia move so fast, though I supposed the extra inches of leg she'd put on since the last school year helped her cover more ground.

"You just had to say something," Cathy griped at me as we yanked the kitchen door open. We stumbled into the foyer to find Lizzie huddled on the ground, covering her ears with her hands and wailing. She was crumpled near an overturned glass vase. It looked as if she was putting roses into the vase when she collapsed. It was something she enjoyed, "making the house pretty" with flowers from the greenhouse when Miss Lockwood dismissed them for lunch.

Our headmistress was crouched next to Lizzie's form as other children filtered from various corners of the manor. Mrs. Lumpkin was fluttering near the dining room entrance, but seemed willing to let Miss Lockwood handle the crisis. Miss Lockwood stiffened as Lizzie climbed into her arms, nearly toppling under the weight as the girl sobbed into her shoulder. It was a movement that would have been unheard of at Miss Castwell's. But Miss Lockwood merely patted her awkwardly on the back. "There, there."

Mrs. Lumpkin arched her brow, but to her credit, said nothing. The other children muttered amongst themselves, but didn't seem particularly surprised to see Lizzie in this state. I looked to Cathy, who only crossed the foyer to pull Lizzie gently from Miss Lockwood's grip.

Lizzie took Cathy's cheeks between her hands and whispered, "There's an army of them. She's making an *army* of monsters to come after us. I saw them. They're looking for us, right now. They were people, but there was nothing inside them. They were just empty shells."

All that hope had made way for a frightful cold, nausea. Revenants. Lizzie was talking about Revenants, re-animated corpses controlled by Miss Morton and her necromancy. And we did not want Revenants coming to Hazelcliffe. Unlike Mr. Crenshaw, whom Miss Morton was occupying directly, the "remotely controlled" Revenants were mindless, shuffling terrors. The shock of seeing them was enough to steal your breath and the will to fight.

And yet, somehow, Miss Morton's foul intelligence, talking through some other person's form, was even more frightening.

I whispered to Robert, "She couldn't really know that, could she? Just from looking into flower water?"

"Lizzie has always been particularly good at divination," Robert explained. "But it doesn't seem to work when she's *trying* to look for something. Most of the time, her visions catch her off-guard. And really, she's predicted more from less."

I'd only seen one Revenant and it was a nightmare – a difficult-to-kill nightmare. I'd had nightmares of more, but if what Lizzie saw was real – how would we deal with an entire army of them? I tried to keep the stress and fear from my face. Lizzie was already frightened by what she'd seen. She didn't need me scaring her further with my own anxieties.

"I saw Ivy with a blond boy, holding a horn," Lizzie continued.

"An animal's horn?" I asked.

"No, a horn, like you would play in a band," she said. "Ivy and the boy were being attacked by the dead people. And when the horn made a noise, the monsters died."

Well, that was unexpected.

Ivy's head tilted as she mulled over what Lizzie told her. "Do you think she means Owen?"

"Most likely," Alicia mused. "Who else would help you wield a musical instrument against the dead?"

"Are you sure it was a horn?" I asked Lizzie.

The little girl leveled me with her frank brown eyes. "That's what you think was strange about what I saw?"

I pursed my lips. "All right then. Any idea where that horn might be located? Because it sounds like it would be a helpful instrument to have around."

Lizzie shook her head. "No, sorry. But Ivy has it, so I think you'll find it eventually."

"That's not very helpful, Lizzie," Cathy told her, smirking at me.

Lizzie shrugged. "It's not my job to be helpful. I just see things. Can I get some lunch now?"

Mrs. Lumpkin bustled from behind me, holding out her arms. "Of course, you can, poppet. I have sandwiches and cakes ready. Come on, you lot. Let's leave Miss Lockwood to talk with Robert and the young ladies."

The younger children filed past us while Miss Lockwood walked into the library. We arranged ourselves around the table, each of us unsettled.

"I think I speak for all of us when I say, 'What in the world does that mean?'" Alicia said. "Why would Lizzie have a vision about a magic trumpet that defeats the dead?"

Robert noted, "Sarah's the one who's always going on about magic being a living thing."

"Why does everybody phrase it that way? I don't 'go on' about anything," I protested.

"You're one who says that magic is a living thing," Robert amended. "What if magic is trying to help us by sending messages to Lizzie, to give us a weapon we need in this fight?"

"In general, magic isn't that direct in communications," Ivy noted.

"How would we even go about finding such a thing?" I asked, looking to Miss Lockwood. "Have *you* heard of a magical anti-necromancy trumpet?"

Miss Lockwood shook her head, as if this was a completely normal thing to ask. "No, but magical music instruments aren't precisely my specialty."

"It would be worth looking into," Alicia said. "There has to be a reason Lizzie saw what she saw."

"Or it could be a trap," Cathy suggested. "Somehow, your Miss Morton could have found a way to send Lizzie a vision to lead us out of the safe place we've managed to make for ourselves. I'm sure our teachers gave her information about each of our talents."

"Or it could be a trap," Robert agreed, nodding.

"Don't just agree with me because I could be right," Cathy snapped at him. Robert looked vaguely offended, but said nothing.

I was starting to wonder whether Robert tended to agree with us as a running joke or as self-defense.

"With the 'trap' possibility in play, do you think we should leave, try to get out of the house before Lizzie's vision comes true?" I asked the others. Miss Lockwood frowned, most likely because I sought the opinions of the adolescents in the room instead of her. While Cathy was quick to shake her head, Ivy and Alicia mulled it over.

"There's no reason to go running after something that may not exist, that we may not be able to locate if it does exist, and may not actually help us if we find it," Ivy said.

We looked to Miss Lockwood, who nodded. "Miss Cowell makes a reasonable argument."

"Do you think you can trust the librarian at Miss Castwell's to write to her and ask her to look it up?" I asked. "The school has a much more comprehensive library than any of our homes would contain."

"After your experience with Miss Morton, trusting another librarian seems ill-advised," Miss Lockwood muttered. "Am I to assume that your second attempt to raise the Mother Book was unsuccessful?"

All of the enthusiasm whooshed out of us as if carried by a swift wind. Cathy's lips pinched together in an unhappy line while Alicia and Ivy rubbed at their reddened hands.

Robert shook his head. "I don't think we're ready to talk about it."

4

Researching what we'd come to call the "death horn" distracted us from the dismal (second) failure of raising the Mother Book. Unfortunately, we didn't find much. Magical musical instruments were apparently a niche interest, one that even the research-obsessed Mr. Winter didn't care for. But we had a goal, which was important. None of us were ready for a third attempt with the Mother Book after we'd come so close and still failed. Almost making contact with the Book only to lose it had left me sort of bereft and adrift. Searching for the horn was a distraction that we needed, even if we ended most of our days without having found anything helpful.

I devoured every page of *The Rise and Fall of the Grimstelles.* There was no mention of horns or even a Grimstelle who had a passing interest in the piano. It was all death and destruction and ruined lives, so... that was delightful late-night reading.

I'd risked Mrs. Winter's wrath, writing to her about the horn, even though she made it clear we should limit our communications. I did what I could to hide our location, enchanting the mirror to appear as if it was located somewhere in the Scottish

Highlands. I even had Robert write it, so my handwriting would be obscured. (His penmanship was much neater than my own.)

"Dearest Annie.

Thank you so much for the unexpected parcel. You were right. I don't know how we lived so long without the contents. Your thoughtfulness is simply overwhelming.

The country is quiet, which is quite conducive to my research project. There's no rest for the wicked, you know. And my Guild expects results by the fall. In my reading, I've come across a reference to a musical instrument that might be connected to our shared interests. Have you ever heard of such a thing? Unfortunately, my library is limited regarding this topic. If you have any titles you might recommend, I would appreciate it greatly."

After including an inordinate number of paragraphs dedicated to the weather and road conditions, I had Robert sign, *Your Friend, Agatha Pennythorn*. I'd probably enjoyed referring to my former employer as "Annie" a bit more than was wise, but to be fair, she *had* started it.

"That is the vaguest letter I've ever read," Robert told me after I dictated the closing. "You're not really saying anything."

"That's the point," I replied. "I'm trying to include enough meaningless pleasantries that it seems like a normal letter between society ladies. I can only hope Mrs. Winter connects 'our shared interest' with Miss Morton, the Grimstelles or at least, the Revenants. If not, I'm sure she'll write me an equally vague reply scolding me for my vagueness."

"Women are very strange," he sighed.

I snorted. "It's sad, that this is news to you."

We waited days for Mrs. Winter's response, beyond the immediate, terse, *"Agatha, Unfortunately, there is nothing in my library on the subject. That is not a particular area of interest for me. And you're very welcome, dear. No further thanks necessary. Sincerely, Annie."*

I took "no further thanks necessary" to mean, "don't write me again, you disagreeable girl." So I didn't.

Between our confinement to the library and the lack of progress, I supposed it was only a matter of time before tempers became frayed. It was a perfectly lovely day, and once again, we were stuck inside, with our noses buried in books that probably wouldn't help us. We'd been doing so for days and our necks were starting to ache from being hovered over desks for hours at a time.

"Have we considered using a location spell?" Alicia asked one afternoon, rubbing at her eyes as she slumped against a shelf. We were arranged in the little sitting area of the library, sprawling over the furniture in a way that would have deeply upset Mrs. Winter, surrounded by stacks of discarded books.

I rubbed the back of my neck, asking, "For the book that we need?"

"No, for the horn," Alicia suggested.

"We're going to use location magic for an object we've never seen?" Cathy scoffed from her seat near the window.

"Lizzie has seen it," Ivy noted. "Maybe we can find a way to use her vision?"

"You're not going to *use* Lizzie for anything!" Cathy replied hotly.

"That's not what Ivy meant," I assured her. "We would never do anything to hurt Lizzie, not even a little bit."

"You're not *doing* anything!" Cathy shot to her feet, slamming the book she was holding shut. "All we do is sit around this stupid library while you try to figure out what you're going to do! First, the stupid book and now this stupid horn! And I'm sure in another week, some other bright shiny idea will come along and you'll have us chasing *that*!"

I swallowed thickly, breathing deeply through my nose because... she had a point. I was so frightened of making mistakes, of getting someone hurt, that I wasn't making the decisions I needed to make. And we were all stuck in place because of it.

"Cathy, Sarah is doing her best," Ivy said, standing and crossing to her.

"Her best isn't good enough! And you just follow along with everything she does because you don't know anything either! We never should have come with you!" she yelled at me. "We should have struck out on our own once we left the mountain."

"That's not fair!" Robert protested. "We're far better off here than we were at the school."

"Oh, shut up, Robert, you're just scared of upsetting your *sweetheart*," she spat the word as if it was a curse, glaring at Alicia. "By being anything but the agreeable little puppy toddling after her."

"I beg your pardon!" Alicia gasped. "I want Robert to tell us what he thinks!"

"If he did, he would tell you that we should be out there, seeking out this Miss Morton, rather than sitting around here, reading about some horn!" Cathy shouted.

"I don't think that!" Robert yelled. "*You* think that. I don't want to aimlessly chase after some villainous necromancer just because you don't like the countryside!"

Cathy turned on me. "You're only in charge here because you got *lucky*. You weren't trained to serve as a guard to some Guardian who wouldn't care what happened to you unless it was some inconvenience to them. You weren't told to feel *fortunate* that this was your place in life because the government could lock you away for what you are. You were turned into a *lady* and you act like we should follow you because of it."

After a long moment, I nodded. "You're right."

She froze, her hands suspended mid-air, as she blinked at me. "What?"

"You're right. I didn't even realize how lucky I was," I told her. "If my parents hadn't realized what was happening to me and found a way to protect me, I could have ended up in the same place as you. And the only reason I have anything resembling authority here is that Alicia and Ivy believed in me and helped me. And Mrs. Winter was willing to provide us with a place to stay."

Cathy's shoulders sagged as all of the steam seemed to seep out of her. She sank into the nearest chair. "Oh, all right, then."

I slid into the chair next to her, exhausted. "Cathy, I don't want to be in charge. I don't know what I'm doing. I am terrified someone is going to get hurt and it will be my fault. I'm practically immobilized with fear from the moment I wake up until the moment I go to sleep. I worry *constantly* that I'm doing the wrong the thing. I have *dreams* about worrying. If I wake up in the morning, without feeling that nagging sense of dread, I have to remind myself of what I'm supposed to be worried about, because it feels so wrong *not* to be worried. If you want to take over and lead the group, be my guest. It would be a relief."

"No," Cathy said, her expression warming from icy rage to disbelief. "It sounds terrible."

I blinked quickly, because I didn't think Cathy would be impressed by the tears heating in my eyes. "It is."

Cathy flopped back in her seat. "I'm angry because I'm just... *angry*. There's nothing personal about it. It's not even about you. I'm angry because I've never controlled anything about my life. Nothing. And now, I feel even more out of control because I don't know what to expect. I cut my hair because I *wanted* to and I'm wearing these old dresses because I *want* to. I don't even know if I like wearing my hair this short–"

"It suits you," Alicia assured her. "It really brings out your eyes."

"And it's very easy to take care of, rather than spending all morning brushing it and pinning it, but that's not the point," Cathy said, raising her hand. "The point is that I did it because I wanted to and it felt good to just do what I wanted. I've never done anything like it before, and it's *frustrating* to take a step like that, only to be held to the whims of you three, just because you happened to have a boat to take us off the mountain."

"If it makes you feel better, many of us have very little control over our lives," Ivy told her. "We're told what to do from the moment we're born. Our parents tell us where we'll go to school, who we can be friends with, how we'll dress, what we'll study, who we'll court, who we'll marry, which Guilds we should join. And one simple misstep, walking in the wrong door, saying the wrong word in front of the wrong person, could ruin your reputation and your entire life."

"Actually, that does make me feel a little better, thank you," Cathy said, brightening a little. "I suppose if I was born into a Guardian family, I would probably be angry that as a woman, I would have little control over my marriage or profession."

"Oh, the boys have a bit more control over their lives, but not much," Alicia supplied helpfully. "Gavin only survives by blithely ignoring our mother's instructions for every aspect of his life and existence. And in return, she makes his every waking moment a living hell."

Though my heart caught at the mention of Gavin – Gavin, who I missed so much, even though we hadn't really spent much time together, strictly speaking – I patted Cathy's hand. For once, she didn't recoil away from me. "Just do us a favor, if that anger develops into feelings that could derail our efforts or result in a total and utter betrayal, could you give us a warning?"

She pursed her lips together before she finally nodded. "Absolutely. I can do that."

I felt the strange knot of tension in my belly give just a little. So much of Cathy's behavior made sense now. She wasn't angry at *me*. She was angry at *everybody*, and that was something I understood. I'd spent so much of my childhood so irritated with my family, my circumstances, the weakness of my body. It wasn't personal. It just *was*. And now that I'd explained that I didn't think I was doing a particularly good job leading the group, she would try to fill in the gaps I was leaving open. Maybe we could all understand each other a little better. Or at least fight each other less.

"Well, did we get that out of our systems?" a voice asked from the doorway. We turned to find Miss Lockwood, watching us with her arms crossed over her chest. She smirked slightly, as if she'd been expecting this particular explosion for a while.

"This is a very normal part of growing up, you know," Miss Lockwood told us as she moved closer. "Being angry. Feeling helpless, like a world you didn't help create is stacked against you, because frankly, it is. Even with the power you have, your life is dictated to you by the adults around you, the generations that have come before you. I've seen enough young ladies go through this as they study at Miss Castwell's. But you can only spend so much time feeling this way, feeling sorry for yourself. It's natural, but not necessarily useful or a productive use of your time – time that, quite frankly, you don't have because of your unique circumstances."

Robert's dark brows lifted. "So, you're saying?"

Miss Lockwood's tone was crisp. "What you're feeling is normal, but you need to snap yourselves out of it. There will be time to process it all when our work is done."

Miss Lockwood was smiling, genuinely smiling, at us, as if she'd figured out a secret about us and couldn't wait for us to catch up. "I have tried to allow you the space you needed to find your footing, and for students your age, you've done as well as can be expected in the circumstances. However, I believe you need some guidance now. You're floundering, rudderless, distracted by each new idea."

"Is this meant to be an encouraging speech?" Ivy asked me under her breath. I shrugged.

"Each young person here is a strong magical practitioner," Miss Lockwood said. "Even you, Cathy, for all your reluctance to be a part of things."

Cathy jerked her narrow shoulders. "Thank you, I suppose."

"But as a group, you're a bit of a danger, to yourselves and others," she sighed. "You've skipped a stage in the development of this little enterprise. You're trying to build something together, but you never learned as a group to create magic *together*. You've never been taught how. I believe we should remedy that."

I tilted my head, staring at Miss Lockwood, wondering how something so simple hadn't occurred to us. Group spells weren't exactly a specialty at Miss Castwell's. Yes, we participated in some group activities, like dance rituals, but our training was meant to promote our individual power. That's what magical society at large valued, singular achievement, individual gains. Even the participation in research guilds, the end-all, be-all of magical careers, was dedicated to individual research and promotion within that group. In general, magical practitioners were not good at sharing.

I'd managed that sort of connection with Ivy and Alicia, but that was extraordinary magic, done under duress to defeat an evil librarian with aspirations to rule the world. It was difficult to recreate that with people we didn't know that well. Our efforts to make another Mother Book proved that.

"And you can teach us to do that?" Robert asked.

Miss Lockwood smiled. "I can."

"Why didn't you teach us to do that at Miss Castwell's?" Alicia asked.

"Have you ever tried to teach a gaggle of well-to-do adolescent girls to do anything that might not be in their own self-interest?" she scoffed.

She had good point. I didn't think that would have gone well for Miss Lockwood's career.

"Honestly, I've already started the younger children on a regimen that will lend itself to cooperative magic," she added. "We were just waiting for you to be ready to join us. We start after breakfast tomorrow. Best to try these things for the first time on a belly full of Mrs. Lumpkin's bacon and eggs."

Cathy's eyes widened as Miss Lockwood swept from the room. "Was she like that at the school?"

Ivy nodded. "Yes, but sterner and with less gentle humor."

Cathy gave a shudder that wracked her entire body.

~

THE NEXT MORNING, Miss Lockwood herded us out of the house into the mid-morning sun. She took us into a clearing between tall oak trees and arranged us like hands on a clock around her. She closed her eyes and stood absolutely still and silent for so long that it was actually a little unnerving. Geoffrey and his most-likely-to-be-induced-into-mischief friend, Joseph, stood next to each other, elbowing each other in the ribs and giggling.

"Do you think she fell asleep on her feet? She does stay up awfully late at night, reading," Joseph whispered, wide brown eyes twinkling. Geoffrey chortled through his nose, which was a frankly, terrifying sound.

"No, young Joseph, I am not asleep, I can hear *everything*," Miss Lockwood called, her eyes still closed tight. "Children, while I value the enthusiasm and exuberance of youth, there is value in silence and stillness. If you're going to forge your magic into one force, you're going to have to stop running amok like a group of rabbits, each in your own direction – Lizzie, even with my eyes closed, I can tell that you're sneaking sweets out of your pocket. I can hear the wrapper rustling. Please wait until after we've finished and I promise you can enjoy them to your heart's content."

It said much about Lizzie's comfort with Miss Lockwood that instead of flinching, she simply smiled, flushing guiltily, and shoved her lemon boiled sweets into her skirt pocket.

"If you're going to forge your magic into one force, one intention, you have to start from a place of calm. Breathe," Miss Lockwood intoned. "Close your eyes and breathe."

I followed her instructions, letting her voice move over my mind in a soft caress. "Clear your mind of sweets and jokes and what Mrs. Lumpkin is going to make for lunch. Focus on your breathing, the movement of air in and out of your lungs. The sun on your face. The soft rustling of your hair blowing in the wind."

For the longest time, we simply stood there, and I believed I *could* fall asleep on my feet. It was longest I'd stood in one place, not worrying, not chasing after a solution to our many problems, and I didn't think I'd ever be able to thank Miss Lockwood for this morsel of peace.

I breathed in and I could feel Alicia and Ivy breathing on either side of me, inhaling in unison. That breath echoed around the circle until it was a singular breath. We had so much in common, still so young, so uncertain in this world that was changing around us. But we were here, together, and we had one purpose... which we would eventually figure out.

We cared for each other, as much as people forced into a strange camaraderie could. I knew as much about these children as I knew about any friend of mine. I knew that Lizzie wanted to have her own dress shop one day – or just to own as many dresses as possible. Either was fine with her. Geoffrey adored cats and slept with a little grey stuffed kitten that Mrs. Lumpkin knit for him on his last birthday. May loved to draw and spent much of her time sketching the house where she'd grown up. And Cathy... I wasn't sure what Cathy loved, besides doing what she wanted. I could feel her anger burning across the circle, the anger that always seemed to be bubbling under the surface. But underneath it, I could feel... fear and hope. I could feel her fear that she felt hope. I could feel her magic. I could feel the magic of every other person in the clearing, bumping against my own experimentally. That magic *felt.* The magics wanted to merge, to create something together. They were happy to be in this one place, to be stronger as one force. And I, for one, wanted to see what they could do.

"Now, open your eyes," Miss Lockwood said softly. She was

still standing in the middle of our circle and there was an unusually large squash at her feet. Rather than giggling or fidgeting, the children stayed perfectly still as they stared down at the squash. "Take out your blades."

When we followed her instruction, she said, "Make it float. Don't speak, just concentrate on the squash rising from the ground. I would ask you to choose amongst you, which spell to use, but I think we can agree that could go very badly. So let's just use a basic levitation charm."

I glanced at the others. They raised their blades and drew the simple, flowing serpentine shape that burned pale green against the air from a dozen points around the circle. The shapes floated across the space and collided mid-air. The squash exploded up from the ground as if it was shot out of a cannon. Miss Lockwood, having expected this, cast her own charm towards the sky, slowing the squash's meteoric ascent into the heavens.

"All right, children, all right," she said, sounding pleased. "While I appreciate the effort you've put into the spell, perhaps relax those intentions just a bit, so we might bring the squash back into the lower atmosphere."

No one laughed, we simply breathed out, a soft, unified sound. The squash slowly descended until it hovered at our eye level.

"Can you change it into something else?" she asked. "You must agree between you, or we'll just have a mess on our hands."

"How do we decide what to change it into?" Robert asked.

"That's the point," Miss Lockwood replied. "Your magic knows. You just have to let it do the work. Magic–"

"Is a living thing," we all finished for her.

I closed my eyes and let my magic reach out to the others. I could feel the individual flavors of each person in the circle, and yet, I could sense it as one blended sensation as well. It was like a magical soup… I would never repeat that aloud so that the others could hear it. And I hoped they couldn't somehow sense it through this shared experience.

I shook off this distracted thought and tried to sift through the feelings in my head. What did our magics want to make? A doll? No, that felt like too far of a transformation for our first try, from vegetable to porcelain and cloth. I had a feeling that wish was coming from Lizzie, who loved dolls in all forms. What about a shield? But the squash could make a beautiful boat, the bottom of it was already sort of hull-shaped, and we could transform vegetable material easily enough. This was coming from Joseph. I could feel his glee for all things nautical in this idea.

I opened my eyes and glanced around the circle. All the other children were thinking of a boat, too. I could see it in their faces, feel it on the air. We raised our knives like paintbrushes, prepared for a downward stroke and began a sweeping arc to counter-clockwise.

Miss Lockwood intoned, "Remember, move your blades as one – No, Geoffrey, not faster than Joseph, it's not a race. You can't 'win' a spell."

Geoffrey and Joseph wore twin mischievous expressions, which was… disconcerting. I shook my head, concentrating on the fibrous squash and how similar it was to wood grain, the amount of energy it would take to transmute it from one to the other. The squash swept across the circle, bulging and shaking as our magic pulled it apart to remake it. It darkened to an oak brown and elongated. One end sharpened into a bow and I could actually see the masts starting to form on top.

But it felt like the more we managed to change the squash, the more unstable its movements around the circle. It ducked and it dodged, nearly striking Alicia in the head before zipping across and skimming the grass.

"Let's calm it down," I muttered. "Squash-related injuries would be very difficult to explain to a surgeon whose services we can't quite risk seeking out."

Just as I spoke, the squash-boat shot up into the sky. We watched it rise out of sight and then, just as suddenly, plummet to

Miss Lockwood's feet. It exploded in a shower of orange-yellow vegetable bits and splinters. Fortunately, most of what landed on Miss Lockwood's face was squash.

To our credit, we did gasp and clap our hands over our mouths in unison.

"It's all right," Miss Lockwood told us, wiping at her cheeks. She smiled brightly. "I have another squash."

IT TOOK us another two hours and three squashes before we managed a completed boat. It was a thing of beauty, though, complete with little linen sails and a figurehead that looked like a mermaid. Joseph, Annie, Lizzie, and Geoffrey immediately snatched it out of the center of the circle to launch it in the stream that flowed east of the orchard. Cathy had rolled her eyes, but dutifully followed to make sure none of them fell in after it.

Bidding a limp goodbye to the others, I slumped into my room and fell face-first into my bed. Somehow, working spells as a group was far more exhausting than trying to work magic alone. It took more concentration to control the flow of my own magical energy while it joined with others. I could only hope it would get easier over time. Unable to breathe through my mattress, I rolled onto my side and saw Mrs. Winter's handwriting scrawled across my mirror.

It glowed a pale pink, meaning it had been waiting there for some time and was in danger of disappearing from the glass all together – another security precaution from Mrs. Winter. "*Dearest Agatha, Having mentioned your inquiry at a few afternoon teas, I was directed to a book entitled* History's Musical Magic, *printed in 1723. Helene Alston remembers reading it in her grandmother's library when she was a child. She said it listed several instruments worth noting, but the volume was donated to some worthy cause years ago. She can't remember which. Sorry I couldn't be more help to you. Just for the sake of proper post, I'm thinking of traveling north for a visit to my Irish cousins. Apparently certain neighborhoods near County Shannon are becoming quite chic. Sebastian Crenshaw himself is said to have sent agents there, searching for the right property for a holiday home. I suppose the rest of society will follow. Sincerely, Annie."*

I stared at the mirror for a long time, before yelping, "Someone! Help! New information!" as it began to fade entirely from the glass.

Miss Lockwood, Robert, Ivy, and Alicia came running into my room. They stopped as a unit, staring at the words on my mirror as they dissolved from sight. I wondered at the mention of Ireland. Was it to throw anyone who "eavesdropped" off of Mrs. Winter's trail? I doubted very much she would be doing any traveling for the time being.

"Helene Alston *must* remember donating her grandmother's books to the Miss Castwell's library," Miss Lockwood scoffed. "She practically took out a newspaper ad announcing it when she delivered those book crates to my office."

"Mrs. Winter is trying to throw any spies off of our trail, should they intercept the message," Alicia informed her.

"Clever," Miss Lockwood conceded before her brow furrowed. "Mrs. Winter lets you call her *Annie*?"

I shook my head. "Decidedly not."

"I don't remember any volume like that in the library," Ivy said. "And I spent most of my time there, hiding from Callista and her lot. Do you think Miss Morton read it while she was working in the library? Could she already know about the horn?"

"Most donated collections go to a special depository within the library," Miss Lockwood said. "We get so many books donated and not all of them are particularly useful, but we're not so gauche as to destroy a gift. So, we store a good deal of them discreetly and hope that no one asks after them. Mrs. Alston's donation was only memorable in that it contained an astounding number of books about lacework. There was nothing of note in the three cartons of volumes we examined. Eventually, we gave up searching through them, boxed the books up carefully and put them in the depository.

"How does that help us?" I asked. "Miss Morton had access to the depository during her time at the school."

"The storage and maintenance of those books was considered above her paygrade. We didn't want anyone beyond the headmistress to know which donated books had been relegated to the depository," Miss Lockwood shook her head. "As headmistress, keeping track of those discreetly discarded titles fell to me and every headmistress before me. Unfortunately, I didn't have time to inform my successor of that room's existence."

"That seems a little petty," Alicia told her.

"So does a dismissal after decades of loyal service," Miss Lockwood countered.

"I don't suppose there's any way to magically transport that specific book to us from the library?" I asked. "Bypassing the wards and the various magical protections put in place there by some of the finest practitioners in Guardian history?"

The look Miss Lockwood shot me was both pitying and indignant.

5

"Are you sure about this?" Cathy asked me for the tenth time that evening.

It's very irritating to be repeatedly asked if I was sure of something when I was sure of nothing. However, since Cathy was finally talking to me with an unprecedented level of civility, I decided not to take that frustration out on her.

It was strange, trusting Cathy more. But ever since our failed experiments with the Mother Book, I got a much stronger impression of what Cathy was feeling. Maybe it was her confession about her anger or the fact that she had relaxed a bit around us, but it was pleasant – especially when we were leaving her behind with the children while a small group of us returned to Miss Castwell's. Cathy had elected to stay behind with Mrs. Lumpkin, to defend the children or even evacuate them if needed.

"Of course not. I'm not sure about any of this," I told her as we talked down the sweeping front stairs of the house. "But we have to do something productive. And finding the whereabouts of a weapon that could help us defeat Miss Morton's army is the closest thing we have to being productive."

"I didn't quite mean that you should run headlong into the

lion's mouth," Cathy scoffed, and for a moment, she actually seemed concerned for my safety.

"We'll be careful," I promised. "If we don't return in twenty-four hours, take the children to the rail station and head for Mrs. Winter's house in Dover."

"I still don't love that part of the plan," Cathy sighed, as I tied a navy blue scarf over my hair.

"Well, I don't love the part of the plan where Alicia assured me that she has transportation in hand, but refused to tell me how that will happen," I retorted as we entered the darkened foyer, where Robert, Alicia, Ivy, and Miss Lockwood were waiting for me. Our "mission team" had dressed simply, in dark clothes, so that we wouldn't be easily spotted. The younger children didn't even know that we were leaving or where we were going. It seemed safer that way.

"But you're trusting her as you're trusting me, and it's not lost on me," Cathy said, quietly. "I know I haven't given you much reason to do that."

"You care far more about those children than you care about me or even yourself," I told her.

"You're not wrong." Cathy nodded as we trooped out of the house. "Take care of yourselves. Don't do anything irreversibly stupid."

"Just our normal level of stupidity, then?" Robert asked.

Cathy snickered. "Exactly."

Mrs. Lumpkin hadn't been able to bid us farewell. She was so nervous about her only child leaving the farm, the tearful goodbye had been heard all around the house, despite the fact that we'd all dutifully closed ourselves off in our rooms to give them privacy. Then Mrs. Lumpkin locked herself in the kitchen and made approximately three hundred raspberry muffins, many of which we were taking with us on the journey to sustain us.

I couldn't precisely blame Mrs. Lumpkin for this reaction. The idea of leaving our little haven was distressing. It was so lovely here in the south, warm and soft – none of the smoky sooty crowded streets we had to deal with in Lightbourne. It was easy to relax here and forget about the chaos and danger we'd left behind in the "real world." I was very reluctant to take that away from any of us.

Robert took her arm and squeezed it gently before she shut the front door behind us. We heard her lock it tight and the hum of a ward, a magical barrier that could keep out most intruders.

"Are you certain about the transportation, Miss McCray?" Miss Lockwood asked as we marched across the estate's south field, the closest route toward town.

"I am," Alicia said, her voice resolute. We followed her down moonlit country lanes, across orchards and fields. It felt like we were walking for hours, though I'm sure it was only forty minutes or so. The stress of being out in the open for the first time in weeks, along with the darkness and unnerving silence, was tugging at my nerves. When we finally arrived at a clearing just beyond a wheat field, I thought those nerves had me imagining the familiarity of it.

"Have we been here before?" I asked, staring at a small circle of stones near a stand of birch trees. I could swear I've seen it before. Alicia raised her blade and a shimmer of the air indicated a cloaking spell lowering. A tidy little barn materialized before our very eyes, the wood so new I could smell the sawdust.

I turned in a circle, my mouth agape. "This is the clearing where Gavin landed the *Aventurine* and dropped us off."

"Precisely," Alicia turned to me, smiling, "Gavin left this for us. He thought we might need it at some point."

"How did he know the farmer who lived here wouldn't stumble onto an invisible barn?" I asked.

"Oh, he bought this farm the day after we landed here," she said dismissively, opening the barn door.

For a second, I hoped against hope that Gavin would be standing there, waiting for us, his tall frame bathed in crayfire light. But all was darkness, and the empty, cold feeling inside me was staggering. I'd never missed someone so much, not even my family. What did that say about me as a person? That I missed a boy I knew so little, compared to my own parents. I could only say that Gavin made me feel safe. He made me feel hopeful. He made me feel something besides the worries I'd been saddled with for so long.

Alicia touched her blade to two crayfire crystals flanking the door and the barn was ablaze with light. Inside was an air-gondola, a recent invention of the McCray family that used magically charged crystals to levitate a small ship to wherever you might want to fly. We'd used one to locate and spy on the Crenshaw school. Suddenly, my stomach dropped, because we were going to have to fly that thing all the way to Miss Castwell's and Alicia had a reckless hand on the tiller.

"So this has been here, all this time?" I asked. I stepped closer to the gondola, noting a small yellow rose comprised of a rolled-up silk ribbon, tied to the handle of the gondola door. It was just like the first gift Gavin had ever given me, a bouquet of ribbon roses to replace the ribbon I'd given to Alicia. And just like that first bouquet, when I touched the tip of my blade to the rose, it unfolded itself and then reshaped into a butterfly. The ribbon butterfly fluttered a few circles around my head and then landed as a neat coil in my palm.

I swallowed thickly, shaking my head. Gavin had left this for me. In the midst of building this escape plan for us, he'd taken the time to leave something simple and pretty for me. Somewhere out there, he was thinking of me, fondly. I clutched the ribbon to my chest and smiled, before shoving it into my handbag.

"I thought this plan would be safer, the fewer people who knew about it," Alicia said. "Especially when we first arrived and Cathy seemed ready to bolt at any moment."

"We are going to have a discussion about information and being more forthcoming," I told her as I climbed into the gondola.

"What is this thing?" Miss Lockwood breathed as I helped her and Ivy climb into the narrow ship.

"Do you get sick on trains, Miss Lockwood?" Robert asked as he unmoored the gondola from stakes buried in ground.

"Never," she scoffed, sounded mildly insulted.

Grinning, Robert climbed aboard. Alicia touched her blade to the crayfire crystal mounted near the tiller.

"Good," he said as the gondola rose sharply and flew out of the barn, into the night sky. Miss Lockwood stumbled and then landed on her rump on the floorboards, sputtering words I definitely had not heard her say in the company of proper Guardian young ladies. I peered over the hull, watching as the trees disappeared under the cloud bank

"How many days will it take to reach the school?" I asked.

"Oh, we should be there in a matter of hours. When we were searching for the mountain facility, we were sort of aimlessly wandering, and therefore not taking full advantage of the gondola's speed and agility," Alicia told us, a manic, gleeful expression spreading across her face as we rocketed through clouds. "But now that we know our destination, we can really test her limits."

"I do not like the look in her eyes," I told Ivy, as Robert took his place beside Alicia. He watched her maneuver the ship with genuine wonder in his eyes. It would have been delightful to watch if my dinner wasn't climbing up my throat.

"I've lived through two encounters with an evil necromancer and I don't think I was this frightened," Ivy said, bracing herself against the hull.

"A reasonable response," Miss Lockwood mumbled, turning slightly green.

It was just after midnight when we landed in the wooded area just behind Miss Castwell's. Though the school was hidden by darkness, I knew the building like the back of my own hand. It was one of the first places I'd felt like myself, one of the first

places I'd felt accepted, even if it wasn't the real me that people were accepting. I knew each darkened window and curved roof tile. The grass was wet with dew beneath our feet and even that felt like a welcome. A sense of longing that I hadn't expected filled my chest, but I had to shake it off and focus on the task at hand.

Robert jumped off the boat and tethered it to the nearest tree. I waited, for some alarm to sound or for Miss Morton to spring from behind a tree, unleashing hell itself. But all I could hear was the sound of night birds and insects.

Alicia cloaked the boat, and I wondered how we were going to find it again. But I was too afraid of making noise to ask. Miss Lockwood, who may or may not have kissed the ground, straightened up with all the grace of a queen. She jerked her head towards the school and we followed across the rolling lawn we'd once used for dancing lessons. I remembered those days fondly now, even though I groaned and sweated my way through them every time. Alicia, who was frankly, a little too generous with the cloaking spells at this point, cast another over our heads like a bubble.

"It's helpful now, Miss McCray, but the school's wards won't allow for cloaking spells once we reach the doors. A security precaution. Keep an eye out for guards," Miss Lockwood whispered as she removed a comically enormous ring of keys from her skirt pocket. "They'd be fools not to have someone patrolling the grounds, what with an inexperienced simpleton overseeing the safety of society's most ransom-able girls sleeping behind these walls."

"That is a very sinister way of looking at it and I'm very glad you're on our side," I told her.

"You don't think they'd know you might come back?" Ivy asked. "What if they changed all of the locks?"

"Oh, they took my keys before my departure, but they didn't seem to think I would have the presence of mind to make copies," she said, smiling as she dangled the heavy keyring. "Besides, there are too many keys for them to replace *all* of them."

We approached the far west side of the building, the kitchen entrance. We believed it would be the weakest point of the school's security, as very few Guardians worried about their potatoes and pots being burgled. Still, we had expected *some* form of magical protection, instead of Miss Lockwood simply waving her blade, Persistence, over the knob without any warning flash of a ward. Frowning, she inserted the kitchen key into the lock and the door popped right open.

"Incompetence of the highest order," Miss Lockwood whispered, though she looked faintly smug.

The kitchen was cavernous, filled with shiny cooking equipment reflecting the low light, but silent. I'd expected to encounter at least one servant, but it seemed like the administration still respected Miss Lockwood's edicts about reasonable hours. The fire burnt low in the grate, barely casting a golden glow over the room. The next morning's bread was cooling on the countertop under cheesecloth. The school had always served the *best* bread, snow white and soft as a cloud. My mouth watered, but I kept focus... because otherwise I could be caught breaking into my former school and possibly be imprisoned. A warm slice of toast seemed unimportant by comparison.

We trooped toward the door to the hallway and Miss Lockwood stopped us. Her hand sliced through the air with a decisive motion and the air rippled with a faint violet light.

"Wards," she whispered, casting off Alicia's cloaking spell. "Lull the intruders into a false sense of security by letting them into the kitchen and then by the time they reach an interior door, you catch them. It's nice to see some of my policies haven't been abandoned."

"I can help with that," Robert said. He raised his blade, making a fluttering motion before slashing through the air. The ward split in half, as if he'd cut a bolt of muslin, and fell to the floor in a shower of fading sparks.

Miss Lockwood's brows rose. "Very nice. You'll have to show me how that's accomplished some time."

"Breaking wards was my specialty at the school," he said. "They'd planned to use me as a sort of 'problem solver' after I graduated. Accessing the homes of well-protected families would be part of my duties."

Alicia and I shuddered simultaneously. I could only imagine who or what those "problems" might have been and how they would be solved.

"Not another word after this point, unless it's an absolute emergency," Ivy told us.

We nodded, filing into the hallway. It was a bit of a shock, to see these familiar halls so dark and empty, long shadows stretching across the black and white tiles. The citrus smell of floor polish and fragrant flowers was comforting, but at the same time, I missed the sounds of dozens of girls trooping through the hallways. The bustle and movement of all of us rushing to class, all certain we were late and that our coursework was covered in incorrect answers.

It had hurt to hear Miss Lockwood refer to us as "intruders," even if we were sneaking to potentially steal from the school. So much of me wanted to rush back to my cozy suite, evict the girl sleeping in my old bed and pull the covers over my head. I would wake up the next morning to a day full of classes and social machinations. The worst thing that could happen was spilling my breakfast down the front of my day dress. But alas, that would leave my companions bewildered, and decidedly annoyed, so I pressed on.

We stopped every few steps to check for wards, but it seemed that once we got through the kitchen, little thought was given to the school's security. We headed towards the library wing, stepping carefully so we would make little noise. A slightly more complicated ward guarded the door – it took Robert several slashes as opposed to one – and I supposed that was fitting, given that the library contained one of the largest repositories of magical knowledge in the world.

The doors opened and I was overwhelmed by the dry smell of old books. Even in the dark, the full scope of the library was impressive – multiple floors of bookshelves spiraling around staircases leading up to a bright blue stained-glass ceiling depicting the sigils of the major houses as stars in the night sky. I couldn't see them well in this low light and that was another disappointment. I wasn't sure why exactly. It was seeing an irregularity in that starry glass that had first drawn me into the mystery of the Grimstelles and Miss Morton's web of lies. I scanned this level for the new librarian or other students who might be sneaking around, but we were utterly alone in this palace of books.

Miss Lockwood started towards the rear of the library. I stopped her, laying my hand lightly on her arm, and pointed to the door marked *"depository"* just across from Miss Morton's old office. She gave me a pitying look, nodded her head towards the far back wall. Miss Lockwood passed towering bookshelves until we reached the far wall and began lightly dragging her blade in wave patterns on all sides of a small marble bust of Athena. I exchanged glances with Ivy and Alicia. What was Miss Lockwood doing? Was her plan to tunnel through the wall as an escape? There were perfectly good windows and doors–

She tapped the wall one last time, and then slid her blade between the folds of Athena's gown, just over her heart. The bust *moved,* bowing its head reverently as the wall just disappeared into nothingness, revealing a hidden room. Sconces on the walls of the little room sprung to life, lighting the rows of fully stocked bookshelves. Cobwebs draped in soft waves along some of the shelves in the back, while some items looked like they'd been moved around recently... as in the last five years or so. We stepped through the entrance and Miss Lockwood closed the wall behind us.

"You think we kept books that we didn't consider well enough to display on the shelves in a room marked *depository,* where anyone could wander in an see how little we thought of their gifts?" Miss Lockwood said in a normal voice now that we were enclosed in a soundproof space.

"Well, not *now,*" I said, shaking my head.

"Besides, we don't just keep the undesirable books here, but the *dangerous* titles. There are a number of volumes involving spells far too advanced or dark for the talents of young people. And yet, the knowledge must be respected and maintained. That little optical illusion is a safe way to keep these books contained but accessible."

"It just seems unfair," I muttered.

"Pardon me, but I saw the damage you could do with the books you *did* have access to," Miss Lockwood reminded me.

We divided the room into quadrants and began our search. Unfortunately, the headmistress of Miss Castwell's hadn't spent much time organizing the stored titles. It seemed she'd simply shelved them neatly and occasionally checked the room for water damage. My section of the room was filled with periodicals. Someone had taken the time to bind years and years' worth of *Rumors and Mysteries of Magical England* in stiff leather volumes.

I certainly understood why Miss Lockwood chose not to keep these where the girls could find them. *Rumors and Mysteries* was a bit of a scandal rag, tracking the social rise and fall of luminaries in magical England. Instead of reporting on Senate votes and trade regulations, the newspaper reported on party disasters, unhappy marriages, and dwindling financial prospects. Mrs. Winter considered reading the publication to be bad luck, as the editorial staff seemed to be rooting for the worst possible outcome for magical society in general. On the rare occasion that a copy blew into the garden, she asked my father to mix the shreds into the compost pile.

As I had no other option, I skimmed the pages of the newspaper, taking in headlines about debutantes tripping down the stairs of their first ball or wealthy sons gambling away the family fortune on hippopotamus racing. My hands were thoroughly stained grey with newsprint when my eye caught on the name "Silas Morton."

"Morton" wasn't a common name in magical society. In fact, Miss Morton had been the only Morton I'd ever met. I opened the book wide to read the story of Silas Morton completing construction of a new "Grecian ruin" in his garden at his newly acquired Stonethistle House, an estate in County Shannon. The event was considered quite the scandal as Mr. Morton had purchased the estate specifically to host "wild and debauched" parties. But it was difficult to gauge what might have been considered wild and debauched almost a hundred years before. Couples dancing within two feet of each other? Women showing their ankles? I probably didn't want the answer to that question, honestly.

Could Miss Morton be a descendent of Silas Morton? Clearly, he'd enjoyed considerable financial resources to be building unnecessary ruins at his fancy country house, while Miss Morton spoke of the dire social and financial straits her family recently suffered. Then again, maybe Miss Morton considered only having *one* country estate to be a dire financial problem.

The author of the article spent an inordinate amount of time describing the "great lengths" Morton had gone to excavating the site, which seemed odd to me. How much digging could be involved in putting up a few pillars and a fountain? Behind me, I heard Alicia squeak excitedly. My hand jerked in surprise and I was very thankful that Alicia's whispering, "I found it!" covered the sound of the page ripping in my hand.

Oh, Miss Lockwood was not going to be happy about this.

I'd ripped most of the page, including the entirety of the Morton article. I guiltily shoved the paper into my skirt pocket. With apologies to magical knowledge and books in general, I shoved the damaged volume back onto the shelf. I dashed around the shelf to join the others and found Alicia waving a copy of *History's Musical Magic* in triumph.

Alicia opened the book and after a few moments perusing a chapter marked "Grimstelle Lore," read aloud, "Musical scholars have long debated the ability of sound to unmake so-called 'core magic,' particularly magic related to a family's magical specialty. Could an instrument crafted by one of their own affect the magic central to a family's core? Sound affects magic across the spectrum. Sound waves can make metal vibrate, shatter crystals, disrupt spells as they travel across the air. But what of the dead? It has long been rumored that renowned researcher Charles Throggle-Grimstelle, a patriarch of the dreaded Grimstelle family – before that house met its end – sought to settle in-fighting between family members by neutralizing their numbers. Numbers, of course, being the armies of undead Revenants the families were raising against each other. Silas sought to end these skirmishes by crafting a weapon that would simply undo their magical thrall over the dead by use of sonic waves. The necromancy performed by the Grimstelles is of a cyclical nature, necessary to repeatedly enforce the caster's will over the dead. As sound travels faster than magic, the tones produced by Throggle-Grimstelle's weapon could disrupt that cycle and end the spell permanently. He called this instrument the Horn of Silence. Sketches of the Horn's design are unavailable as Throggle-Grimstelle was notoriously secretive."

"So, we're looking for something called the Horn of Silence," I sighed. "Of course, we are."

"I found something useful, I think," Robert said, holding up a copy of *Lineage of Mother Houses Throughout the Ages.* "There might be something about the Grimstelle family lines in here."

"But we don't have time to read all of these books," Ivy said. "It could take hours to get through them and we need to be out of the school by sunrise. I think the other girls will notice if we try to sneak out at lunchtime."

"That depends on what's being served for lunch," I noted.

"Well reasoned, Miss Cowell – and only Miss Cowell – so, what shall we do about it?" Miss Lockwood asked, in her best classroom tone. I couldn't help but think she saw this as an extracurricular educational opportunity for us. I dropped the books into my shoulder bag and smiled sweetly.

"A simplistic, but effective, solution," Miss Lockwood said, grinning broadly. Apparently, I'd redeemed myself for the lunch menu comment. "This is rather fun, isn't it?"

"I think we've corrupted her," Ivy whispered to me. "In ways that make me uncomfortable."

I couldn't help but agree with her, but it seemed more important to stay silent as we closed the wall behind us and made for the library exit. As soon as we entered the hall, I could feel a ripple in the air, someone's magic was present in the hallway. Magic that I was familiar with.

"Do you feel that?" Ivy whispered.

Panicking, I grabbed Miss Lockwood's arm and shoved her into the nearest janitorial closet, one that was, unfortunately not large enough to fit all of us. Miss Lockwood squawked in protest as I pushed Robert in with her. He was far more pliant than Miss Lockwood, only shooting me a confused glance as I closed the door.

Alicia and Ivy turned as Jeanette Drummond's tall form rounded the corner. It was all I could do not to shriek in joy at the sight of her. Dark-haired with an angular and elegant sort of beauty, Jeanette was one of our close friends at school before our departure, having helped us create a study group with other girls who were struggling with their classes. That vulnerability and the act of helping each other had built bridges between girls from different social circles and age groups. It had been one of my favorite things about school, something I'd truly regretted losing.

In the shadowed hallway, Jeanette clapped her hand over her mouth to prevent the startled shriek from escaping. I rushed forward to hug her, which she returned with a fierce squeeze. I opened the closet door and pulled a perturbed Miss Lockwood and a blushing Robert into the hall with us. Jeanette's eyes went wide with surprise, but she managed to stay silent.

Holding her finger to her lips, she ushered us toward the entrance to the solarium – a glassed-in room crowded with potted plants and chaises where girls might take in the warmth of the afternoon sun. She closed the door and threw her arms around Alicia and Ivy, who wore twin expressions of relief.

"What are you *doing* here?" Jeanette asked quietly. "You have no idea the sort of things the other girls are saying about you."

"I can only imagine," I chuckled.

Jeanette shook her head. "Honestly, Callista's contributions alone are simply–"

Ivy held up her hands. "I think we get the point, Jeanette, thank you."

Meanwhile, Robert goggled at the sheer number of potted plants in the space. It did seem like a bit much now that we'd enjoyed the natural beauty of Hazelcliffe.

"Miss Drummond, what are you doing out of your room at this hour?" Miss Lockwood asked sternly.

Jeanette's eyes went the size of saucers as she whispered, "Headmistress Lockwood? I thought you retired. And is that a *boy* with you?"

Robert inclined his head awkwardly. "Nice to meet you."

Jeanette managed a curtsy while pulling her robe tighter around her throat, but only just.

"Yes, yes, it's a banner evening for rule violations committed by former faculty," Miss Lockwood deadpanned. "But my presence doesn't explain why *you're* breaking curfew, Miss Drummond."

"I'm in charge of setting the wards for the school each night at this time. Headmistress Bonhomme is not quite up to speed on the latest techniques," Jeanette said, prompting a snort from Miss

Lockwood. "So, she entrusts this task to senior students. I felt a disturbance a while ago and thought I should check the halls."

"Why wouldn't you report this disturbance?" Miss Lockwood asked.

"Because it felt familiar?" Jeanette suggested. "I could sense that the energy present was magic that I knew. Or at least, magic that had cooperated with my own at some point. And it seemed premature to raise the alarm if it was a student walking around at night. I didn't want them to get in trouble under the new system, if I could prevent it."

"And do you feel the need to report this disturbance now that you know it's us?" I asked carefully.

"Absolutely not. It's not the same school, without you," she said, glancing at Miss Lockwood. "We're not learning anything useful anymore. The girls are all stressed because they're convinced they're not going to be ready for their Guild interviews. And there's a new 'senior girl,' who just appeared out of nowhere. Headmistress Bonhomme created a new position this year, a 'student liaison' who keeps watch over us girls for the faculty. I've never heard of such a thing at a proper ladies' school. And this girl, Jennifer, she doesn't even seem like a student. She's not taking classes. She's not socializing with any of us. She's just always *there,* watching us, frowning. She looks quite a bit like your former ladies' maid, actually."

I glanced at Alicia and Ivy, who'd gotten to know Jenny extensively while we traveled together to Coventry – before Jenny turned on us. Why would Jenny come anywhere near the school? Jenny hadn't wanted to get *more* involved in Miss Morton's schemes. She'd wanted Miss Morton to take away her magic so she could live a "normal" life.

Outside, in the hall, I could hear footsteps. I pressed a finger to my lips. Miss Lockwood seemed to recognize right away what was happening and shoved all of us towards a nearby fichus. Our former headmistress pushed us *into* a wall and it was like falling through a cold mist. She'd pushed us into a side room, that had only looked like a plain wall from the solarium. It looked very much like the girls' lounge, but the chairs were cushier, each with its own little side table and low crayfire lamp. It was a plush space with bookshelves and a display of elaborately decorated sweets next to what looked like well-stocked bar.

"Is that a wine rack?" Jeanette asked.

I shushed her, but Miss Lockwood shook her head. "It's quite all right. This room was designed to be an oasis for the faculty, where we could not be detected by the students when we needed a moment's peace. It's 'soundproof,' so to speak."

"How many secret rooms does this school *have*?" Robert asked.

We watched as a petite blond girl in a fine linen nightdress carried a crayfire lantern into the solarium. It was indeed Jenny, and she looked to be no happier than she was the last time I saw her. Her usually peaches-and-cream complexion was sallow with purpling shadows under her eyes. While it was petty of me, there was some comfort in that. She'd literally handed the Mother Book over to Miss Morton.

Jenny scanned the solarium, an annoyed expression on her face. She walked right up to the wall dividing the solarium from the teacher's lounge, squinting at it in the low light, as if she could sense there was something not quite right with the invisible magical barrier.

"Can she get in?" I whispered.

Miss Lockwood shook her head. "A faculty member has to give her admittance, and she doesn't seem aware of the entryway."

"To be honest, it seems more like 'Jennifer is in charge of the headmistress than the other way around," Jeanette muttered. "You never would have tolerated such disrespect."

Miss Lockwood smirked as Jenny gave the solarium one last sweep and then slumped out of the room. Through windows of the lounge, we watched the light from Jenny's crayfire lamp travel up the windows of the stairway, towards the dormitory floors.

"Do you think it's safe to leave?" Ivy asked.

"Let's give the girl a few minutes to go to bed," Miss Lockwood said, watching out the window.

"I rather wish I could go with you," Jeanette sighed. "I always thought I would be eager to graduate because I would want to start my life. But now, I want to leave because I'm miserable here. I can't sleep. I don't enjoy classes the way I used to. I just feel something... something is coming, isn't it?"

"It is," Ivy said. "It wouldn't hurt for you and the others from our study circle to pick up the practice again. Defensive magic would be a useful area to brush up on."

Jeanette's face went ashen, even in the low light, as if we were confirming her worst fears. And while I felt bad for frightening her, it was only right to give her and our other friends some warning. We couldn't tell them everything just yet. It was too dangerous. And I wasn't sure they would believe us. Or worse, they might believe us and then panic, and then they might get hurt. Or they might inadvertently tip our hand to Miss Morton and all our plans could be dashed.

"When the time comes, we may call on you for help," I told her carefully. "Will you answer?"

She smiled, her familiar steel returning as she clasped my hand. "I'll keep my eyes on my mirror."

Alicia said, "Talk to the other girls that you trust. We might need them."

"But keep your conversation away from Jennifer," I told her. "You're right not to trust her."

She nodded sharply, eyeing Robert as she curtsied to us. Then she crept out of the teacher's lounge, looking around for signs that Jennie really departed.

"I will miss this room," Miss Lockwood sighed.

"I don't blame you," Alicia said, looking towards the cakes and wine.

Jeanette turned, motioning for us to follow her out of the

teacher's lounge and towards the hallway door. She walked into the hallway, checking again and then motioning for us to exit. We shared one last hug and hurried down the hall towards the kitchen.

"While useful, she shouldn't be sneaking around the school like that," Miss Lockwood muttered as we trooped towards the back door.

"A little perspective, please?" I suggested as we tested the door for magical alarms.

"If the school is so worried about security, why would they put students in charge of defenses?" Robert asked.

"Maybe they think we couldn't possibly be stupid enough to try to break into the school?" Alicia suggested.

"Well," Ivy scoffed. "We showed them, didn't we?"

6

Walking out of Miss Castwell's was considerably easier than walking into it. We simply opened the kitchen door and strode out into the quiet night. No alarms sounded. We heard no shouts of warning from guards. We didn't even see Jenny looking out of a window for us. Frankly, it made me worry for the friends I had sleeping under the school's roof. They were not protected in the least.

As we crossed the lawn, I glanced over my shoulder at the school building, a tired lady reclining against the moonlit dark. And in my heart, said goodbye to it. As much as I missed Miss Castwell's, I didn't belong there anymore. And I wouldn't ever again, which broke my heart a little. I had too much to do. What good were grades and academic guilds when there was a world to save?

Maybe I was being a little dramatic.

Probably.

I was eager to go "home." I missed the farm. I missed the other Changelings. I felt safer with them, even if we did occasionally make things explode. We were together. I had a family there. I'd had parents before, but never a family.

Alicia took the tiller of the air gondola with a little more gentleness, but I thought it was in deference to Miss Lockwood's emotional state than anything else. Our former headmistress looked down at the shrinking image of the school with the expression of someone bidding a beloved parent goodbye. She sat near the back of the gondola, as far as possible from us all, which I took as a cue that she wasn't up for our usual lively, somewhat irritating, chatter.

Robert settled near Alicia, reading over the books we'd filched. Exhausted, Ivy and I slumped against the hull, summoning the will not to fall asleep. Heaven knew what Alicia would do to the boat if she thought we needed a jolt of adrenaline.

Ivy laid her head against my shoulder, sighing deeply. "That was… disheartening."

I nodded. "A sort of shocking splash of reality to the face, wasn't it?"

"We've been separated from our everyday lives for so long, it felt a bit like a dream," Ivy agreed. "But Miss Castwell's, it was our life for so long, and I don't know if we can ever go back. At the same time, I don't know how much that bothers me when we have all this to contend with." She stopped to gesture at the boat in general.

"I was just thinking the same thing," I noted as Robert rose and crossed the boat to show Miss Lockwood something he'd found in his reading.

"I know," she said. "Isn't that strange? I know what you're thinking sometimes, and Alicia, too. Occasionally, I get something from Cathy, but it's pretty easy to tell when she's annoyed with us… which is almost constantly."

When my eyes went wide with alarm, she added quickly, "Not true phrases of thought or anything like that, just impressions. I can feel them, in my head, like my magic is communicating with yours."

"Ever since the attempts with the book?" I asked. "I've felt a flicker of the same with Cathy. But with you, all I sense is how much you miss Owen. It's shocking really, how sincerely you miss someone so loathsome."

Ivy elbowed me in the ribs, making me grunt. "I do miss Owen," she sighed. "I know that sounds silly and sad, but just hearing from Lizzie that she saw us together in her vision. . . I just miss him."

Nodding, I put my arm around Ivy's shoulders and leaned my head against hers.

"I understand," I told her. "I've spent more time away from Gavin than with him, and yet, I spend so much time thinking about him, even in all this mess. There's so much unfinished business between us. He's only just found out that I've been *lying* to him from the moment we met. What if he's decided that I'm not worth the strain of secrets and social upheaval, combined with inherent dishonesty on my part? What if he'd found some other girl who is exactly as she seems? I wouldn't blame him."

"I think you're underestimating my brother," Alicia commented from the tiller. "He quite likes a bit of trouble."

"Thank you, Alicia," I snorted, but I laughed, despite it all. "It doesn't feel right, carrying on a courtship when you two are separated from your... what do we even call them?"

"Special boy... friend?" Ivy suggested.

"Friend who is a boy?" I countered.

"Male companion... malepanion?" Alicia said, smiling and shaking her head.

"This is perhaps why we're too young for relationships," Ivy said, snorting.

"I think I miss my mother," Alicia confessed quietly after a few moments. "Which I never thought would happen. I am still very angry with her, for how she's tried to control every movement in my life since the moment I was born. But I miss the good parts, like the way I felt protected by her. Does that make sense?"

I nodded. There was a lot about my relationship with my

parents that was troubling, but I missed them all the same. I missed my mother's cooking. I missed the way she kept our family going. I missed the way my father never stopped trying, even while it wore him down. I missed Mary's liveliness, the way she threw herself into her enthusiasms headlong, even when they were extremely foolish. Even with her betrayal, I missed my sister. Well, parts of her.

Not for the first time, it struck me that I hadn't spoken to my parents since leaving Coventry. I couldn't imagine what they were thinking now. I hoped that Mrs. Winter was giving them some consolation.

"Your beau lives right down the hall, so we don't want to hear about it," Ivy told Alicia quietly, so Robert couldn't hear.

"Yes, right down the hall… near his mother," Alicia muttered. "Who doesn't think I'm good enough for him."

I laughed, clapping my hand over my mouth and glancing at Robert. He was still going over the books with Miss Lockwood, seemingly unaware that we were talking about him. "That must be very odd. A McCray is considered quite the catch among society's matchmaking mamas. I'm sure your own mother would be quite insulted."

Alicia scoffed. "My ill health always kept me from being a consideration when it came to matchmaking mamas. But it is a little insulting, yes. If Robert likes me, why should that not be enough for his mother?"

"Mothers very rarely take their children's feelings into consideration in these things," Ivy reminded her.

Alicia sighed. "I wish there was a way to get a message to Mother, to Gavin, that was safe, but I know we can't risk it right now."

"I'm sorry, but it will be worth it," I promised. "We end whatever plans Miss Morton has for the world, and then we can try to figure out what the rest of our lives will look like."

Ivy laughed. "Is that all?"

We joined Ivy in her chuckles. We hadn't had such a "quiet" evening since leaving the McCray's home in Coventry. There had been the children to take care of and the chaotic noise of the house. We'd been wrestling with so many life-altering issues lately, it was nice just to sit there and talk about something like boys. Even if that conversation was mixed with concerns about parents, safety, and possible magical world domination.

There probably wouldn't be that many more evenings like this for some time. If we were going to find this Horn of Silence, we were going to have to leave the farm again. It was as simple as that. Could we leave the children behind? Would they be safe? Would that be fair? They had just as much at stake as we did and it seemed wrong to just run off and leave them to wait for us to succeed or fail. I doubted Cathy would be content to sit by and twiddle her thumbs. I'd become so used to others being in my room, at the table with me, running and yelling and laughing.

Mary and I weren't close. The Changeling children had become the siblings I'd wanted, even if they were very, very loud. But we couldn't exactly move swiftly in such a large group. I didn't want to leave them behind, but I didn't want to put them at risk, either.

They reminded me of exactly why I felt that way when we arrived at Hazelcliffe to receive a hero's welcome at the farm, even if we felt like we accomplished very little. We were so tired from the trip that we didn't have the energy to lock the gondola up again. Alicia promised she would do so, before dawn, when she was less likely to be seen at the neighboring farms. We all received hugs and kisses from the children as Cathy hung back, watching the fray. Mrs. Lumpkin attached herself to Robert like a lamprey, fussing over his wind-reddened cheeks. She swore he'd lost weight in the mere hours since she'd seen him last.

"The others thought perhaps you wouldn't come back," Cathy said as she sidled up beside me. Ivy was being overrun by Meggie and Lizzie, who insisted on showing her new dresses they'd made for their dolls. Geoffrey and Joseph were explaining to Alicia how an "incident" with a frog and Miss Lockwood's inkwell was *not* their fault. And they needed Alicia to help explain that to the headmistress, who was sort of slumped in a nearby parlor chair, apparently exhausted by the events of the evening.

"It would have been much easier for you to travel where you needed to go to next without us," Cathy added.

"Cathy thought that, the rest of us didn't," Lizzie protested as she hugged Ivy's side.

Rolling her eyes, Cathy informed me, "I've been thinking, while you were gone. I finally had time to think, without you around, bothering me."

I lifted my brows. "Really?"

"You're always going on about magic being a living thing, yes? Well, maybe we *ask* it for help," Cathy suggested. "We left that bit out, while we were preparing. Maybe the reason magic hasn't been on our side when we've been putting your book together is that we haven't been very polite about it."

I blinked at her, feeling very foolish. "That's a brilliant idea."

"Well, there's no reason to be sarcastic about it," Cathy retorted, clearly insulted.

"No, you're absolutely right," I cried, throwing my arms around her. "We left out the most basic step in any partnership, asking politely for help!"

"Oh, no," Cathy shuddered, struggling against me. "No hugging! Absolutely, no hugging!"

Over Cathy's shoulder, I saw the beveled mirror over the side table glow to life. Mrs. Winter's handwriting was scrawling across the glass in bright orange – the most urgent of colors. *"Incoming. Do what she asks. – A.W."*

What in the world did that mean? I turned to Miss Lockwood, who was also frowning at the message. A knock sounded at the door and the room froze.

Miss Lockwood turned towards the door, her shoulders set

and her blade in hand. Alicia, Ivy, and I followed suit like nosy, well-armed ducklings. Robert and Cathy ushered the children to their pre-assigned "stations" – strategic positions all over the house where they would be safe in case of invasion.

Mrs. Lumpkin grabbed a heavy saucepan from the kitchen and looked very put out that our happy reunion was being interrupted.

Miss Lockwood opened the door to find a striking woman on the other side. Tall and stately, with brown skin set to striking lethality by a well-cut black silk gown. Her jet-colored hair was piled dramatically around a black silk hat with a long quail tail feather curled rakishly under her chin. She wore leather gloves on long-fingered and elegant hands. Her face was carved in lines that were as regal as they were severe.

"I know you," Miss Lockwood whispered. "How do I know you?"

The woman smirked at Miss Lockwood, but only had eyes for me and the other girls.

Well, that didn't make me feel better.

"You must be Miss Smith and her associates," the stranger said, her tone lazy and slightly amused as she took in the way we were gripping our blades. "I am Miss Larkspur Wrathburn. Mrs. Winter sent me here."

I'd never heard of a House Wrathburn, and given how intimidating the name was, I was sure I would have remembered it. There was no hint of her sigils on her clothing, something all well-to-do ladies hid about their wardrobe as a visual reminder of their social clout. This was all very odd.

"How would we know that?" I asked, my blade still raised. "You could be sent by someone else."

Miss Wrathburn chuckled, a note of approval in her voice. "Mrs. Winter said you wouldn't trust me, and good for you. So young Mr. Winter told me to remind you of an incident, only you and he would know about, involving a swing and a book."

I snorted, very indelicately. Technically, Mr. Winter knew about that incident as well, but I doubted Owen wanted to relive that. Ivy looked to me, her dark eyes questioning.

"And what was the result of the swing and the book?" I asked, lips twitching.

Miss Wrathburn winked at me and touched to the tip of her finger to the bridge of her nose. Despite myself, I giggled. When we were little, Owen had left of a copy of a book on his swing in the garden. I'd found it and had begun reading. Owen had been so annoyed that he'd knocked me off the swing. In return, I'd smacked him across the face with the book, breaking his nose.

"What did you do to Owen's face, Sarah?" Ivy asked, though she was snickering. Maybe she felt my mirth, through this newfound link of ours. "How dare you endanger that beautiful face?"

"He said much the same thing," I told her with mock solemnity.

"This place will hardly remain a secret if Mrs. Winter keeps sending every tourist in England to Hazelcliffe," Miss Lockwood muttered as she opened the door just a little wider to Miss Wrathburn.

"She makes a reasonable point," Robert said, pointing at his thumb at Miss Lockwood.

"Why didn't our wards keep you out?" I asked.

Miss Wrathburn gave me the sort of look you would give a puppy, one that you felt sorry for. "Oh, my dear girl, please."

I was left, blinking away the sting of the insult, while Alicia demanded, "Why would Mrs. Winter send you here and why wouldn't she tell us until you arrived on our doorstep?"

"It was a rather sudden decision," Miss Wrathburn informed us, her tone cool and unperturbed. "Sebastian Crenshaw has died."

Miss Wrathburn extended a copy of one of Lightbourne's leading newspapers, *The Beacon*. The headline screamed, "**Senate Luminary Sebastian Crenshaw Dies in Sleep**."

I reached out and caged Alicia's hand in mine. While Miss Lockwood brightened at the news, this was terrifying to us. Eliminating Sebastian Crenshaw didn't mean that the threat of Miss Morton was gone. Miss Morton could change vessels at will, simply hopping into the nearest dead body. This meant that we no longer knew who to guard against. She could be anyone.

Was that why she'd done it? The whole point of Miss Morton burning the first Mother Book and consuming the ashes was to anchor herself in Mr. Crenshaw's body. Perhaps she knew that we were planning something? Maybe she was trying to disguise herself in some new form? Or maybe she'd only destroyed the book to taunt us, make us feel powerless?

This news certainly made me trust Miss Wrathburn less. Her sudden appearance, bearing news like this, didn't make me trust her *more.* For all we knew, Miss Morton could be disguised as Miss Wrathburn, having intercepted her on the way from Mrs. Winter's.

"We're being very rude," Ivy said, shaking her head and giving Miss Wrathburn her best hostess smile. "Please come in, Miss Wrathburn."

"Wait, wait, this still doesn't make sense," I protested. "I'm sorry, but the safety of the people in this home comes before manners, Miss Wrathburn. Why did Mrs. Winter send you here?"

Miss Wrathburn smiled at me, the sharpness of it making me take a step back. "Because you're a Changeling, Miss Smith, just like me."

My mouth dropped open. "Wha–"

"Girls!" Mrs. Lumpkin yelled from the dining room window. "Something is moving out on the lawn!"

We nudged Miss Wrathburn aside and stared out into the darkness. I could barely make out shapes moving in the distance. They weren't walking with any swiftness or purpose, just sort of stumbling through the field, their necks bent as strange listless angles.

I'd only seen one body move like that... a gardener at school who had been murdered, cursed and re-animated by Miss Morton to attack me.

"Oh, no," I whispered. I glanced at Ivy and Alicia, who seemed to understand immediately what we were looking at. Revenants were ambling towards the house, their arms outstretched towards us.

"They're coming from this side too!" Robert yelled from upstairs. "They're approaching from all sides of the house! I count ten on this side!"

"Fourteen from the east!" Cathy shouted.

"What's approaching from all sides of the house?" Miss Wrathburn asked quietly, having drawn her own blade.

For a moment, I was frozen. I didn't know what to do or where to run and I was in a numb state of panic. I'd struggled to kill, well, to re-kill, *one* Revenant. And that had been blind stupid luck, grabbing a random birch branch from the ground to stab it, rather than some other piece of wood that wouldn't have magically purged the parasitic magic from its body. I didn't have any birch branches on me. They were all out in the woods, where branches belonged.

What was I going to *do?*

"Why aren't the wards keeping them out?" Robert shouted. "Is it because the new lady broke them?"

"It's Miss Wrathburn," the lady in question retorted. "And no, I closed them after I came through."

"Have *you* ever designed wards for the re-animated dead?" Ivy yelled.

"No!" Robert confessed in the distance.

"It requires a few adjustments," Miss Wrathburn told us kindly.

"Oh, don't act like you've done it before!" Cathy snapped at her as she thundered down the stairs, which only made Miss Wrathburn smirk.

Meanwhile, I was still in my breathless panic. My hands were frozen. I couldn't seem to feel my feet. I felt the others around me. Alicia and Ivy and Robert and Mrs. Lumpkin and Lizzie. They needed me. I couldn't stand here frozen while they were frightened and in danger. I needed to *move.*

"Everyone, get your escape bags!" I shouted. "Robert! The supplies!"

"What bags?" Miss Wrathburn asked calmly. "What supplies?"

"Miss Wrathburn, with respect, I would suggest you stop asking questions and come along with us. It's going to get quite ugly in the next few minutes," I told her. We ducked inside and closed the door behind us.

Upstairs, I could hear the children running into their rooms to fetch their emergency bags filled with clothes and food. We'd run so fast from the mountain school they'd left with practically nothing. We didn't want them in that position again. After a few minutes, the others trooped down the stairs just as we practiced.

"The air gondola," Alicia cried. "We get everyone into the boat and fly away. This house is clearly no use to us anymore. They know we're here."

"Oh, Mrs. Winter is not going to like us abandoning her house to undead, uninvited guests," I said, shaking my head. "Where would we go?"

Across the house, against the garden doors, I saw pale hands claw at the glass, not quite able to grasp anything like the doorknob. If nothing else, seeing it was a primer for everyone on how these creatures moved. I'd been so panic stricken when I'd faced the gardener, that I hadn't learned anything about them. Revenants might be mobile, but their dexterity was limited. The only good thing about Miss Morton's awful magic, was that Revenants were more blunt instruments than weapons of finesse. Still, it was only a matter of time before they–

We flinched at the sound of a pane of glass shattering in the dining room. More hands reached through the opening of the broken window, clawing at empty air. The sounds they made were horrible – rasping groans like they would speak if they still had the breath in their lungs. Alicia gasped, looking to me.

"We've seen worse," I assured her. She nodded, drawing breath deep into her nose. "Remember that. We've seen worse."

"We need to leave now," I told Miss Lockwood.

"What if it's a trap?" Robert asked, tossing labelled canvas emergency bags to Alicia, Ivy, and myself. "Your Miss Morton could be waiting for us outside the property. The minute we leave, she could pounce."

"Would it be better to stay here and wait for another attack?"

Alicia asked. "Besides, she'll be expecting us to run on foot. She won't expect escape by air."

"You're right." Robert took Alicia's hand and pressed it to his chest. His broad, ruddy face was shiny with sweat, but he was fighting to stay calm, for all of us. It reminded me that I would have to do the same. I took a deep breath and tried to think of the next few minutes as a series of tasks, simple tasks I needed to accomplish to get to the next task of finding shelter for us all – not a terrifying ordeal I needed to survive whilst somehow dragging the others to safety with me.

"Have you stopped to consider that this Miss Wrathburn brought the Revenants with her and she's the reason they've attacked?" Miss Lockwood asked, escorting Lizzie down the steps.

"Yes," I confessed. "I have considered that several times over in the past few minutes."

"Birch!" Lizzie yelled, handing each of us a sharpened birch stake. Birch was used for purifying and made for a handy weapon against Revenants. Robert had prepared these and stockpiled them in the kindling basket in the girls' rooms. We figured we were less likely to accidentally stab each other with them than the boys.

We gathered in front of the kitchen door, the one cozy space we'd shared, where Alicia and Ivy and I regularly found the others gathering for late-night biscuits and milk at the long wooden table. Miss Lockwood watched our every move, her eyes apprehensive. She hadn't been with us long enough to have seen our drills for this situation. On the other hand, Miss Wrathburn simply stood back and watched us, and I had a sinking feeling – adding to the already sinking sensations in my belly – that this was some sort of test. I much preferred Miss Lockwood's watchfulness.

"Joseph?" Robert pulled little Joseph toward the front of the group. He was pale, lanky for his age, with dark curls that always fell over his eyes. Joseph's particular talent was a sort of defensive spell that literally created a concussive bubble that displaced anyone and anything that stood in its way. If "displaced" meant dissolved at the molecular level. Whatever he hit just disintegrated into nothing.

Joseph brandished his branch and his blade in both hands, nodding with too much purpose for such a young boy to bear. The spell required Meggie to cast a counter-bubble that protected us from the blast. I considered asking Meggie to "forget" to include Miss Wrathburn in that protection as she was an unknown, potentially threatening element, but that seemed unethical and cruel.

"The gondola is anchored just past the kitchen garden," Ivy told everybody, her voice quivering a bit. "Stay together, under Meggie's protection. Don't panic. If you start to panic, just look at Mrs. Lumpkin. No one is more terrifying than Mrs. Lumpkin with a saucepan in her hand."

The little ones tittered nervously as Mrs. Lumpkin twirled the pan by the handle. Miss Lockwood looked at us like we were all insane. With a plaintive chirp, Phillip fluttered over the stairs and landed on my shoulder, burrowing into my hair.

"Is this really your chosen weapon?" Miss Lockwood asked. "A saucepan?"

"Well, it's not essential to the plan, but it makes everybody feel better," Cathy replied. "Do you have a better one?"

Miss Lockwood shook her head. "No."

"All right," I said, glancing around at the faces before me. I had to work to ignore the pounding at the glass, the groans, my own fear crawling up my throat like a living thing. "We stay together. It's just a brisk walk across the yard, yes? We're going to be just fine."

The little ones nodded, while the other older children just gave me meaningful looks followed by gulping breaths. I didn't know if I was re-assured or guilty that the others seemed to believe in me so easily. I ignored the dread that fear sparked in me. And I ignored the strange surreal quality of standing in this kitchen, where we'd felt so much at home, knowing there were monsters outside of the door. I took Lizzie's little hand in mine. It was warm and she winked at me. She was confident in my ability to protect her and keep her safe. I wished I had the same confidence in me.

"On three. One," I said as Robert took hold of the doorknob.

"What happens when you reach three?" Miss Lockwood asked.

"Two," I counted. All the children gripped their birch branches like the weapons they were.

"That's a reasonable question," Miss Wrathburn noted. "What happens when you reach three?"

"THREE!" I yelled.

Several things happened at once. Robert flung the kitchen door open. Several corpses stood just outside, wavering on their feet, their gray skin mottled by the grave. They looked to be farmers, possibly locals, given the relatively fresh state of their clothes. Had Miss Morton stolen them from a nearby graveyard? Or had she actually murdered people to enlist as her pawns?

Joseph lobbed a spell at the space just outside of the door. The coiled symbol was blazing red and landed on the flagstones outside with a deafening crash. Meggie raised her blade, casting a calm, sparkling blue shield over us, which protected us from the rippling red energy that exploded from the ground up.

The same could not be said of Mrs. Winter's kitchen, which lost its door, quite a few hanging pans, and the stove. They just dissolved into dust, just as the energy struck them. The bodies outside did the same, collapsing into neat little piles on the ground. This seemed to catch the attention of the other Revenants gathering in the garden. There were eight of them, wavering between us and the gondola. We moved forward as one unit, the bubble staying over us like an umbrella. Miss Wrathburn smiled under its glow, as if she found the whole thing to be quite charming... while we were surrounded by the wandering undead.

As we moved, a few Revenants shuffled towards us, but as long as we stayed under the bubble, we were protected from other magics. Meggie just had to keep up her concentration and we had to avoid breaching the shield with so much as an elbow. In the distance, one of the Revenants, a heavy-set man who'd had white muttonchops that covered his large ears, was batting at the ropes securing the gondola to the ground, as if he was trying to unmoor it. That would leave us stranded here.

It would be simple enough to remedy. We just had to make it to the gondola and force him away from the ropes. I was confident we could accomplish it because Mutton Chops didn't seem to have much luck with knots. But I could see the plan forming in Miss Lockwood's head before she even raised her blade.

"Miss Lockwood, no!" I cried just as she flung a searing yellow symbol shaped a little like a U at Mutton Chops. The good news was it sent the Revenant tumbling to the ground like a western tumbleweed, rolling on and on out of sight. The bad news was that Meggie's bubble had burst and we were left without protection. And the Revenants were creeping closer.

"Oh, no." Miss Lockwood looked stricken as the shield faded into a sizzle of light. Meggie flicked her blade, but her attention was drawn to a slight woman in a worn blue wool workaday dress. The woman's thinning dark hair had partially fallen over eyes that were filmy and grey. I tried to turn Meggie's face away from the sight, but she resisted, whispering, "Mum. I know my mother is miles from here, but she looks like Mum. The hair. It's the same color as my Mum's."

"Meggie, we need you to concentrate," Ivy whispered gently as the Revenants shifted closer. "If you don't cast another spell, we're going to have to fight."

Meggie nodded, but no matter how many times she tried to cast the symbol, it just wouldn't light – like a matchstick in a stiff wind. And the dead were growing closer and closer, their feet dragging through the grass. I could smell them, all mold and grave dirt, as the wind shifted towards us. Miss Lockwood cast another charm overhead, but it just didn't have the strength of Meggie's unique talent. After a minute or two, just as we passed the kitchen garden, it faded away.

"Birch!" Lizzie yelled again. The children gripped their sharpened branches and pointed them outward. We moved like a Spartan phalanx, each ready to defend the person at our sides. It was the first time I'd seen the other Changelings work defensive magic together. They were so young, it was easy to forget that they'd been trained as a fighting force.

"I'm running for the boat. I'll have it ready by the time you reach it," Alicia said.

"I'm staying with her," Robert added. We nodded our assent and suddenly, Robert threw Alicia over his shoulder, hauling her across the ground at twice the speed she could have managed herself. In a normal day, I might have spared a thought for compromise and how if this had happened in public view, Mrs. Lumpkin and Mrs. McCray might have spent the next day discussing engagement plans. But tonight, I was too busy watching Alicia stab at any Revenant that approached them. She hit one well-fed farmer in the center of its chest as they passed. The birch wood did its job and the Revenant crumpled to the ground in a heap. Miss Morton's magic rose out of it like a cloud of dirty kettle steam.

We closed the space they'd left in our ranks just as we reached the Revenants standing between us and the gondola. The remaining six.

It was horrible. I would have given anything to spare the children those next few minutes of violence. We took a step and stabbed out, striking whichever Revenant was the closest. Took another step and stabbed out, and so on. It wasn't the most efficient way of walking as a group, but it kept us from losing our nerve and bolting. Miss Wrathburn fell into formation. I would give her that. She didn't betray us or make it easier for the undead to get us, so I supposed that was a point in her favor, in terms of trusting her.

But if I had Mrs. Lumpkin behind me, armed with a heavy pan, I wouldn't endanger her son, either.

By the time we finally reached the boat, Robert and Alicia had it ready to lift off. Robert practically threw each of us into the gondola, only to have his hands batted away by his mother when he tried to help her.

"I'll manage this nightmare on my own, thank you," Mrs. Lumpkin sniffed.

"What is this?" Miss Wrathburn asked, climbing into the gondola. Behind her, the remaining Revenants moved closer. Miss Lockwood smirked.

"That's everyone! Go now!" I cried, counting the heads in the craft with us. I closed the gondola door. Alicia nodded and touched her blade to the crayfire stone. The gondola shot up in the air, far from the grasping hands of the dead.

Miss Wrathburn dropped to the deck, eyes wild as we rose. She shouted, "What is *this thing*?"

"Just try to look at the horizon," Geoffrey told her solemnly.

Miss Lockwood smashed her ruffled hair back from her face and tried to appear as if she hadn't just had the wits scared out of her. "Well, while I can't take away marks for effectiveness, that was a disorganized muddle of magic. There was no cohesion. There were quite a few moments where members of your own ranks were in danger from your spells."

"That wasn't something our teachers prized, ma'am," Cathy told her. "We weren't meant to work together in the future, so they didn't see the point in us learning teamwork."

"Well, I suppose it's up to me to further supplement your education," she sniffed.

The younger children groaned.

"And I could be of help there," Miss Wrathburn offered.

"Having completed my training years ago, I know what sort of magic they will need to defend themselves."

"It couldn't hurt," Cathy replied.

"You're advocating for us to trust someone?" Robert asked, smirking.

"She did know the story about Sarah and the book violence," Cathy shot back.

"I don't know if I would call it 'violence,'" I protested weakly.

"And Mrs. Winter had to have sent her to us for a reason," Cathy added.

"Well-reasoned, Cathy. Now, is everyone all right?" Miss Lockwood asked, glancing around the boat. "Any injuries?"

"Only emotional," Ivy grumbled, hugging Meggie. "I'm so sorry you were frightened."

Meggie bobbed her little shoulders. "It could have been worse."

"How, exactly?" I asked.

"I don't want to think about that," Meggie said, shaking her head.

I watched Hazelcliffe fade as the clouds gathered between us and the house. It was much sadder to bid this place goodbye, than it had been leaving school. At least tonight, I had a bag of clothes with me, though Mrs. Winter wouldn't thank me for blowing up her kitchen or leaving several bodies wandering around her property.

Wait.

"We forgot the book," I moaned. "The blank book we made. We're going to have to start all over again. I'm so sorry, Robert."

"It's all right," Robert said, smiling softly. "Better that we all got out safely."

"You didn't forget anything," Mrs. Lumpkin told me. From her own bag, she drew out the book comprised of blank pages. "Robert worked so hard to make the covers again, it seemed a waste to leave it behind."

"Mrs. Lumpkin, I could kiss you," I told her. And then I

decided to kiss her plump cheeks anyway. She batted her hands at me, too, but looked pleased.

"You silly girl," she grumbled, plopping down next to Robert on the deck.

"I brought the material we 'liberated' from the school as well," he said quietly, opening his own bag.

"Where are we heading?" Miss Lockwood asked, her arm around Lizzie.

"I have a back-up plan," Ivy sighed. "But you're not going to like it."

I was just so happy that we were all together, relatively safe and unhurt, and that we'd managed to get one thing right. I clutched the blank book to my chest. I missed the Mother Book so much in moments like this. While I was proud of how we'd handled ourselves so far, it was a relief to be able to trust adults to help us, who could give us some guidance. But ultimately, they were just as lost as we were, just as clueless.

I missed the *wisdom* of magic practitioners who had come before me. I wanted it so badly, not just for myself, but for the others, too. I wanted them to be protected, to be guided. I wanted it with everything in my being. I sniffed, hoping the flood of relief and longing coursing through me wouldn't lead to tears. I didn't think the children needed to see that right now. Ivy put her hand on my shoulder, patting it. I could feel her sympathy, flowing from her hand, how much she wanted us to achieve the goal of recreating the Mother Book.

Against my chest, the book began to warm. Alicia slowed the gondola to a hover and stepped forward, placing her hand on my other shoulder. Robert clasped his hand on her arm, and then Lizzie slipped her little hand into his. And then Meggie wrapped her arm around Cathy and on and on around the circle, until all the Changelings were linked. Each of us wanted the book to be reborn, even if the little ones didn't fully understand why. They knew we needed it and they trusted us.

I felt a sort of contraction inside the book, like it was pulling our magic in, and then it expanded. The book jerked away from my chest and hovered over our heads. Miss Wrathburn pushed to her feet and moved towards us.

I grasped Ivy and Alicia's hands. We watched as the book pulled itself apart and the pages began circling in the now-familiar bird patterns. But this time, strands of golden energy began to swirl from each of our hearts, towards the pages, wrapping around the paper like cobwebs. The pages re-assembled between the covers and Lizzie's hair ribbons wound through, securing them. The strands wrapped themselves around the completed book and began to form letter shapes, magical cuneiform, older than the spoken word. I laughed, delighted as I watched the letters flash across the pages, adhering to them, as they had before, when I was chosen as Translator.

The book spun overhead. Miss Wrathburn approached Alicia from the left and placed her hands on Alicia's shoulder and then Robert's. Suddenly, the energy circulating amongst us came into focus, like we'd been blinking into the sunshine and suddenly, we could see clearly. As a Changeling, Miss Wrathburn's magic was like ours – at odds with what was supposed to be – but firmer, decided. Her magic was fully developed and we needed it to balance us out. My dragonfly mark hummed, almost contented, while every other person in the circle flinched – even Robert. Each of them hunched around their hands in pain, as if they'd touched a hot stove. But they never broke the connection with the rest of the circle. We were connected. We were together. We were magic.

The book glowed golden and complete, then floated gently to the deck. We took a breath in as one and the glow faded. Lizzie stepped forward to scoop the book up. She opened the book to a page I recognized, about familiars and how they helped stabilize a practitioner's power.

I burst out laughing, finally breaking contact with the rest of the circle to clap my hands over my mouth. Tears formed in the corners of my eyes and, after the night we'd just had – breaking into the school, fleeing the farm, accidentally re-discovering my long-lost friend – I couldn't stop them from falling.

The book was back, in all its former glory. Joy warmed me through to my toes, even as the cold winds whipped at my hair. We had help, some direction. Like the mentor we needed, the book was *back.*

Cathy hissed in pain, and reddened lines in her palm bloomed black and silver until a dragonfly formed on her hand. Each of the others shook out their own hands, showing the same mark on their palms. Each and every one had a dragonfly on their hands.

"I couldn't resist approaching," Miss Wrathburn murmured, peering down at the book. "You needed me. I could feel it. Is that strange?"

"Not in the group," Alicia assured her.

"It's pretty," Lizzie mused, holding the book up so I could see. "Is Phillip in here?"

The little blue bird peeped lightly as he poked his head out of the hiding place under my hair. I took the book from Lizzie. "Why do you ask?"

"Well, this spells 'familiar,'" Lizzie said, dragging her finger across the letters. "F-A-M-I-L-I-A-R? That's what Phillip is, right?"

"You can read this?" I asked.

Lizzie scoffed, clearly insulted. "Of course, I can. Cathy hasn't had to help me spell out the big words in a long time."

"No, Lizzie, it's not that I don't think you can read, it's just you're not supposed to be able to read this book." I laughed. "The Translator is supposed to be able to read the book, and only the Translator."

"Well, that's stupid," Lizzie informed me.

I couldn't disagree with her.

"I can read it, too," Cathy said, sounding vaguely frightened as she rubbed her palms together.

"Me, too," Ivy whispered.

"And me," Robert said, eyes wide.

Geoffrey and Joseph raised their hands, each showing half of the dragonfly mark. "Us, too."

My mouth opened to reply, but I could only make confused sounds. Very inspiring. We'd all revived the book, so I suspected that we were all Translators. And I was *glad.* It was the one thing I had that separated me from the rest, but I found I didn't want to be separated from them. We were all the same now and there was a considerable comfort in that.

"I can read it, but it's less clear for me," Miss Wrathburn said. "It's as if the words are waving, floating around the page. Perhaps because I remained standing outside of the circle? But I did receive one of your lovely marks."

She held up her palms to show us the now familiar silver dragonfly. The Mother Book wouldn't have allowed her to help us if she'd had bad intentions. She was one of us, whether she liked it or not.

"I will have to get out of the habit of wearing gloves," Miss Wrathburn mused, staring at her palms. "The metal would wreak havoc on silk."

"You just created the Mother Book from nothing," Miss Lockwood marveled, shaking her head at us. "Without casting a single spell, you raised a legendry magical book from the proverbial grave. To be honest, I wasn't sure it was possible, but I wanted you to have a project to keep you occupied and unified. I would tell you 'well done,' but I'm too busy being terrified by the implications."

I flipped through the pages. All the spells that had been Translated before, were back. There were still some pages left blank.

"I'm going to go back to flying the boat," Alicia said, brushing her hands against her skirts, even though it must have stung. "Try not to do any more world-changing magic while I'm over there."

Ivy snickered.

"You really don't plan *anything* that you do." Miss Wrathburn marveled, though her tone wasn't derisive. "Aneira was right. You just bump along through life, crashing into everything you accomplish."

"Technically, we did plan this," I protested. "Just not particularly well."

7

Alicia obviously knew where she was piloting the boat, because she asked no questions as she sped the gondola through the skies. The others piled together on the deck for warmth, slumping from exhaustion. Robert stood by Alicia's side, watching her steer the gondola as if it was the most fascinating thing in the world. To be honest, it probably was, I'd just become immune to the dubious charms of air travel.

I sighed, leaning my head against the hull. The encounter with the Revenants had reminded me of the nature of our enemy. They had brute strength. They didn't fear. They didn't get hungry. They didn't get angry or distracted from their goal. They only did what the necromancer bid. We wouldn't be able to fight that strength with cleverness or social cache. We were going to have to find some new weapon. I only hoped the book could point us in the right direction.

I hardly noticed when we started to descend. I peered over the hull. We were dropping towards a patchwork of fields that were deep, dark green even in the growing pre-dawn light. That patchwork surrounded a large stone manse, with extensive gardens. From the top, the slate roof looked like it had once been a merely "suitable" manor that had been added onto over the years, as the family gained the money and means to become grander. I found I liked the look of it. It seemed more interesting than a house built all at once, by a family that had *always* had means.

Robert and I helped Alicia guide the gondola to the ground as the adults helped get the children to their feet. The house was even more impressive from ground level. It was far larger than Hazelcliffe, with three stories and multiple wings spiraling off the central hall. The windows, dozens of them, glowed with warm welcome. It wouldn't have shocked me to see staff lined up on the elaborately carved stone steps from the garden to greet us – which was a startling thought, considering we were supposed to be in hiding. Surely, the staff didn't greet fugitives like honored guests.

"Alicia, where did you take us?" I asked.

Behind us, a resonant female voice announced, "Welcome to the Bellflower Folly."

I turned towards the gardens and was once again, face to face with one of the most intimidating women I'd ever had the chance to meet. Ivy happened to call her "grandmama".

Mrs. Eugenia Dalrymple was a stately lady with shining silver-gray hair piled high on her head and piercing dark eyes. She was wearing a formal evening gown of dark aster purple, the perfect shade to display her still-smooth, brown skin to perfection. It looked as if she'd just walked out of a dinner party to find a good dozen children crash-landed on her croquet lawn. At least, I thought it was her croquet lawn. I'd never had the chance to pick up the game.

Out of habit, I dropped into a curtsy, and wobbled on my tired legs, nearly dropping the Mother Book. Alicia caught me by the elbow and lifted me, something that would have been impossible when we left school. Mrs. Dalrymple's brows rose, but she only said, "I warned my granddaughter that a friendship with you might be trouble, young lady."

Standing to full height, I turned to Ivy, who flushed guiltily. "I may have been communicating with my grandmother... privately. Alicia and I agreed to the Folly as a contingency shelter, just in case."

I stared at her, slack-jawed. First Alicia and her secret plans with Gavin and now this? "And you didn't think to tell me?"

"You've had so much on your mind," Alicia said, wincing. "We just wanted to take something off your shoulders. Also, the fewer people who knew about it, the more secure the plans would be."

I bit my lip before exhaustion and hurt made me say something I would regret. I couldn't help the sense of betrayal that coursed through me. Yes, I'd kept things from Alicia and Ivy before, but they knew my every thought now. I'd come to understand the importance of it. The fact that they'd kept these contingencies from me because they were concerned that I couldn't handle it? I couldn't decide if I was more disheartened or insulted.

"I don't think I appreciate that," Miss Lockwood sniffed.

"Me, neither," Mrs. Lumpkin muttered.

Oh, no. Mrs. Lumpkin and Miss Lockwood were joining forces. This could only be very bad for us.

"There is room enough for all of you here," Mrs. Dalrymple said. "You are welcome and will be well cared for, I promise you."

Suddenly, Mrs. Lumpkin straightened to her full height. "I know the children best," she insisted. "I should instruct the staff as to their needs."

"Of course," Mrs. Dalrymple said, nodding and inclining her head to Mrs. Lumpkin. "My housekeeper, Mrs. Newton, will meet with you shortly."

Mrs. Lumpkin brightened, because I supposed she expected more of a fight from this grand lady, over control of her household. "I would appreciate that."

"Has anyone else been communicating with people in the 'outside world' without my knowledge?" I demanded, turning to the other children. "I know you're entitled to privacy, I just don't think I can stomach any more surprises or secret agendas."

"I suppose we deserve that," Alicia whispered to Ivy.

"I haven't, because the only person I really know is here," Robert said, nodding toward his mother. She preened and ruffled his dark hair, making him scowl and re-comb it with his fingers.

"I haven't but only because I don't know how," Meggie said.

I closed my eyes and dropped my head. "Thank you, Meggie."

"Now, if that little temper tantrum is done, let's get you all inside and in bed, I assume you've all had a bit of an ordeal," Mrs. Dalrymple said, as Mrs. Lumpkin herded the children towards the house's enormous back door. Cathy and Robert, Ivy and Alicia stayed at my side, but I assumed that it was because they didn't want to miss anything.

"Mrs. Dalrymple, the staff, they can't know who we are and why we're here," I warned her. "And I can't vouch for Miss Wrathburn. I've never met her before. She just showed up to… the house we just occupied."

"That's a rather mean description of Hazelcliffe," a familiar voice said from the direction of the doorway. I turned to see Mrs. Winter standing there in equally formal attire, with her son, Owen, at her elbow. Tall, with his mother's golden hair and the pale skin and aquiline features of his father, Owen broke into a grin at the sight of me. But when he saw Ivy, all that troublesome mirth seemed to melt from his expression and he ran to her. Ivy gasped and threw her arms around him, shrieking with laughter.

Owen Winter had been a frustrating, sarcastic part of my life since I was a small child. My sister, Mary, had been obsessed with him, convinced that somehow, despite all their differences – like Owen not realizing Mary was alive – that they would get married and Mary would one day be the mistress of Raven's Rest. But a lot of that had changed since I'd discovered my magic. Owen definitely took perverse pleasure in deceiving society at large, presenting me as his beloved cousin. Even while he helped me, for the most part, I still considered him the smarmy, conceited spoiled prince he'd always been. But then he'd fallen in love with Ivy, and he'd made her happy. Ivy, well, she just glowed when he was near her, so I was willing to forgive a lot of the irritating behavior of his youth.

Mrs. Winter watched her son embrace Ivy with an oddly conflicted expression. For a woman who liked to control the people in her life like chess pieces, it was disconcerting that her son had formed a relationship without her arranging it. Ivy was from an old Guardian family with plenty of wealth, but not quite the same level of political power as the Winters. At the same time, I was sure that even Mrs. Winter could see that Owen was happy. For all his advantages, Owen was rarely happy.

Theirs was a highly improper greeting, and it did my heart good to see it. Even Mrs. Dalrymple could only clear her throat to remind the two of them that there were witnesses present. I scanned the darkness for some sign of Gavin. I couldn't help it. If Mrs. Winter decided to join us, bringing Owen with her, why not Gavin? Apparently, he was just as much a secret ally to us as the Winters, hatching escape plans and providing the means for us to fly away. And if Alicia and Ivy had their sweethearts along on this adventure – if constant tension and terror constituted an adventure – why not mine? It was a shallow, selfish thought, and I could only blame my low reserves for thinking about it, or for being disappointed that he did not, in fact, appear, smiling before me.

"Mrs. Winter has been here some time, awaiting your arrival," Mrs. Dalrymple told me. "When my granddaughter made arrangements for this contingency, I issued an open invitation."

"Frankly, it was safer for us to be far away from the city at the moment," Mrs. Winter commented.

"It's the fancy lady!" Lizzie squealed, throwing herself at Mrs. Winter's skirts. Mrs. Winter had made quite the impression on fashion-conscious Lizzie when she'd helped us escape Coventry. And to my surprise, Mrs. Winter didn't scold Lizzie for her lack of decorum or regard for her dress. Mrs. Winter only smiled ever so briefly, and patted Lizzie's back, before Mrs. Lumpkin scooped her up.

"Where are we anyway?" I asked Alicia.

"Ireland," she said, grinning at me. "My mother would be *furious* if she knew."

When I titled my head and gave her an irritated look, she grimaced and said, "I'm going to go inside now."

"Um, if you will pardon us, we'll help Mrs. Lumpkin see that the children are tucked in for the night," Ivy said, dipping a curtsy to her grandmother and then Mrs. Winter.

Apparently, fear of missing information wasn't enough to keep my friends nearby for the lecture sure to follow.

Owen cleared his throat. "What she said. Hello there, Sarah."

I lifted a tired hand to wave, but he was already turned and walking towards the house. Mrs. Winter rolled her eyes slightly, but focused her energies on me as her son actually scampered into the house after Ivy. Owen Winter. Scampering.

She asked dryly, "So, you've run into a spot of trouble, have you?"

"Oh, just a surprise visitor – who, for all I knew, could be an agent for Miss Morton, but as you're not physically attacking her, I assume she's expected – showing up at the farm, claiming to be our ally right before an ambush by the shambling undead," I said dryly, making Miss Lockwood snort.

I was so tired, I didn't have time to wonder more about the timing of Miss Wrathburn's arrival and what it meant. How had Miss Morton known our location? Would she be able to find us again here? Would we ever feel safe again? Anywhere? I pinched the bridge of my nose, hoping to ward off the headache forming behind my eyes.

Mrs. Winter glared at our former headmistress, her adversary since the pair of them attended Miss Castwell's together. I sighed. Could nothing be simple anymore?

"Oh, you must admit, Aneira, all of this secrecy has become rather tiresome," Miss Lockwood huffed. "How was poor Miss Smith to keep up with all these schemes within schemes? It was enough for *me* to arrive on her doorstep without warning."

"My doorstep," Mrs. Winter corrected her.

"Then you send this *stranger* into our midst, just as crisis strikes," Miss Lockwood said, nodding towards Miss Wrathburn.

"The crisis being the shambling undead," I added.

"And then *you* show up unannounced with your son in tow?" Miss Lockwood sighed, putting her arm around my shoulders. I wasn't sure, but somehow, I was pretty certain my position was being undermined here, just so Miss Lockwood could needle Mrs. Winter. "You ask too much of her."

"I think you're underestimating your *former* pupil," Mrs. Winter said, putting extra emphasis on reminding Miss Lockwood she was no longer headmistress. "I've noticed she seems to have re-created the Mother Book. How lovely."

"Yes, well, she also managed to completely re-order the way Translators interact with the Mother Book," Miss Lockwood retorted. "Once again, turning magical history on its ear."

"Well, it's not like I did that all on my own," I muttered, clutching the book to my chest.

"Yes, she and her companions drew me into the enterprise," Miss Wrathburn said, raising her hands.

Mrs. Winter shot me a censuring look. "Oh, really?"

"Can we all stop posturing in my garden before the bile you're spewing kills off my perennials?" Mrs. Dalrymple asked. "Let us retire to the library for a hot drink. It should prove quite restorative."

Ivy's grandmother took my arm. "No need to worry about my staff, my dear. Their numbers are minimal and they're paid enough to be very, very loyal. . . And this far out in the country, it would be very odd indeed for them to see a soul to tell of your arrival anyway. That's why we call this place the Folly, you know, because my foolish husband's even more foolish father spent so much money improving a property in the middle of nowhere. Though I will admit the place has its charms."

She opened the doors and we walked into a grand landing of carved double staircases that led to three stories above and another below. To the right, sat a dining room large enough to accommodate even our motley group. To the left, double doors opened to a library I didn't trust myself to enter, for fear of endangering the books. The walls and furnishings were lavish, comfortable, and subtly colored in hues of ivory and rich maple. All was warmed with candlelight instead of the more efficient crayfire lamps. It was a dream home, and I found myself offended on its behalf that it was called a "folly."

"Mr. Winter?" I asked of my former employer.

"Being watched very closely," Mrs. Winter told me quietly. "We can't afford for anyone to suspect that he's anything but a loyal and enthusiastic government appointee, so he stayed in Lightbourne. With Mr. Crenshaw's 'passing,' things are even less stable. I have tried to warn my friends. But the moment I imply that the Grimstelles might have returned or that society as we know it isn't quite as stable as we like to think it is, they change the subject and turn away from me. Katarina Benisse said I was making it up so that I might draw attention from your *debacle.*"

"That sounds very uncomfortable," I conceded. "I'm sorry that you've had to go through that."

"Oh, please," she scoffed quietly. "I couldn't give a fig for what Katarina Benisse thinks of me. Besides, your ordeal has hardly been a stroll through the park."

Mrs. Dalrymple directed us all to the comfortable, red-upholstered chairs situated around the fireplace. I placed the Mother Book in my lap, still unwilling to let it out of my sight. There was a white and gold tea service painted with the Dalrymple sigil, an axe slicing through an oak tree. Mrs. Dalrymple poured a dark liquid from the pot into tiny cups. It smelled a bit like coffee, a drink my mother had occasionally let me try, though mine was mostly milk. I'd felt very grown up while sipping it in the kitchen on a winter's morning.

I took a taste of the cup Mrs. Dalrymple offered me. I blanched at the bitter flavor coating my mouth. I yelped, gagging and cried, "What sort of evil magic is this?"

"It's called *espresso*," Mrs. Dalrymple informed me. "It's Italian."

"A bracing but effective beverage that has aided us in staying awake long enough to greet you," Mrs. Winter noted, smirking.

"Augh," I shuddered, clutching my hands to the chair arms, so I wouldn't wipe at my tongue with a napkin. Mrs. Winter snorted into her cup, sharing an amused look with Miss Wrathburn and Miss Lockwood. Mrs. Dalrymple was smirking as she handed me a cup of plain milk. I was too tired and too disgusted to object. So much for appearing to be mature or worldly.

Ivy and Alicia knocked at the door and I found myself annoyed with them both all over again. How could they hide these plans from me? Had they not considered I might have felt *better,* had I known we had somewhere to run if things went badly at Hazelcliffe? Particularly when things always seemed to go badly for us, given enough time?

"Owen is helping Robert and Cathy put the children to bed," Ivy told us.

"My Owen?" Mrs. Winter commented. "Helping with the children?"

"He's really very good with them," Alicia assured her. Mrs. Winter frowned, sipping her cup without a twitch of her countenance.

When the girls took seats next to me, I didn't bother warning either of them when Mrs. Dalrymple served them both piping hot cups of *espresso*.

"So, how did Mrs. Winter know you were a Changeling?" I asked Miss Wrathburn as Ivy and Alicia recoiled from their own cups, sputtering and waving their hands at their faces. I snickered, making them both glare at me.

I glanced over to Miss Wrathburn, who only seemed amused by my lack of confidence. "Oh, I don't take that personally, my dear. I would do the same in your position. Trust no one, that's how I've stayed alive this long."

"While you may not trust Miss Wrathburn, Sarah, please believe me when I say I vetted her quite carefully," Mrs. Winter said.

Miss Wrathburn smiled. "After you staged your rather clumsy rescue attempt at the mountain facility, where I myself was trained – cold, awful place that it was."

Alicia, Ivy, and myself were united again in tilting our heads quizzically, simultaneously. While Miss Wrathburn had informed me that she was a Changeling like the rest of us, it had quite slipped my mind in all the chaos. Miss Wrathburn had trained at the so-called Crenshaw school? I'd assumed the school was a recent development, but Miss Wrathburn was a bit older than Mrs. Winter.

"Oh, yes, Sebastian Crenshaw's family has 'sponsored' that particular endeavor for some time," Miss Wrathburn said. "Mrs. Winter took the time to review the rosters of politicians' security staff close to retirement and found my name."

"I found a woman who had very little to lose," Mrs. Winter noted. "And asked the right questions. She had rather the same energy about her that you do, Sarah. It was almost familiar, having a conversation with that barely restrained power and unruliness."

I wasn't sure if Mrs. Winter meant that as a compliment or not. Miss Wrathburn didn't look particularly insulted.

"Our clumsy attempt was *effective*," Alicia noted sourly.

"Oh, I applaud your efforts," Miss Wrathburn assured us. "But I simply wish you'd put more thought into them before launching your offensive. Though having seen how you operate for just a few hours, I can see that strategy is not your strong suit."

"I prefer to think of us as flexible and spontaneous," Ivy noted. "There are no training courses for the challenges we have faced."

I looked to Mrs. Winter to defend us, but she simply shrugged. Owen chose that moment to enter the room. There appeared to be a great glob of raspberry (or possibly strawberry) jam splattered across his shirt.

"Oh, that reminds me, I put a bit of toast and tea in each bedroom, just in case the children were hungry," Mrs. Dalrymple said, smiling.

"Why is it always jam?" I muttered to myself.

"I asked Robert and Cathy if they wanted to join us," Owen said, flopping into a chair next to Ivy. "But they said no very quickly and shut their doors in my face."

Mrs. Dalrymple's lips twitched over her cup. Between Ivy's responses and Owen's shirt, this was shaping up to be quite the evening for her. Mrs. Dalrymple served Owen a cup of plain milk. I supposed she didn't have the patience for more *espresso*-based complaining.

"It seems like a waste of our time to keep you up even later for a review of what skills you have and don't have. If you wish to strategize, now is the time, because given the mood in Lightbourne, time is the very thing we are running short of," Mrs. Dalrymple commented, giving Miss Wrathburn a pointed look. "Should we not direct our conversation to a more useful topic?"

"The artifact that you mentioned, in your very cryptic communication, have you found more information?" Mrs. Winter asked.

Alicia nodded, pulling the copy of *History's Musical Magic* from her bag. She turned to the page showing an illustration of a strange horn. It looked like the sort of horn that would be used to start a hunt, with a large ebony bell that led back to a shiny silver mouthpiece. "The Grimstelles called it the Horn of Silence."

"Well, that makes very little sense," Mrs. Dalyrymple noted.

"It's a horn that raises the dead," I reminded her. "Well, technically, it's a horn that lowers the dead. The horn was created as a failsafe. If the elder Grimstelles felt one particular family member was amassing too much power, they would use the horn to permanently dissolve their Revenants."

"As in literally dissolve the bodies?" Mrs. Dalrymple asked, frowning.

"From what I've read, the Grimstelles valued the ability not to leave evidence behind," Owen said.

"You read?" I said, raising my eyebrows, making him roll his eyes.

"Mother, are you going to let her talk to me like that?" Owen asked, gasping in feigned insult.

"It's a reasonable question," Mrs. Winter replied. "I happen to recall your grades from last term."

The indignation on Owen's face was real. Alicia summarized the rest of our findings from the library, including the horn's ability to take away a Grimstelle's power to make Revenants.

"We could neutralize Miss Morton," Alicia said, her voice rising. "Mr. Crenshaw is 'dead' and we assume she's rooted in a new host. If that body is … dissolved through using the horn, she wouldn't have anywhere to go."

"Unless she has another body waiting somewhere in the wings as a contingency?" Owen suggested, prompting a shudder from the rest of us.

In my lap, the Mother Book squirmed like a cranky cat and fell open. The others froze as symbols began to ripple across the blank page, in a wave of gold-turned-to-black. The words "*Magical Archeology*" appeared at the top of the page.

"Can you read it?" I asked Miss Lockwood. She shook her head.

"Why would Miss Lockwood be able to read it?" Mrs. Winter asked.

"It's a long story," Miss Wrathburn sighed.

Ivy's eyes followed the script as it formed across the page. "*Magical Archeology is largely considered to be a fool's errand, in terms of career planning. Magic practitioners across the ages and cultures have delighted in setting elaborate puzzles and traps to prevent others from accessing their treasures. It is not considered a field for those who wish for a long lifespan. However, if you find yourself in a situation where you are solving a riddle set forth by previous generations, remember the founding principal of magic and life – Sometimes, the simplest answer is the correct one.*"

"Are all of these entries so maddeningly unhelpful?" Owen asked. "It feels like we're being mocked."

"It does feel like that, fairly often," I replied.

"How is my granddaughter able to read the Mother Book?" Mrs. Dalrymple demanded.

"We did say it was a long story," Miss Lockwood reminded her.

"My granddaughter is the Translator?" Mrs. Dalrymple exclaimed, smiling broadly.

"She's *one* Translator of many," Miss Lockwood said. Mrs. Dalrymple frowned.

I stared at the pages in my lap. The book had never written anything so direct before. Previous entries had been coy, indirectly leading me to information I needed. This felt like the book was communicating to me, without the contribution of previous magic practitioners.

"What is the book trying to tell you?" Owen asked Ivy, looking at her with awe. Well, more awe than usual.

"That we would be fools for trying to find the horn?" Ivy suggested, peering at the page. "It says right here, 'Some items would be best left lost to time immemorial. It could be considered a kindness to leave them in that state.'"

I chewed my lip, considering. Maybe this was why the book chose to return tonight? We hadn't been able to raise the book before. Maybe the book knew we needed this nudge from it to find the information we needed, during this conversation. Or maybe it just was blind, stupid luck. I wished I could drink the espresso. It might have tasted like liquid evil, but I was sure I would be more alert.

"All of this discussion of the artifact is fascinating, but how is *anyone* to make use of something that's 'lost to time immemorial'?" Miss Lockwood asked.

Mrs. Winter glared at her old schoolmate, and there was heat in it. "I believe this is where I could contribute."

Mrs. Winter paused to flick her wrist towards her bag. It was wordless, bladeless magic. Even though all she was doing was moving a book across the room, it was something we would have difficulty managing. That was advanced level magic.

"The author claims the item is lost because the author didn't have a great-great-grandmother who tracked all of the financial misfortunes of her social class," Mrs. Winter said, motioning for another book out of her bag. It was an old leather-bound journal with gold-stamped letters on the cover, *Clarissa Brandywine.*

"Do you always have to make such a production of things?" Miss Lockwood sighed.

Mrs. Winter rolled her eyes and read from a page of the journal. *"Young Gregory Ramsley turned out to be such a disappointment to his poor parents. Imagine, the scion of one of the most successful families in Hertfordshire having to resort to pawning his belongings in order to pay his debts!"*

"It would appear you and your great-great-grandmother had much in common," Miss Lockwood muttered.

"While young Ramsley had to sell many of his family's treasured heirlooms to settle with creditors, it was particularly distressing to know that he parted with a certain musical instrument from a family line better left unnamed. Ramsley tried to keep his transactions a secret, of course, but I happen to know – on good authority from my ladies' maid who is cousin to the Ramsley housekeeper – that he sold it to old Silas Morton, who is known to collect items of a macabre nature. He's said to be very pleased with his prize and hiding it under lock and key. Tis' fortunate old Silas isn't a stronger practitioner. Should he have the skill or power to make use of such objects, it might spell disaster for society in general."

"A family line better left unnamed certainly sounds like the Grimstelles," Ivy said. "And the bit about the musical instrument seems significant."

"I read an article about a Silas Morton in the library," I said, pulling the page I'd ripped from *Rumors and Mysteries* from my pocket. Miss Lockwood made a strange clicking noise, as if she'd sucked air through her teeth. I gave her an apologetic shrug. "I only noticed because Morton isn't name you see very often in magical society and I wondered if he could be any relation to Miss Morton. Look how much the author wrote about the construction of the ruin near Stonethistle. He goes on forever about all the digging involved. If I was going to hide a priceless, diabolical musical instrument, an underground vault would be my first preferencc."

"So you think that somehow, Silas Morton tracked down an ancient Grimstelle artifact, one that technically belonged to his ancestors, but didn't have the skill to use it, so he just locked it away?" Miss Wrathburn asked.

"Maybe he just liked knowing it was there," I said. "Some people like knowing they have power in reserve, just in case."

"It seems Silas was the last successful Morton," Mrs. Winter told us. "The family fortunes plummeted after his death. His ownership of Stonethistle was all but wiped from the public records. Afterall, the Cavills wouldn't have wanted anyone to know that they bought an estate *second-hand*. After a few generations, people forgot."

"Aneira only found out because she knew which clerks she could demand information from in an imperious manner," Mrs. Dalrymple noted.

"If Miss Morton isn't aware of Silas's former holdings, there's the possibility that Miss Morton is aware of the horn, but not its specific location," Mrs. Winter added. "I mentioned in our last correspondence, Mr. Crenshaw was sending agents to County Shannon, searching for 'property.' Mr. Winter tells me he'd sent search parties there for a few weeks. That seems like a rather large coincidence."

I put my hand on the Mother Book. It would make sense that the book would try to warn us about such a move from Miss Morton. But somehow, if just didn't fit. I shook my head. "Miss Morton is nothing if not thorough, even in non-corporeal form. If she knew there was a weapon that could undo her entire army?

She would have found it and destroyed it by now. And then mocked us to our faces that she managed to find the one thing that would have helped us. She's thorough, but not very subtle."

"That makes sense," Mrs. Winter conceded.

"Wonderful, everything is pandemonium and dire straits," Owen drawled. "What do we do about it?"

"Well, if Miss Morton has been unable to locate the horn, that would be a good place to start – the location. Which Cavill does Stonethistle belong to now?" Ivy asked, giving Owen a light poke to his arm. My eyes darted to Mrs. Winter. I didn't think she would appreciate Ivy laying hands on her boy, but the lady was only looking at Ivy with approval.

"William Cavill," Mrs. Winter said. "He's an odious little man with a completely overblown opinion of his own importance. He's never even served a term in the Senate."

"Callista's father's name is William, isn't it?" Alicia asked.

Ivy made a sour expression at the mention of our own school rival. Callista Cavill and her cronies, Millicent DeCater and Rosemarie Drummond, took great pleasure in bullying Ivy. They mostly ignored Alicia, and after I rejected their one-sided, mercenary brand of friendship, they spread some fairly awful rumors about me. But to be fair, I hadn't done much to save Millicent from a flesh-eating unicorn that attacked our dance class... so... I wasn't sure how to follow up that thought.

"Yes, I believe he's your classmate's father," Mrs. Winter said.

Alicia's smile grew to frightening, manic proportions. "So you're telling me that we get to burgle Callista Cavill's house?"

"I don't think we're going to burgle anything," I said. "I'm certain the ruin is outside. At best, we'll break their wards and violate their expectations of proper guests."

"Maybe we could break into the house, just in case?" Alicia suggested, her eyes wide and hopeful.

"I can't take her back to her mother like this," Mrs. Winter told me.

"This part isn't my fault," I replied, sweeping my hand towards Alicia. "This happened on its own."

"Well, young ladies," Mrs. Dalrymple said, clapping her hands. "I believe we've had enough discussion for this evening. You've given us much to consider. And now, I think you should head off to bed and get some rest."

The "young ladies" all looked at each other, confused.

"And what will you do, Grandmama?" Ivy asked.

"I told you, we have much to discuss," Mrs. Dalrymple informed her. "In the morning, we'll all talk about our plans. Don't worry, dear. We will have things well in hand before you know it."

"If you're going to be discussing plans, I believe we should stay with you," Ivy replied. "We're not going to be sent off to bed like troublesome little children."

Mrs. Dalrymple's chin drew up. "I beg your pardon?"

"With respect, we're the ones who have been taking all of the risk up until now," I told her. "And we're the ones who will likely take the risk in any action going forward. We should have a part in any planning that takes place."

"We are *capable* of planning," Alicia added. "It just happens that so many of our plans go awry because of changing circumstances, in the moment."

Owen stayed silent. It seemed the wisest course of action, honestly. Miss Wrathburn was also quietly watching the proceedings with interest. It occurred to me that Mrs. Dalrymple was still accustomed to the Ivy she'd known before, the quiet Ivy who'd attended Miss Castwell's. Mrs. Dalrymple was in for some surprises.

Mrs. Dalrymple frowned at us, but Mrs. Winter patted my arm. "They have earned the consideration, Eugenia."

"Very well," Mrs. Dalrymple sighed. "We shall *all* retire for some rest."

Ivy rose to kiss her grandmother's cheek.

"Your usual room is ready, my dear," Mrs. Dalrymple told Ivy. "I'm very proud to have you home again." But as she drew close to Ivy, I heard Mrs. Dalrymple whisper, "I told you she was trouble."

We bid the other ladies goodnight and walked up the stairs. Owen had taken Ivy's arm and I missed Gavin all over again. Alicia threaded her arm through mine and squeezed it.

As we walked to our rooms on the luxurious guest floor, I whispered to Ivy, "I thought your grandmother liked me. She was the one who introduced us at school!"

"Well, yes, because you were the talk of the school at the time and she thought perhaps a friendship with you would bring me some social cache," Ivy said as we walked to our assigned rooms in the lengthy guest hallway. "But she also warned me that you were a strange and unconventional girl who seems to cause chaos wherever you go."

"I am oddly hurt by that," I grumbled. "Even if it happens to be true."

8

Despite our cozy surroundings, we didn't have time to get comfortable at the Folly.

To my surprise, the Guardian ladies, and Miss Wrathburn, listened to us and waited until the next afternoon to start planning our next move. And so began a very long and tedious debate regarding exactly what we were going to do, who was going to participate and how we would go about it. This protracted discussion, involving a lot of bickering between Miss Lockwood and Mrs. Winter, only reminded Alicia, Ivy, and me why we didn't involve adults in our plans so far. So far, Mrs. Dalrymple was the adult who was annoying me the least, and she had served me the beverage equivalent of liquid evil.

Miss Lockwood wanted to accompany us to Stonethistle, but Cathy insisted she was needed by the children. Mrs. Dalrymple wanted to accompany us, but Ivy and Mrs. Winter protested, stating that it was too dangerous and she was needed to oversee the safety of her home. Mrs. Dalrymple assumed we meant the safety of the children, and we just let her have that, even though we meant the ability of the Folly to remain standing with the children in it. Mrs. Winter insisted that she *would* accompany us, considering that Owen was planning to go, but both Owen and Miss Lockwood agreed that was a terrible idea – for entirely different reasons.

Eventually, it was decided that Miss Lockwood, Miss Wrathburn, and Mrs. Dalrymple would stay at the Folly with the children. Owen and Mrs. Winter would accompany us to Stonethistle. Cathy had seemed determined to be part of the second "mission," but, as we were packing the gondola to leave for County Shannon, she pulled me aside.

"I don't want to leave them," Cathy said, her face more vulnerable than I had ever seen. She watched as the children played in the gardens, thrilled to find yet another place they could consider "safe."

"It feels like we're leaving them unprotected," Cathy added. "I feel better, knowing Miss Wrathburn is here. Ever since she helped us with the book, I've felt more settled, knowing she's with us. It's nice having adults we can trust, but …"

"There's nothing like seeing to it yourself?" I suggested.

She nodded, relieved. "Exactly."

"Then stay here, work with the Mother Book," I replied, trying very hard to keep my voice casual. "Help the others Translate as much as you can so we have what we need when we get back."

"You would trust me with the Mother Book?" Cathy exclaimed, as Robert nudged past her with a barrel-sized bundle Mrs. Winter had packed for us.

"Of course, I do!" I exclaimed. "You're a Translator, too. You have just as much right to it as I do."

A strange metamorphosis took place on Cathy's face and for a moment, I was afraid she was going to cry. She threw her arms around me and for the first time, I felt like I'd actually connected with her, as surely as I was with Ivy and Alicia.

"Thank you," she whispered as I awkwardly patted her back. I didn't think Cathy understood how relieved I felt, being able to share the burden of the Mother Book with other people. I hoped I could help her see the joy I felt in not being alone with it.

We tried not to make a production of leaving, quietly taking off in the air gondola as Miss Lockwood was overseeing bedtime. It was better to leave under cover of darkness anyway. As we rose, I could see Lizzie and Meggie sitting at Mrs. Dalrymple's side in their room, reading over a fairy story. I smiled at this image, so calm, so *normal*, blinking quickly as it faded away.

"You've grown quite attached to them, haven't you, my dear?" Mrs. Winter asked quietly as Alicia carefully piloted us upwards. None of us wanted to test how air-sick Mrs. Winter might become.

"What happens to them after this is over?" I asked her. "Lizzie hasn't seen her family since she was taken to the school. She says they live in Liverpool, but it's been years. What if they've moved?"

"I will make sure each child is returned to their parents," she assured me. She nodded to Robert. "For the older children, if they wish to find positions, Mr. Winter and I will help them find them. If not, we will help them find a way to finish their education properly, to find a trade, if they wish it. They will be taken care of, Sarah."

"And what of me?" I asked, leaning against the hull. "I don't know what I will do. I'm not a servant anymore. I'm definitely not a lady. I'm not a child. What do I *do* with the rest of my life? Open a shop? Go back into service? And if I did, what family would have me?"

"I'm not sure there will be research guilds when all of this is over," Mrs. Winter replied. "You would certainly be asked to join one."

"I don't think I would be welcome," I replied.

"Surely, you knew there would be consequences for all this. Changes. Did you honestly think the world will be the same if you defeat Miss Morton?" Mrs. Winter scoffed.

"I hadn't thought ahead that far," I confessed. "I only thought of keeping myself, my friends, the children safe. I haven't had the luxury of long-term planning, even though I do believe this world needs to change. I'm just not sure I'll be around to see it. I'm not sure I'll survive the confrontation with Miss Morton. Every time we meet her, she seems to get stronger and I… I could die in the attempt, Mrs. Winter. We all could."

"And you've simply accepted this?" Mrs. Winter demanded.

"No, it's just–" I suddenly changed the topic. "Do you ever regret the decision to send me to school, to create this false life for me?"

She blinked at me. "Well, I won't lie. There have been moments when I wondered if it would have been worth the risk to my reputation to just hand you over."

"I knew it," I muttered dryly.

"And yet, you're correct, this world needs to change," she said, sighing. "And not just because the way you're treated is wrong, but because we Guardians have become far too comfortable in the way things are. And Miss Morton can't be allowed to continue this assault on our way of life. She's hurting people. She abuses magic. She's betraying everything we're supposed to stand for. And we'll never grow if we just keep doing things the way we always have, never advance. Look how we derailed technological developments because of our own fear. It will be better this way. This new world will be different, but it won't be boring."

"Well, I'm not going to give up," I swore "I wouldn't be here if I had. I'm just saying, I don't think it's going to go very smoothly."

"And yet, you're trying anyway," Mrs. Winter said.

"Yes."

Aneira Winter reached over and squeezed my hand, and she actually smiled at me. It was unnerving. "You're a very brave girl. Rash and occasionally silly. But brave. And if you have trouble finding a place after this is all over, you'll always be welcome in Raven's Rest."

"Really?"

"It would just be so boring without you," she drawled.

I chuckled as the whisps of clouds covered the boat and we sailed into the skies.

~

I WASN'T EVEN aware that the Winters owned property in Ireland. I certainly hadn't expected this modestly-sized limestone house in a quiet corner of Limerick – just a few hours ride away from the Cavills' estate. We landed quietly in the back garden and carried our bundles in through the smoke-stained kitchen. The doors were open and I could see all the way to a small, practically casual dining room. It was nicer than my own home back in the Warren, but still a far cry from the cold, formal rooms of Raven's Rest.

Why would the Winters need something so unassuming and comfortable? And why couldn't we stay longer? We were only planning to be there a few hours, using it as an operating base while we raided the Cavills' country home. I thought it was shame.

"No one knows we own this property," Mrs. Winter told me, locking the backdoor behind us. "We only purchased it last month, just in case we needed a place to retreat to, given all the … kerfuffle. But it has been prepared for our arrival."

Before I could ask what that meant, we stepped into the dining room and found my parents waiting in the nearby parlor. I shrieked and Robert pivoted himself in front of us, as if my father was some sort of threat.

Papa looked better than I had seen him in years. His eyes were clear and his cheeks were flushed with a healthy glow. He looked years younger. Both he and Mum were dressed in the clothes they only wore when they weren't working, their "summer fete outfits." I was touched that they took the time, and shoved Robert aside to throw my arms around them.

"I've missed you so much!" I exclaimed as they hugged me

tight. While they were dressed up, they smelled just as I remembered, of soap and liniment and exhaustion.

"We've been so worried," Mum whispered into my hair. "Mrs. Winter has told us what you've been up to."

I snorted into Papa's worn wool jacket. I couldn't help it. The way she'd said, "what you've been up to," like I'd been embroidering inappropriate samplers. It made me giggle.

I cleared my throat. "I've been very careful, I promise."

"Well, we don't like it at all, young lady," Papa told me.

"I'm sure that you don't," I said. "But it has to be done. There are far too many Changelings out there. Like Robert, here."

I waved Robert forward, motioning towards the hulking teen standing by the door, not quite sure where to look during this emotional exchange. "He's like me. There are a lot of children like me."

"Hello," Robert said awkwardly, shaking my father's hand.

"It's so hard to believe that," Mum sighed, pushing my hair back from my face in a gesture so familiar it made my heart ache. "We thought you were the only one. If we had known, maybe we wouldn't have panicked."

"Well, there were a lot of reasons the Guardians didn't want us to know," Papa interjected. "It doesn't go along with their whole 'special bloodlines' story, does it? We'd be a lot harder to bully around if we knew that they weren't the only ones with magic."

My brows rose. Behind me, Owen cleared his throat.

"How are you, Mr. Smith?" Owen asked.

It was a marked difference from how Owen normally spoke to my father. He'd never been rude exactly, but like most Guardians, he'd always just called both of my parents "Smith." I didn't know if he was trying to be more polite because of Ivy's presence or influence. But I chose to see it as a step in the right direction.

"Just fine, Mr. Winter, thank you," Papa said, tugging uncomfortably at his collar. "How was your trip?"

My father was not accustomed to parlor small talk.

"Oh, just fine, just fine, thank you," Owen said. "May I introduce Sarah's companions? This is Miss Alicia McCray and Miss Ivy Cowell."

I turned and realized that while they'd known my secret for some time, Ivy and Alicia had never met my parents.

"Yes, I'm sorry," I said, putting my hands out to my friends "Mum, Papa, these are my dearest friends."

I motioned them over. Alicia and Ivy eagerly moved in close and my parents visibly stiffened. Mum began to drop a curtsy and Ivy shook her head. She took Mum's hands in hers and squeezed them affectionately. "Oh, please don't bother with that."

Alicia grinned up at Papa. "We feel like we know you already. Sarah is like family to us."

"Just don't ever tell your mother you said that," I muttered, making my own mother frown.

Overhead, there was a noise, as if someone dropped something on the floor of the room above us.

Oh, no.

"Who's upstairs?" I asked carefully, though I was pretty sure I knew the answer.

"Mary is here," Mum told me carefully.

"What?" I whispered. "What's she doing here?"

I hadn't quite forgiven my older sister for acting as an agent for Miss Morton-slash-Mr. Crenshaw, believing that she would be elevated to her own place in magical society's first circles. Over the last few months, Ivy and Alicia had tried to talk me through my angriest moments, reminding me of the weight that my condition had put on Mary for her whole life. She'd never been the center of attention. So she created this fantasy world, where she and Owen Winter would live happily ever after. But it still stung that my own sister had tried to hurt me so badly.

"Well, Mrs. Winter couldn't exactly leave her at Raven's Rest, could she? She knows to keep to her rooms while you're here," Mum whispered, glancing at her employer.

"Sarah, dear, we really should be going," Mrs. Winter said, checking her pocket watch. "I've packed some appropriate clothing for you. Robert just carried them into an upstairs bedroom for you girls to change."

I nodded. Right, clothing. Because I was carrying out a mission that was essential to magical society and didn't have time to worry about sibling betrayals. Priorities.

"We'll be back in a few minutes," I told my parents.

As Alicia and Ivy and I walked up the stairs, I heard Mrs. Winter tell my mother. "For the time being, you will be the only occupants of this house. I know it will be difficult without help, but it's imperative that your location be a secret. If Sarah thinks you're in danger, she won't be able to concentrate on what she needs to accomplish."

My mother scoffed at Mrs. Winter. "Compared to Raven's Rest? I could run this place in my sleep."

It was the most dismissive, disrespectful thing I'd ever seen my mother do in her employer's presence, and Mrs. Winter didn't even bat an eyelash. Things were changing between them, between all of us. The boundaries were blurring. I couldn't help but think it was a good thing.

I walked onto the landing to see my sister standing outside one of the guest rooms, wringing her hands. My first instinct was to plant my fist in her perfect, pink-cheeked face. How dare she? How dare she stand there healthy, whole, and beautiful when she'd done everything she could to pull the rug out from under my already precarious life?

"Um, we're going to go… somewhere else," Alicia whispered, disappearing into the guest room. Apparently, they didn't want to be witnesses to violence.

I stalked towards Mary, who raised her hands. "I know that you're angry with me."

"Oh, good, you can detect the anger in my face and voice," I shot back.

"I know I was wrong," she said, shaking her head. Her blond curls fell out of the knot at the nape of her neck and it occurred to me that this was the messiest I'd ever seen Mary. Her dress was only half-ironed and her fingernails were bitten to the quick. She had to be aware that Owen was in the house and yet, she'd taken no care with her appearance. She hadn't bolted for the stairs, and she had to have heard his voice earlier.

I eyed her suspiciously. "Go on."

She swallowed thickly. "You don't know what it was like. If Mum wasn't praising you for being so brave, she was clucking at me for not doing enough to take care of you. I never could work hard enough, be good enough to suit her."

My mouth dropped open. "She praised me?"

"Of course, she did," Mary said, rolling her eyes. "Sarah, who never misbehaved. Sarah, who did her best, even when she was sick. Sarah, who was always so polite–"

"Well, she never said those things to me!" I exclaimed. "She used to brag on all the work you could get done in a day, when it took me all day just to clean one room."

"Well, she never praised me, either!" she shot back. "At least, not in front of me!"

I burst out laughing, clapping my hand over my mouth. I wasn't even sure why I found that funny, but I didn't want her to see me laugh. I wasn't ready to be that vulnerable in front of her yet, but it seemed to encourage Mary, who forged ahead.

"I know, I went too far. I know I did things that are unforgiveable," she said, glancing at the staircase. "I can't even explain what I did back in Coventry. I just wanted something that was for *me*. Something that showed that I was special too. It just seemed so unfair. All your life, you were set apart, and then you get magic, too? You get to go to school with the fancy girls and become a lady? I was angry, and stupid. And I didn't realize how angry and stupid I'd been until Mrs. Winter brought me home and I saw the look in Mum and Papa's eyes. I thought I knew what disappointment looked like before, but it was nothing compared to them knowing that I'd hurt you on purpose."

"I haven't exactly been thinking kind thoughts about you, either," I muttered.

"I've spent these months thinking about all the stupid things I'd done," Mary said. "I'm sorry, Sarah, truly. I know you'll probably never forgive me. But I just need you to know how sorry I am."

I considered that for a long moment. Mary hadn't bolted for Owen. (Ivy would have had a great many things to say if she had.) And Mary hadn't made excuses. She'd given her reasons for doing what she'd done, but she seemed to recognize that she wasn't justified. I reached forward and took her hand.

"I'm not ready to forgive you entirely just yet," I told her. "And I'm sorry if that's not what you want to hear. I'm just not ready yet. One day, I may be ready, but just not now. I'm sorry that I hurt you, even if I wasn't trying to hurt you. I'm sorry I didn't realize it. There's no excuse for it. But I think we can move forward, if you continue to think about what you've done and what you can do differently now, so we don't hurt each other."

She smiled tremulously. "I agree."

"The best way to start is to stay up here for the next hour or so," I told her.

She nodded, retreated to her room, and closed the door behind her.

I didn't know if I would be able to speak freely with my sister again. I didn't know if I wanted a relationship with her, but she'd apologized. And that meant something.

AFTER SOME TIME, the three of us trooped down the stairs, a little disoriented by our "breaking and entering" costumes. None of us had

ever moved so freely, without skirts or heels to slow us down. We were wearing dark breeches and black jackets, so we were less likely to be spotted while moving around the estate. I could only assume Mrs. Winter and Mrs. Dalrymple had raided the attics of the Folly to find clothing in our sizes. Having been given caps, we all tucked our hair up, so if anyone saw us, they wouldn't realize we were female.

Robert was sharpening fresh birch branches from the garden with a large utility knife. Alicia and I joined him at the table, making additional weapons for Mrs. Winter and Owen. Robert very deliberately kept his eyes trained on his knife, though I wasn't sure whether it was to show respect to Alicia or prevent the loss of a thumb. My mother bustled in from the kitchen with a pot of tea and nearly dropped it.

"Sarah, what on Earth are you doing?" my mother exclaimed. "Your ankles are visible!"

"Preparing for a life of crime?" I suggested, adjusting my cap. Owen came running into the room, wearing his own dark clothes. When he saw Ivy standing near the table, his face went pale and he actually had to grip the doorframe for support.

"I don't think this venture is a good idea, poppet," Papa said, eying Owen balefully.

"I quite like it. If I'd known how comfortable they are, I would have put them on years ago!" Ivy exclaimed, turning this way and that, enjoying the freedom of movement. "I wish we could *only* wear breeches!"

Owen looked like he was about to faint at the very idea. He cleared his throat, looking for some distraction.

"What are these?" Owen asked, nodding at the stakes. "Are you planning on taking up carpentry as one of your many ladylike accomplishments?"

Alicia laughed. "If only. These will come in handy during out excursion to Callista's estate."

Owen turned to me, his expression confused, and I told him,

"A sharpened birch stick is what saved me when a Revenant attacked me at school. I want us to be prepared."

"You're frightened, aren't you?" Owen commented. "You've been so quiet since we arrived at the Folly. You've only taken half of the opportunities you've had to mock me. That's a shockingly low percentage."

"I think it would be foolish not to be afraid," I replied quietly. I didn't want my parents to know exactly how frightened I was. That certainly wouldn't help them.

"My father, for all his faults, has always told me that brave people aren't the ones who lack fear," Owen told me. "They're the ones who try to do the right thing, the difficult thing, even when they could lose. They try, even when they're afraid. I've always thought he was wrong, that those people are idiots. But I'm starting to understand his way of thinking."

"Are you telling me that you're an idiot?" I asked. "Because I've always known that."

"Sarah! I'm trying to be emotionally mature!" Owen groused. I snorted with laughter as Ivy giggled and kissed Owen's cheek. He flushed bright red.

Mrs. Winter practically floated down the steps, wearing a black bombazine gown with full skirts. She looked like she was ready for a night at the opera. Simultaneously, our eyes traveled from our own simple outfits to Mrs. Winter's ensemble.

"One has to maintain some standards, even under unorthodox circumstances," Mrs. Winter sniffed. "Besides, I've maneuvered more difficult situations in these clothes than you girls could ever dream of. These *are* my comfortable clothes."

"She does realize we're probably going to have to cross several pastures, doesn't she?" Ivy whispered.

I shook my head. "I don't think she does."

9

For the rest of our "adventure," we took to land. Robert carefully guided our wagon out of town and into the countryside. Owen sat on the driver's seat next to him, a cap pulled low over his face.

It occurred to me that Owen had no idea how to help. He'd never driven anything before, but he was too proud to be left in the back of the wagon with his mother. What a strange experience that had to be for him, I thought, being helpless and not in-control. Not being of use. It was amusing really, but not a helpful thing to tell him.

"Do you think they have wards on the entire property?" I asked as we passed the main gate for Stonethistle. It was an elaborate iron affair, all curlicues and flourishes, perfectly suited to metal workers like the Cavills.

Mrs. Winter shook her head. "Only a Drummond could cast wards on an estate covering this much ground, and Drummonds charge too much for William Cavill to invest such an expense in a country estate."

"Even with an object like the Horn of Silence buried there?" Ivy replied.

"I'm not entirely sure that William knows it's here," Mrs. Winter said. "I think he would make it known if he did. He likes throwing his weight around, impressing people with his wealth. There was a dinner party a few years ago, oh, something hosted by the Benisses. I was unfortunate enough to be partnered with William and he bored me near tears talking incessantly of a painting he'd found of one of his ancestors. Because it highlighted what he called 'the noble Cavill chin.' Five dinner courses of nothing but 'the noble Cavill chin.' A man like that wouldn't be able to keep possessing a highly prized magical artifact to himself."

"That stands to reason as much as anything else we've experienced in the last few days," I mused.

"Would we know right away, if we set off a ward?" Alicia asked. Robert stopped the wagon near a low stone wall that appeared to protect a sheep meadow, far from the house. We climbed out, again astonished by the ease with which we could do so in pants.

"Without risk, young ladies, there is no reward," Mrs. Winter told us as we helped her down to the ground. True to her word, she was just as nimble climbing around in her voluminous skirts as we were in our pants. "You can't be afraid of a little thing like breaking and entering when you've already survived Revenants and necromancers."

"And Miss Shelton," Alicia added, shuddering. "Our literature teacher. She was such an awful stickler for grammar."

Mrs. Winter, for once, didn't know how to respond to that.

"This is what she does when we're about to do something ill-advised," Ivy told Mrs. Winter, making our "chaperone" smile. "She makes non-sensical jokes. It helps her cope."

"As if I'm the only one who does that," Alicia sniffed.

"All right, all together now," Mrs. Winter said, grinning as she raised her blade. She cast the symbol that loosely translated to "un-hide" at the fence line. If there were wards there, we certainly couldn't see them. Alicia raised her blade and cast a cloaking spell over us. The faint silver light rose over our heads like a dome and shimmered down to the ground. When we moved, it stretched outward to maintain our space inside. Owen and Robert followed us silently, and I felt better, knowing they were at our backs. Well, they had Alicia and Ivy's back. I felt rather alone.

In that moment, I truly missed Gavin. It would have been so comforting to have him here, making suggestions, calming me with his gentleness and his sense of humor. I missed him in a way I didn't think I'd ever miss anyone. I felt appropriately vulnerable, out here in the dark, especially after the incidents with the Revenants. I didn't know what I would do if I'd had to do this alone. No amount of magical light would have made me feel better. I adjusted my grip on Wit, grateful for my weapon and its magic. I noticed that Mrs. Winter was watching me, out of the corner of her eye.

Stonethistle came into view as we walked over a rise in the landscape. The mansion seemed to match Callista's personality. Even in the moonlight, we could tell it was hewn from dark stone and slate. The design involved a lot of decorative iron-and-stone statues of griffins holding hammers on the corners of the roof. It was somehow both fussy and foreboding. I knew that Callista hadn't grown up here, but it certainly reflected what I'd expected of her family. All show, no softness.

Silently, Ivy and Alicia and Robert moved towards me and together, we cast the symbol for "FIND." Alicia thought it was very important that we thought of the spell in all capital letters. We hoped that through the unified magic we developed from raising the Mother Book, we could focus on the Horn of Silence and its location would be revealed. We didn't know what would happen if we mixed our magic with the Winters', so for now, we held them in reserve. I felt my magic bumping against the other Translators' as surely as I could feel Alicia's elbow in my ribs. I could even feel Robert's, though it was less sure than my two close friends. Our magic was one living force and we could do anything with it. It was a gift, to be able to feel them in the dark. I *wasn't* alone in this.

There were lights on inside the house. Even if the family wasn't home, the servants were, and we certainly didn't want to have conflict with them. Fortunately, the magic symbol we cast was a sort of light misty gray, something that could be mistaken for fog if they happened to see it. The symbol sank into the ground with a fizzle.

"Is that all?" Owen asked quietly. "A bit anticlimactic, isn't it?"

"Just wait," Mrs. Winter murmured.

"Ow!" I hissed, as Wit heated up in my hand, sending burning pain along my mark.

"Shh!" Robert cautioned me.

"I'm sorry! It burns!" I whispered back, just as Alicia and Ivy sucked in their own pained breaths. Their blades were glowing in their hands, just as Robert's was now. I could feel the blade pulling at my hand, like an agitated mother guiding me safely across the street. We were being led toward the house, to my horror, but just as we reached the outer edges of the overly formal gardens, our hands were collectively jerked to the left and we were guided towards a false Grecian ruin.

It seemed odd to me that one would take the time and expense to build something that was supposed to look like it was falling apart, but there it was, broken statues and a fake broken edifice of a fallen palace. The only thing that was intact was a fountain, a rotund Greek man holding a bunch of grapes, spewing water into the air from his mouth.

"That's just strange," Owen commented. We all nodded in unison.

Suddenly, a line of low grayish flames sparked from Robert's blade. It zipped along the ground about six feet until it split and formed a rectangle the size of a manor door. We managed not to make any noises as we jumped back, but it was very close.

"This is it? But it just looks like grass," Owen objected under his breath.

I looked to Ivy and Alicia, who merely shrugged. Unsure of what else to do, I raised my hands, spreading my fingers and mimed pushing a heavy object away from my body. The patch of grass outlined by flames sank and moved with a soft grinding noise.

Mrs. Winter's pale brows rose in the moonlight. "Bladeless magic. Quite the advancement."

I shook my head. I hadn't even had a spell in mind. I just wanted the ground to move. It felt… effortless. I didn't have to make sigils or think of spells. I simply willed an object to do what I wanted. The very idea was intoxicating… and terrifying. This felt like too much power, too soon. If we could move earth embankments with our minds at fifteen, what would we become?

No. I didn't have time to worry about that now. I had a priceless artifact to steal.

I stepped toward the hole in the earth, like a mouse wandering into the open maw of a lion. The stone steps felt raw-edged under my feet, as if they'd never been trod over before. The air was musty and cool, with the underlying scent of something… not quite right. I had a sudden horrible suspicion that Silas Morton had somehow managed to leave a Revenant in the vault with the horn as some sort of trap. The cloaking spell remained over the door like a bubble, protecting us from being seen from the house.

The chamber was octagonal shaped with a large mirror occupying each wall. The stone ceiling, which felt uncomfortably close to our heads, was inscribed with magical runes I didn't recognize. But they made me feel… uneasy. This was not a good place.

I listened, but I didn't hear the shuffling steps of the undead, which I took as a good sign – but that was the only nice thing I could say about it.

The chamber felt airless, even with the hatch open. Mrs. Winter cast a spell for illumination, which landed on the stone floor and cast a faint purple light. It was magnified by the mirrors, giving us an eerie glow to work by. I'd hoped perhaps that finding the chamber would be enough, that we would walk down the steps and the horn would just be resting on some decorative, not-booby-trapped-in-any-way plinth and we could simply snatch it and disappear into the darkness.

But no. It appeared that Silas Morton had designed this chamber as some sort of puzzle, to test whether the person seeking the horn was smart enough or informed enough to take it. Or perhaps this was simply an entrance to the real puzzle that lay behind some other protective layer of magic and traps. I was suddenly very tired, but at least I didn't have the weight of a heavy evening gown dragging at me.

I loved trousers.

Mrs. Winter frowned at her general surroundings. "All of the charm of a tomb."

"I've never liked the Cavills," Owen sniffed.

"Well, they didn't build it. They just own the property over it. Either way, we need to figure out where the horn is hidden in this room," I said, gesturing at the mirrors.

"I don't suppose there's a sign on the wall that says, 'Possibly evil musical instrument here'?" Alicia asked, waving her blade around the room.

"I suddenly understand why your brother is so exhausted all of the time," Owen told her.

Owen nudged her slightly with his elbow as he passed and Alicia looked pleased with herself. Owen had taken to treating Alicia much like Gavin did – like she was something precious, but potentially dangerous and definitely annoying. It was rather sweet. While Robert narrowed his eyes, Ivy just shook her head, snickering. Even in a moment as fraught and potentially lethal as this one, I realized that – if we all survived the coming months – I would dearly miss living and working so closely with my friends. My family.

Right. Potential nostalgia, later. Life-threatening adventure, now.

I had to assume the horn would be hidden behind one of the mirrors. They looked normal enough, just panes of reflective glass you would see in any looking glass. And they all looked the same, except that each had a little symbol carved into the top of the stone frame. The symbols weren't magically significant. A musical note, a lily, a skull, a crescent moon, among others. Other than that, the room had nothing that would indicate how we might choose which mirror.

Somehow, this was even more intimidating. What if I chose the wrong one? What if I put us in danger? What sort of horrors would the Cavills use to protect something so valuable and dangerous?

"This one has a musical symbol over it." I nodded towards it. "Could it really be that simple?"

"*Sometimes, the simplest answer is the correct one*," Mrs. Winter quoted the Mother Book's entry on archeology, peering at the mirror. "I don't see how this mirror is any different from the others. We might as well try it."

"Any volunteers?" I asked. Mrs. Winter sent me a withering look. "I think you should know, technically, I'm not the only Translator anymore."

"Leadership means the risk lies on your shoulders, my dear," Mrs. Winter countered.

"Am I the leader, really?" I asked. "I like to think of us as more of a collective."

Now, Ivy and Alicia were glaring at me.

"All right." I sighed and raised my blade. "Stand back, just in case."

The others arranged themselves behind me. I sent out a sigil for "break" and the mirror splintered as if I'd punched it. The glass fell to the floor in a glittering pile and green viscous fluid rushed out of it like pus from a wound. It smelled like the ocean at low tide, like drowning and decay. The was a large open room behind the mirror, filled to the ceiling with this strange liquid. It was rushing towards us, as if it was sniffing us out.

"Don't let it touch you," Mrs. Winter barked at us. "Move back towards the steps!"

Instead, Alicia flicked her wrist and a barrier formed around us, diverting the flow of the murky green liquid like a geometrically shaped river around the chamber. Robert, Ivy, and I drew the sigil for a Reversal spell together, and it made a much larger single symbol that flew towards the broken mirror. The green fluid was sucked back into broken glass and the pane reformed, as if we'd never broken it.

"Nasty bit of magic," Mrs. Winter mused. "Well, it's a combination of magic and chemistry. Highly corrosive acid, enchanted to seek out and cling to organic material. If it touched your skin, there would be no treatment, only pain and eventual death."

"What sort of person puts that in their garden!" Robert exclaimed. He turned on Owen, who threw his hands in the air.

"I'm not friends with them!" he exclaimed.

"Shh!" Mrs. Winter hissed.

"How did you know we would cast the Reversal?" I asked Robert.

"Seemed like the right thing to do," he said, shrugging. "It was one of the first things they taught us at school. And I just had the feeling that it was what you were going to do, just like I knew that my Alicia was going to make the acid split away from us."

I grinned at him. Owen looked a little put out. And I supposed I couldn't blame him. He wasn't included in our magical bond just yet. He was on the outside, looking in, and that was a new and unwelcome experience for him.

"Yes, yes, well done, all of you," Mrs. Winter said. "But it doesn't bring us any closer to finding the horn."

"Well, I don't think I should pick the next one, I picked the acid death mirror," I muttered. "Alicia, do you want to pick?"

Alicia shook her head. "No…"

"I'll choose," Owen said, pointing towards the mirror with the skull over it. "That one."

"Why that one?" Ivy asked.

"Completely random," he said, shaking his head.

I scoffed. "You can't just pick one at random."

"We have just as much chance picking the right one at random as we do from any clues over the mirrors," he countered. "We tried using clues and they lead to the acid mirror. It's possible the clues are meant to misdirect us towards the more dangerous options."

"That is a very valid point," I conceded. "Your turn, Owen."

He approached the skull mirror and was about to handle the hilt of his blade into the glass when he stopped, considered, and stepped back. Mrs. Winter looked caught between pride and apprehension as her son sent a spell towards the mirror, breaking it quietly. He made a sweeping gesture that cleared the glass away and behind it, was just a room. For a heavy, silent moment, nothing happened, and I relaxed against the wall, thinking maybe the room was empty and we could just move on to the next.

And then I heard something in the dark, the soft sound of limbs dragging across stone.

"Oh, no," I whispered as a dark shape shuffled through the opening in the wall, undulating towards us.

For a moment, I was afraid it would be a Revenant, left behind to do their necromancer's bidding. But when my brain finally stopped skittering inside my skull like a frightened rodent, I realized no re-animation spell could last the centuries it had been since Silas Morton owned this house. Eventually, the body would break down and to put a macabre point on it, there would be nothing left to move.

No, this was something much worse.

A lion's paw slipped into view, the fur blood red even in the low light, iron-tipped claws scraping across the stone. Icy cold flushed through my belly. The feline body came into view and if I hadn't been absolutely quaking in fear, I might have admired the way the light reflected on its fur as it moved. There was something almost human about the face, a terrible intelligence in the eyes that sent a shudder down my spine so thorough that I could hear the bones creak. Its mouth was like a shark's, displaying multiple rows of razor-sharp iron teeth as the thing *smiled* at me.

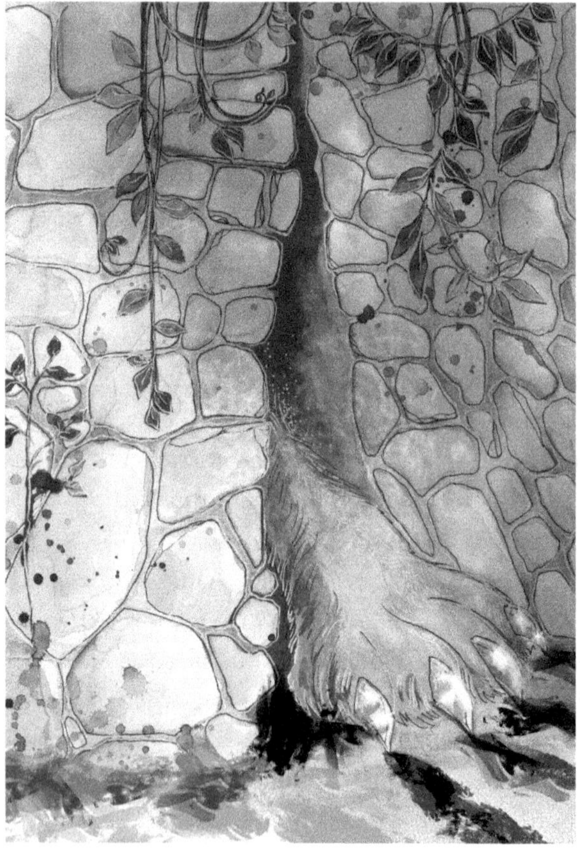

There was nothing more frightening than when a scary thing was happy to see you. And this creature looked absolutely *thrilled* that we were the ones greeting him after so long a sleep.

"What is that?" Robert whispered.

No one had the wits about them to tell him that it was a manticore, an awful collection of creatures pieced together to create a living nightmare. They could survive for centuries without eating, but when they finally did, they feasted on their favorite food – people – until they couldn't eat anymore. How in the world had Silas Morton managed to get one down here?

No one seemed to be able to move. Even Mrs. Winter looked frightened, which I found downright paralyzing.

The creature threw its head back and while I braced myself for a roar, instead, a strange musical blend of noises poured from its mouth. It was a strangely charming symphony. Was it like the hollowhorn we'd clashed with the previous year? Did it lure its victims in with beautiful melodies, only to devour them with those awful teeth?

"That noise! Do you think it *swallowed* the horn?" Owen asked. Alicia shot him a withering glare. He shrugged. "It would explain the sound! It could be some sort of weird riddle-quest thing."

"There's no reason to panic, children," Mrs. Winter murmured, though her voice shook. "Every problem is just a question of finding the right tool to fix it."

Mrs. Winter flicked her wrist and released a bright orange spell that curled toward the manticore like flames. It didn't look like any spell I'd ever seen before, the way it writhed across the air and surrounded the creature. But when it surrounded the manticore, it just sort of faded away like a smoke ring on the wind. The creature shook its lion's mane and it *yawned.*

Mrs. Winter's face went pale as her mouth dropped open. "It can deflect spells?"

"You didn't expect it to just crumble under one spell, did you?" Alicia asked.

"That was my most lethal magic," Mrs. Winter whispered, her hands trembling. "I'm not even supposed to know that spell. It's illegal in fifteen countries."

"You unleashed your most lethal magic with us standing right here?" I hissed, as the manticore licked its chops. "Without any warning?"

"Why start out with *less* lethal spells?" Mrs. Winter replied, clearly exasperated.

I looked to Ivy, who was trembling against the wall, her dark eyes wide with horror. I could see the problem of the manticore turning in her head like tumblers in a lock. Ivy was *terrified*, but she was trying to think through the problem. I would have to do the same or become manticore fodder.

I grit my teeth and sucked in a huge breath through my nose, trying to remember the few bits of trivia I'd read about manticores... but I kept getting stuck at *"their favorite food is people."*

Could we back out of the tomb before it struck? No, I didn't know if we could move the slab back into place in time to trap the manticore inside. And even if we could, would it hold against the creature? That thing was awake and hungry and if it wanted to get out, it would get out. And then we would be responsible for a manticore eating the entirety of this county.

What were manticores known for, I asked myself. Besides anatomical variety and virulently fatal poison tipping the spikes on its tail? A bit of information I'd gleaned during one of those long summer days spent hiding in the garden, reading books pilfered from Owen's collection, bubbled to the surface of my mind.

"Doom!" I yelped suddenly, making Mrs. Winter flinch.

"No, I promise we're going to be all right, Sarah. Don't lose hope now." Owen promised, sounding unusually calm and sure as he moved in front of Ivy. Mrs. Winter watched the movement and it seemed to snap her out of her daze. The manticore lurched forward, stepping over the doorway to its cell. Its lips drew back from its fangs and it seemed to be scanning each of us with those eyes, trying to determine who would be the first course.

"No, manticores are attracted to tragedy," I told them. "They absolutely *revel* in bad news. It feeds their will to live."

"I don't understand," Ivy said, shaking her head as the manticore prowled closer to Robert, sniffing deeply.

Robert swallowed heavily, backing away. As the largest amongst us, Robert seemed to have been chosen as the tastiest morsel. Alicia did not appreciate this, jumping in front of her beau, blade drawn. Robert rolled his eyes, picked her up, and placed her at his side.

"They tend to lose their appetites if you remind them of all the good things in the world. Births and weddings and kindness and generosity, all that." I explained.

"Are you seriously suggesting we shout happy news at it?" Mrs. Winter demanded as the manticore coiled, ready to strike. Robert braced himself, tracing Meggie's shield symbol in front of himself.

"Do you have a better suggestion?" Ivy demanded.

"I have wonderful friends who keep my secrets and support me in all of my idiotic endeavors!" I yelled.

The manticore made a disgusted face and it stepped back, as if my good fortune was repulsive to it.

"I've never been so healthy! I feel better than I have in my whole life!" Alicia called. "And I like Robert very much!"

Robert grinned down at her as the manticore shuddered, its shoulders slumping. All of us joined in, shouting out the bright things in our lives. Well, except for Mrs. Winter, who seemed equally shaken by the ineffectiveness of her magic *and* our absolute lack of decorum. Personally, I found it rather encouraging that we could all *find* something good in our lives to crow about, considering the situation.

Not to be outdone, Owen shouted, "I'm fairly certain I'm in love with this girl!"

"I feel very much the same." Ivy's eyes went wide and soft and she smiled at him.

Mrs. Winter didn't seem to know how to respond, focusing on the way the manticore was retreating back into its cell. Robert struck the hilt of his blade against the wall stones, cracking them into neat squares. As a group, we raised those stones through the air and stacked them in the open mirror space. Sand whirled around the floor in determined puffs and slipped in the cracks between the impromptu bricks. Mrs. Winter stepped forward, a jet of flame shooting forward from the tip of her blade and sealing the sand together in a slick mortar. Alicia and Ivy and I stepped forward. Together, we cast an Indestructible symbol, a spell to create a seal that would never break over that magically formed glass.

We stopped, each of us seeming to realize at once that we had made an enormous amount of noise while warding off a man-eating monster and there was a good chance the bubble hadn't contained it. But we didn't hear anything from the house, only the chirping of night birds and insects.

"We should just go," Owen said. "There's no telling what's behind the next mirror. It's not worth the risk."

"It is," I insisted. "They wouldn't put a manticore down here unless there was something important to protect. If it's this important, there's a chance we need it very badly."

"Well, then at least leave the chamber and let me and Robert open the next mirror," Owen retorted.

All of the softness melted from Ivy's eyes and she looked downright irritated by his attempt at chivalry. "I beg your pardon?" she demanded.

"I only want to protect you," he began to say as she flung her blade at the nearest glass. A sort of magical fog came rolling out of the room behind the mirror and she rolled her hand, a sort of conductor's gesture as she closed her fingers together. The fog rolled back into the room as if blown by an invisible wind and then dissolved all together. Owen's chin disappeared into his neck.

"You were saying?" Ivy asked, her brow arched.

"You can protect me," he said, nodding agreeably.

Mrs. Winter smiled at Ivy. "Impressive, my dear. The three of you are progressing remarkably together."

"They're downright terrifying, they are," Robert snickered.

"You're a Translator, too," I reminded him.

"Well, yes, but not nearly as scary," he protested.

"Could we choose the next room with a bit more care?" Mrs. Winter asked.

There were four rooms left and we all seemed to have a different opinion on how to select the next one. Scrying, numerology, coin toss. But at least Owen had stopped suggesting random selection. When that selection ended in a manticore, it was clearly a bad method.

"Would you all just stop?" Ivy hissed. "For just one moment, stay still and listen?"

"I don't hear anything." I told her.

"Because you're not *listening*."

She tilted her head towards a corner of the chamber, where there was no mirror at all. From the crack in the joined bricks, I could hear a low almost musical hum… like someone blowing over the mouth of a bottle. Almost like a… horn.

The mirrors had been a distraction. What we were looking for was behind a brick wall. We just had to figure out how to break through it.

"You're the smartest of all of us. I hope you know that," I told Ivy.

"Hardly bragging, considering the competition," she scoffed, as I gasped in indignation.

"Could it be another manticore?" Alicia asked.

"I doubt it," Robert said. "The noise is too singular. It just sounds like a horn, not all of the instruments together like that thing did."

"Besides, I'm shocked Morton managed to capture one of those things," Mrs. Winter reasoned. "Two would require a minor miracle."

Alicia drew a door on the wall with the tip of her blade and simply pushed. The mortar seemed to fade away and the wall opened like any door. Behind it was a closet-sized space, completely unlit. Mrs. Winter whispered behind us and a purple light filled the room. On a marble pedestal, rested a black horn that seemed to absorb the light Mrs. Winter cast.

It was such a simple thing. But I could see things reflected in its dark surface, awful things. I could hear screams echoing from its surface.

Robert frowned "What if it's just a copy?"

"I doesn't feel like a copy," I said, shaking my head. "Can't you feel it? It's death. It's the end of everything."

"She's a being a bit melodramatic, but she's right." Owen nodded. "This is it."

"Should we break all of the other mirrors just in case?" I asked. "They could be hiding something else we could use in here."

"They could also be hiding some sort of horrible curse that could kill us all," Robert replied as Owen tucked the horn into a leather tote bag on his back. Frankly, I was happy not to be the one to carry it. The vibrations coming off that thing made my skin crawl.

I smirked at him. "It's your sunny disposition that draws Alicia to you, isn't it?"

10

Our mood on the ride back to the Winters' Limerick house was downright jovial. We just needed somewhere to stop and rest for the night before heading home. We were too exhausted to try to make it all the way to the Folly. Also, we were covered in dust of an unknown origin. We weren't exactly dancing in our seats, but we'd managed to seal the ruin and leave the property with an important magical weapon in hand, without being seen. And we hadn't been eaten by an ancient, evil lion creature.

That was a pretty successful evening, as far as I was concerned.

We should have known it wouldn't last.

We parked the wagon in the back garden of the property. Owen was about to sling the bag on his shoulder towards me, the bag containing the horn. I stopped him, shaking my head, and slowing to a halt as I hopped off the wagon. It felt… wrong, too easy. Something was out here in the darkened garden with us, a presence I hadn't felt on the Stonethistle property.

I glanced at my friends, who were also paused, their heads tipped sideways, listening to faint rustling sounds in the dark. This time I knew, it was the footfalls of the dead.

"I thank you, for taking the trouble to find that little keepsake for me," a deeply feminine voice intoned from the shadows. "It belongs to my family by right, you know."

My heart dropped into my stomach. The voice was different, but I knew it. It was the voice that had haunted my nightmares for months. It was the voice of the only person to ever make me truly afraid.

"Take off," I told Alicia. "Get the… thing and get everybody out of here."

Alicia shook her head. "Your parents."

"I can take care of them. Just get out of here," I told her again.

The trees around us burst into flames, a perfect circle surrounding us, separating us from the safety of the house. A tall woman, wearing a navy blue satin ballgown, a woman who gave Mrs. Dalrymple a run for stateliness, stepped through the flames. She had nearly white hair but dark eyebrows punctuating every movement of her face. Those movements were familiar to me, the way she held her head and neck as she walked. This was not a Revenant. This was a body actively being occupied by Miss Morton.

Wait, she wasn't just familiar because of her possible occupation by Miss Morton. I'd met this woman before. She came to tea regularly at Raven's Rest. Mrs. Winter was always careful to use the best silver service and enchant the parlor door so we couldn't eavesdrop on their conversations.

"Elora?" Mrs. Winter gasped. "What is this?"

I felt energy flex around me and I screamed, dropping to my knees at the pain in my middle. It felt like my magic was being pulled out of me, through my belly button. My friends and Mrs. Winter were all on their knees, too, groaning, in too much pain to do anything but keep from vomiting in the grass. I couldn't move. I couldn't cast. It felt like a total failure of my body.

"Auntie Lorie?" Owen cried, crawling towards the woman. Robert caught his arm and shook his head.

"What's happening?" Ivy whimpered. "I can't move."

"Her name was Elora Delgado-Winstone," I whispered, watching Owen's face crumple. "She was Owen's godmother."

Owen's voice was wavering. "She can't be – she wasn't – We just saw her, right before we left Lightbourne."

None of this was right. We'd spent so much time preparing, hoping that we could build our magic together and it was all falling apart. I was so tired and *so* scared I couldn't think straight. I was failing my friends.

The woman – the grand lady who had once been Elora Delgado-Winstone – laughed, an awful rasping chuckle that echoed across this fiery clearing she'd created. "I'm afraid she is. Heart failure is so common in women of a certain age, especially when their tea is doctored with a little digitalis by a well-known acquaintance."

"No, that's impossible," Mrs. Winter insisted, pushing to a kneeling position. Miss Morton waved her hand and shoved Mrs. Winter back to the ground. "She never would have had tea with Crenshaw. I *warned* her."

Owen tried to rise from the ground, pulling the bag that held the horn off his back. Miss Morton hissed, swiping her blade towards Owen and sending him toppling into the dirt. The bag tumbled over the grass, six feet from him. Miss Morton was wielding a dark silver blade with an owl set in the handle, probably another Grimstelle artifact she'd located. We all reached towards Owen, especially Mrs. Winter, but Miss Morton wouldn't let us move.

"Do you honestly think I'm working alone?" Miss Morton scoffed. "My operatives are everywhere. They may not know I exist. They may have been following 'Crenshaw,' but they're doing what *I* command. They're working for your families, they're working at the school, they're even working for your precious sweetheart at the McCray headquarters. How else could I have found you, so cleverly tucked away in the countryside, without that moonstruck boy leading me to the farm, repeatedly checking on the perimeter of the property? He practically painted a target on your little farmhouse for me. No wonder, really, given how incompetent you are, and how weak his sister is. Young Mr. McCray recognized that you need to be supervised. It's amazing that you've gotten this far on your own, honestly."

I was caught between being touched that Gavin had tried to hover near us, just to be close to us, and despair that his gesture had led to the Revenant invasion. I supposed it was lucky that Miss Morton hadn't had the opportunity to sabotage the air gondola Gavin had stashed nearby. If she had, we probably would have dropped out of the sky like a rock as we tried to escape. Somewhere in this turmoil, I found a moment to feel guilty for blaming Miss Wrathburn for the Revenants' timing, even silently and temporarily.

And Miss Morton was still talking.

"And now my operatives will do what your friend commands, in Crenshaw's absence. We all want the same thing, after all... power. They simply don't realize that I'll be the only one left standing with it in the end. I will not be stopped, not by you and not by your sad little band of compatriots. Now, hand over the horn or there will be consequences."

I glanced towards the house, remembering my family was inside... unless she'd hurt them. My parents, my...

"Augh, did my sister contact you somehow?" My reactionary anger somehow burned through the magic that kept me pinned to the ground, so I could push to my knees and shout. "I can't believe she would do this to me *again!*"

"Oh, please, I didn't give your sister a way to contact me," Miss Morton scoffed. "It was tortuous enough spending all that time with the shallow twit back in Coventry. Your precious family is perfectly fine, Miss *Smith.* I wouldn't waste any more effort on them. Now, stop stalling and tell me where the horn is!"

"I don't know what horn you're talking about!" I cried. I would not glance back at Owen or his bag.

"Don't insult me," Miss Morton growled, sending another wave of magic that flung me back to the ground. "Do you honestly think, after everything my family lost, that my father wouldn't put an enchantment on any Grimstelle artifact that made it out into the open? I knew of its existence. I knew it was located somewhere in Ireland because I could feel it there *somewhere.* I just didn't know exactly where it was until the moment you emerged from whatever horde you raided to find it. And then I knew where *you* were, thanks to my father's magic. Now give it to me."

I made a gesture toward my blade. It wasn't the most subtle of signals, but it was enough to catch the others' attention as the Winters mourned the friend who was standing in front of us, dead.

Silently, I reached out to my friends' magic as we chose which spell to use. I could only think of explosions, which was appropriate, but not very helpful. Fortunately, Alicia kept a clearer head, sending us the impression of calling the bag off the ground, into Owen's hands, and using the horn to dissolve Miss Morton into nothing.

We summoned the strength to reach up simultaneously and I'm sure we would have called the horn to us... if Miss Morton hadn't swept a spell across our limbs with crushing force. We screamed as our arms were hurled back down to the earth. I heard something crack in my wrist. I moaned and cradled it to my chest.

"Ah ah." Miss Morton clucked her tongue at us. "None of your new 'advanced' magic, such as it is."

Smirking, she flicked her wrist towards Owen. Even with Mrs. Winter and Ivy scrabbling to hold onto his arms, Owen was dragged forward, his feet digging furrows into the ground. In the process, the bag strap wrapped around his ankle, dragging it along with him. Howling, Mrs. Winter flung a violently crimson curse at Miss Morton's feet and her ballgown burst into flames.

Miss Morton rolled her eyes and put it out. She grinned evilly as she lifted Owen off his feet to hover before her.

"Where is it?" she hissed at him. "Tell me, young Mr. Winter. Or I start hurting the ladies here until I figure out which one you value most. Your meddling mother? Your feckless friend? Or your insipid sweetheart?"

As Owen struggled against her magical grip, she sighed. "I do love alliteration, don't you?"

"You're insane," Owen wheezed.

Miss Morton snarled. "Fine, if you're not going to play. Let us get to the point."

She turned her wrist, and as she did, Owen's body flipped upside down, so that his ankle – and the bag containing the horn – were dangling at her eye level. She pulled the horn out of the bag and examined with child-like glee. She eyed us speculatively, grinning.

"Should I give it a try?" she asked, gesturing absent-mindedly and turning Owen's feet back toward the ground. She pursed her lips near the mouthpiece. "Who knows what purposes my ancestors had for this precious item?"

Did she really not know? My breath caught in my throat. I had no idea which path was preferable here. If she used the horn, it would eliminate any Revenants nearby, which would solve some problems. And it might even eject Miss Morton from Mrs. Delgado-Winstone's body. But if it didn't, could something worse happen? It was rare that these magical objects only had one side effect.

Miss Morton blew a breath lightly across the mouthpiece. I shuddered as a wave of screams rippled out of the horn and coated my skin like a filmy slime. Miss Morton giggled, and somehow, that was even worse. "No, not yet, I think. I like the idea of you wondering."

She pulled Owen by the collar, closer to her, in an awful imitation of a hug. "Thank you, for this rather timely delivery. It was just what I needed. But just to keep your mother off-balance, you'll be coming with me."

In the distance, I could hear horse hooves clattering over the ground. For a second, I was afraid she had summoned hollowhorns to finish us off. But I didn't hear the telltale pipe music that accompanied them. Miss Morton cackled, walking through the flames unharmed as a black carriage rolled to a stop nearby. A Revenant sat in the driver's seat, listlessly flapping the reins against horses that were very much alive. I imagined the horses were well trained, and could have pulled the carriage without a human driver. But that would have attracted attention Miss Morton didn't want.

"Owen!" Mrs. Winter cried.

"Stay there, Mother," Owen shouted. "Stay back!"

Miss Morton dragged a hovering Owen behind her, his feet barely brushing the ground.

"No!" Mrs. Winter roared, breaking the hold on her long enough to stumble to her feet. Miss Morton threw Owen towards the carriage, which opened the door and seemed to catch him. Mrs. Winter forced her way to the ring of flames, her dress igniting as she shoved her way through to her son. The carriage dashed away with a whinny from the horses and as we watched, faded away like a dying flare. It simply wasn't there anymore, and I didn't know whether it had actually disappeared or if it was simply invisible.

"What was that?" I asked, gasping for breath. I could move again, and stand, though it was difficult with what I was pretty sure was a fractured wrist. "What did she just do?"

"She has the horn. She has Owen," Ivy said, blinking rapidly, her breathing shallow as she walked to the edge of the dying flames. "She has everything."

"No, we have the book," Alicia insisted. "We have people to help us. We're not just going to give up, Ivy."

"What if she *hurts* him?" Ivy seethed at us. "She could turn him into one of those things, Sarah. She could..."

"I know," I put my good arm around Ivy carefully. Meanwhile, Mrs. Winter was kneeling on the ground, her dress still burning. Robert put her out quickly and helped her to her feet.

"Mrs. Winter?" I called quietly. I didn't know what to do here. I didn't know how to help. Mrs. Winter looked lost, and for the first time in my life, I was truly worried about her. "Mrs. Winter?"

She looked at me, her eyes empty, and her mouth opened. A howl escaped her lips and it sounded like the gates of hell opening. A wave of blazing silver energy rippled off her and we were knocked back with the force of it. The leaves of all the surrounding trees flew off in a rush. The last thing I remembered before slumping to the ground, was tiny bits of leaves fluttering down on my face, like green snow.

Miss Morton hadn't lied about my family. They were perfectly safe inside the house, though highly disturbed at the state of Mrs. Winter. The combined losses of her friend returning to her as a corpse and her son being taken before her very eyes seemed to have snapped something in Mrs. Winter's brain. She sat still, staring into space, shaking. She didn't speak. She didn't weep. She only stared. It was frightening.

I didn't feel safe leaving my family at a house when Miss Morton knew where they were, so I sent them by train to the Winter house in Coventry with little farewell or fanfare. It was all I could think to do, to get them far away from me. Mary didn't even ask about Owen, she only hustled our parents onto a wagon bound for the station. Somehow, seeing her act like the near-adult that she was – well, it didn't make me feel better, but it was one less thing for me to worry about.

We practically had to carry Mrs. Winter back into the gondola.

I sat next to her as Alicia piloted us through the sky, if for no other reason than to keep her seated. The sheer impact of what we'd lost that evening couldn't seem to penetrate the denial I'd built around my mind. We'd gone after the horn in the hopes of using it to finally eliminate Miss Morton as a threat, and she'd stolen it right from under us. She used her ancient family's greed for its own lost treasures against us. I should have known better. I should have planned better. I should have *been* better.

But Miss Lockwood and Mrs. Winter had approved of our plans. I hadn't rushed in alone and half-informed. I hadn't trusted people who hadn't proven themselves. How had it gone so wrong so quickly?

Owen was gone. And I didn't care about him being obnoxious and arrogant. I just wanted him back. I was so frightened for him. What was Miss Morton doing to him? What if the next time we saw him, he was... no. I couldn't think about that.

I was grateful that, at least, the Mother Book was left with Cathy and the others. I don't know what we would have done if we'd lost that too.

Mrs. Dalrymple could see there was a problem before we even landed.

"What's happened?" Mrs. Dalrymple demanded, rushing forward to take Mrs. Winter's arms as we climbed out of the gondola. Her eyes searched frantically for Ivy, and she relaxed only slightly when she saw her granddaughter curled against Alicia's side.

"Was anyone hurt?" Cathy asked.

I shook my head and murmured, "Worse."

Miss Wrathburn strode towards Mrs. Winter, taking her arm. "I'll see to her. I'll receive a debrief when she's comfortable."

I watched as Miss Wrathburn helped Mrs. Winter up the stairs.

As we walked into the house, I saw the other children playing games in the library. Everything here appeared to be fine. Perhaps

I could trust the woman after all? I wasn't ready to extend that courtesy quite yet. It was something to consider later.

"Well, I'd hoped this would be more a pleasant surprise for you young ladies, but I invited another guest to attend to us while we make our plans," Mrs. Dalrymple said, gesturing towards the parlor.

Gavin McCray was standing there, tall and whole and perfect in his evening dress, smiling at me from his place in front of the mantle. I was simply too tired to throw myself joyously into his arms as Ivy had done to Owen. I could only move toward him, sinking against him and burying my face against his shirt. I felt him lift me from the floor in an embrace that was certainly not proper. I buried my nose in his shirt, inhaling the strange ozone and herb scent of him.

He pulled back from me, smiling broadly, but winced when he saw me recoil my injured wrist away from him. It was quite swollen now and discolored. He clucked his tongue and took a small metal box out of his pocket.

"I thought to carry one of these around, now that I'll be seeing you more often," he said.

Inside was a variety of small healing instruments, centered around a chunk of obsidian. I let out a watery laugh. The first time I'd met him, under-sized and wearing my servants' garb, I'd bumped into him and went sprawling on the street. I'd scraped my hands and Gavin healed them with a bit of obsidian.

I leaned my forehead against his shoulder as he healed my wrist, allowing myself to breathe for just a little bit before the difficult conversation we were going to have to have.

Mrs. Dalrymple sent the children to bed. They moaned and protested, exclaiming that we'd only just returned "home" and they wanted to play with us. Miss Lockwood sternly, but kindly, informed the children that we could all talk over breakfast the next morning, before lessons. To my surprise, the children simply herded up the stairs without another word.

Miss Lockwood said nothing about my inappropriate display with Gavin, or the absence of the magical artifact we'd been sent to retrieve. Mrs. Dalrymple served us hot tea with plenty of sugar and informed us we all looked like we'd been gravely ill. Gavin simply sat at my side, watching me, watching his sister, but he knew better than to demand answers from us. I appreciated that more than I could say. Mrs. Dalrymple took Ivy's hand and said gently. "Tell us."

"Miss Morton has Owen," Alicia said.

"What do you mean, she has Owen?" Cathy demanded, showing more concern than I expected when she'd shown little emotion for Owen beyond casual annoyance.

"They have Owen," Ivy seethed. "I am going to get him back."

"I admire your confidence, my dear, but do you have any idea how you're going to accomplish that?" Mrs. Dalrymple asked.

Ivy fell silent.

"I'm assuming your Miss Morton intercepted you?" Mrs. Dalrymple asked.

I nodded. "There was a charm on the horn. I think it was protected from her sight as long as it was in that tomb. But as soon as we brought it out into the open, she was able to locate us. She took it and Owen, to neutralize Mrs. Winter. So far it's been very effective."

"I've heard of charms like that before, but I've never seen them practiced myself," Miss Lockwood marveled. "To think that woman worked in my library all those years when she was capable of such horrors."

Cathy exclaimed. "So, you managed to find a precious magical weapon that could have been our salvation and then you handed it over to her?"

"We didn't exactly hand it over," Alicia barked back. "She took it."

"And you just let her!" Cathy yelled.

"And you elected not to come with us, so I would appreciate it if you didn't criticize us," Alicia retorted. Ivy only sat there, quietly, watching us bicker back and forth.

"Cease this pointless arguing, this instant!" Miss Lockwood thundered, standing suddenly. "It does no good to any of us and it disappoints me that you would turn on each other the moment things become difficult. It's a loss but surely, you've learned something!"

All of us snapped our mouths shut and lowered our heads. When someone yelled at you in that tone of voice, you couldn't help but do so. I swallowed with a gulp and gave Mrs. Dalrymple, Miss Lockwood and then, Miss Wrathburn a brief summary of our misadventures, the appearance of Miss Morton in the form of Mrs. Delgado-Winstone and Owen's capture. To my surprise, the adults didn't chastise us for our foolishness or lack of action.

They simply nodded, taking our story in until Miss Lockwood prompted us. "So, ladies, what have we learned?"

Ivy, Alicia, and I glanced at each other. I couldn't feel their magic anymore. We were all too shocked to establish that sort of connection. But I could reach out to them physically, and I did so with my hands. I touched each of their hands. And while Alicia gripped my own hand immediately, Ivy's was loose in my fingers.

"Miss Morton is very frightened of us being able to work magic together," Ivy observed hoarsely. "She worked to keep us from doing so."

"Perhaps she feels the shift in your magic since you resurrected the Mother Book?" Miss Lockwood suggested.

"I don't know," Alicia said, shaking her head. "I'm sorry. I'm just so tired. I know we don't have time to be tired, but so much has happened."

I squeezed Alicia's hand and to my relief, Ivy squeezed mine lightly. I felt bereft without that connection to their magic, truly alone for the first time in a long time. I hoped we would be able to regain it soon.

"It's all right," Mrs. Dalrymple assured us. "You're all

exhausted. You need to get some rest and then we'll talk more in the morning. You're no use to anyone in this state. We'll keep watch over the children and you."

"That's why I'm here," Gavin said. He turned to his sister. "As reinforcement. I appreciate that you've been trying to do things your own way, and you've done remarkable things."

Miss Wrathburn snorted, making it clear that she considered our "accomplishments" to be dubious indeed.

Gavin ignored her. "But it's not very heroic, is it? Sending your sister and your sweetheart off into the great unknown, without protection, to do all the work–"

"You needed to maintain appearances at the business while we were off doing things that could have ruined your whole family's reputation and livelihood," I reminded him, tamping down the thrill at his calling me his sweetheart.

"Well, that ends now," Gavin replied. "If you're at risk, I'm at risk. I was very grateful to receive Mrs. Dalrymple's invitation for a 'visit,' if no other reason than to get away from our mother, who is furious with all of you."

For a second Alicia's expression brightened, probably thinking of how much angrier her mother would be if Mrs. McCray knew her daughter had piloted an airship to Ireland. "I knew she would be."

11

I did not feel rested or restored when I woke more than a day later in my comfortable chamber at the Folly. I stretched into the beam of sunlight that poured over my bed. Phillip was perched on a wooden perch that May had fashioned for him, staring at me with what I preferred to think of as concern.

For just a few seconds, I forgot that Owen was missing. And then I remembered the look on Mrs. Winter's face when he'd been dragged away and my heart felt so heavy, I didn't know if I could get up. But Ivy needed me, so I rose and dressed and walked down to the dining room to find the children at luncheon. It was bad enough that I'd slept more than twenty-four hours after our ordeal. I couldn't be lazy now. I looked out the window to the back garden as I walked down the main staircase. Gavin was outside, going over the air gondola. Given the amount of parts that were laid out on the grass, I supposed that we'd done some damage to it during our travels.

I glanced at the large grandfather clock just outside the parlor. Today was the day the eldest Castwell girls would complete their spring interviews. The term would end soon and the girls would return home. It seemed so far away now, worrying about things like that.

The children were chattering and excited around the table, consuming sandwiches and cakes with gusto, while the older members of the group were somber in their seats. Mrs. Winter was sitting in the parlor, by herself, staring at the fire that we really didn't need given the spring weather. Ivy sat next to her, equally quiet and pensive.

"No change?" I asked Mrs. Dalrymple, who silently shook her head as I took my seat.

I tried to keep up with the children's rapidly changing course of conversation, but all I could do was sit quietly and listen. After an hour, Miss Lockwood announced that it was time for afternoon lessons. The children didn't complain. They simply stood and scampered off towards the nursery. They were very much looking forward to some sort of game involving floating cards that displayed various magical crystals. When the children guessed those crystals' correct magical purposes – divination, amplification, healing – the card burst into a shower of brightly colored sparks. If they got it wrong, their stream turned red and the cards danced out of order. It sounded like great fun and I was a little jealous I wasn't able to play.

Miss Lockwood patted my shoulder as she followed after them, leaving us with Mrs. Dalrymple and Miss Wrathburn. Over time, Miss Lockwood seemed to have… softened towards the children. She was kinder to them. She made an effort to ensure their time here was enjoyable. I was glad for them, that they were finally getting the education they deserved while being treated like children.

"Do you remember any of our lessons being turned into games?" I asked Alicia.

Alicia shook her head. She was paler than usual and her hand shook slightly as she spooned sugar into her tea, but she made an attempt to sound jovial as she said, "I remember that time that I blew up an amethyst in crystallography and Miss Templeton wouldn't let me leave the room until I'd managed to pluck all of the fragments out of the ceiling with a pair of tweezers,"

"Not quite the same," I said, shaking my head. "Are you alright?"

Alicia glanced around and said quietly, "Ever since we took the horn from that chamber, I've felt... weaker. As if my magic is draining away from me," she confessed, her expression crumbling. "I was barely able to sleep, from worrying. I often felt this way before, when I was still suffering the effects of the reverb. What if I'm going back to that state? What if this new power I've achieved while working with the two of you, what if it was only temporary? I don't want to feel like that again, like I wasn't contributing, like I couldn't if I wanted to."

"You're always contributing," I assured her. "You don't let me wallow. You help me see the lighter side of a problem. And if I can laugh at something, I won't be quite so frightened by it. And as for losing your magic, well, we simply won't allow it."

The pair of us grew quiet as Mrs. Dalrymple appeared at our sides.

"Well, ladies, what do you make of this, given your description of Mrs. Delgado-Winstone's condition?" She laid a hastily scrawled bit of parchment next to the marmalade. Mrs. Dalrymple had been invited to a ball at Starworth Manor near Lancaster in just a week's time.

"It's a considerable accomplishment to host a ball when you're dead," Alicia muttered into her cup.

"Yes, the invitation is most strange, considering that it was issued over mirror message," Mrs. Dalrymple sniffed. "Elora Delgado-Winstone *adored* elaborate invitations. She employed a full-time calligrapher. She never would have issued an invitation in such a way. Several of my friends received the same this morning."

"It's a very close window in which to plan an event like this," I said. "I've seen my mother plan balls every season with Mrs. Winter. It takes months to prepare. I'm assuming Mrs. Delgado-Winstone was much the same?"

Mrs. Dalrymple nodded. "And the timing is odd."

"How so?" I asked.

"No one with Elora's social cache really plans a grand ball just as the season begins," Mrs. Dalrymple said. "The young ladies and gentlemen are barely home from school. No one has had time to visit their modiste. Elora always waits until people have become bored with the usual soirees and then puts on a memorable evening that shames any other lady who has fallen short."

It occurred to me that the ladies of magical society didn't sound like people I would want to accept invitations from, but I didn't share that.

"And it's being held on the night of the scaled toad moon," Mrs. Dalrymple commented. "Historically considered unlucky, in terms of social gatherings of any size."

"Why is that?" Alicia asked.

"It's a rare astronomical event that emphasizes intent of a spell. If one was attempting to cast a spell over a large group of people, this would be a good night to do it," Ivy said, approaching the table. "Gathering on the scaled toad moon is considered unlucky because the host could decide to cast a spell on the guests."

"I've never heard of a scaled toad moon," I said, working to keep my face calm. Ivy was participating in our discussion. That gave me so much reason to hope.

"It's an anomaly outlined in the astrological system designed by Norton Entwhistle, a fringe section of the study, at best," Ivy said, sitting on the opposite side of the table, where she could keep an eye on Mrs. Winter. "If you're going to take the design to a new astrological system, it's best not to name all of the signs and events after amphibians, no matter how much you personally love them. Some people find that off-putting."

I frowned. How outlandish did a system have to be for astrologers to call it "fringe?"

"Sarah!" Cathy yelled from the library. "The book is doing... something!"

We leapt to our feet, Mrs. Dalrymple included, and ran into the library to find Cathy holding the Mother Book at arm's length. It looked as if she was afraid it might explode at any moment.

I supposed it was possible.

She turned the book so we could see the words form across the blank pages. Miss Lockwood stood with us, squinting as the ink set itself. My heart thrilled as words began to form on the page. The little fingers of ink reaching towards each other to shape into words.

Suddenly Miss Lockwood straightened and rolled her eyes. "Why am I trying to read this? I'm not a Translator."

"We're among the few non-Translators in the house, dear," Mrs. Dalrymple reminded her.

There was no illustration to the new page, just a brief statement that read, *"Objects capable of removing core magics could have catastrophic consequences to any magic practitioner. While such objects can be prescribed strictly to one family's unique magical signature, they can be manipulated to produce the same effect against all magical signatures. These objects are very dangerous, but could prove quite useful when applied strategically. Explore further – notes to be kept in coded journal."*

The initials CTG formed at the bottom of the entry.

I frowned, remembering the portion of *History's Musical Magic* Alicia had read aloud, about Charles Throggle-Grimstelle and how he designed the Horn of Silence to take away the Grimstelle family's core magic. Core magic, the very essence of our magical being.

Could this passage have come from Charles Throggle-Grimstelle? The book had shown me excerpts from other practitioners' private writings before. Maybe this was a snippet of Charles' notes? If so, the effects of the horn could reach much further than just the Grimstelle family.

I cleared my throat. "Alicia, you said you began to feel your magic was 'affected' from the moment we discovered the horn?"

She nodded, glancing towards the adults with a worried expression. "I thought perhaps I'd pushed myself too far, that the reverb was coming back. I didn't want to say anything because I was scared. And then Owen was taken and it didn't seem so important anymore."

"I'll confess I haven't quite felt myself since the catacomb excursion," Ivy said, putting her hand on Alicia's shoulder.

I thought about my own state since the trip to Stonethistle. I hadn't exactly felt up to par, either, but I thought perhaps it was the stress of Owen's disappearance, or our lack of progress. But what if we'd been infected with something in the catacombs? What had been down there with us? The manticore? Terrifying yes, but none of us were injured by it. Perhaps it had been some sort of fungus that just happened to grow in the catacombs that was affecting us? On occasion, a lurid headline would run in one of the Lightborne newspapers about magical archeologists taking ill after excavating tombs... but that usually had more to do with respiratory distress than magical fatigue.

I tried to broaden my mind's eye and take in all the elements – Miss Morton's determination to get the horn, the information we had about the horn, the sudden and sloppy invitation to a grand ball. The horn was originally designed to take magical influence or "life" from other Grimstelle's revenants. For magical practitioners, magic *was* our life, it was our very blood and breath. What if the horn could steal our magic?

I thought about the horn in a new light, and it seemed all the more evil. Who would think they had the right to take someone's magic?

Well, Miss Morton would. I'd always thought it was rather

strange that Miss Morton told us exactly what she was planning to do with her re-established power, back at Miss Castwell's. For all her evil, Miss Morton was a smart woman. Surely, it would have been smarter to hide her plans from us. But there she was, blathering about her plans to take over magical society and regain the power her family once enjoyed.

Obviously, she wasn't telling us everything.

I turned to Ivy and Alicia. "She doesn't want to just re-order magical society, she wants to take magic away from whoever she chooses."

Alicia nodded. "She's not just worried about protecting her army of revenants. The horn does so much more than that. It can take away core magic. That's why I've been feeling so weak, just from being near the cursed thing. But I still have my magic, thank goodness!"

When my brows rose, she added, hastily, "Well, yes, it's horrible, but at least, it's not permanent!"

"For now," Ivy commented. "But clearly, Miss Morton is planning something, with this sudden large-scale ball to celebrate nothing in particular. It's not an invitation, it's a lure for a trap."

"On a night where the probability of performing a successful ritual on a large group of people is higher. She's going to try to take magic from all of the prominent magical families in England," I marveled. "She could decide who has magic and who doesn't. She may decide that no one gets magic save her."

The other women looked positively ill considering the possibility. It wouldn't just be chaos, it would be the end of the magical world as we knew it. It would be the end of everything we knew. Miss Morton would hold all the power. Having seen the way she worked, I could see how that would appeal to her.

"Not just in England," Mrs. Dalrymple corrected me. "This could be something of an experiment, to see if she could perform similar rituals all over the world."

"Part of me is on her side," Cathy muttered. When I grimaced and shook my head, she shrugged and said, "What? It's not like this lot has done much good with their magic."

Miss Wrathburn put an arm around Cathy's shoulders. "I understand your point. But this is something we simply can't allow. It would make us no better than Miss Morton. Besides, I doubt we would like her manner of running things any more than the current system."

Cathy grumbled. "What do we do, then?"

"What if we warn the Guardian families not to come?" I asked. "Would they believe us if we told them it was some sort of ambush?"

"Probably not," Ivy said.

"Could we start a rumor that would ruin Mrs. Delgado-Winstone's reputation?" I asked.

"You jumped to that very quickly," Alicia noted.

"I'm only saying we could turn this into the party no one wants to attend," I exclaimed.

"If anything, society at large might want to go to the ball even more, to witness a matron-of-legend at her lowest," Mrs. Dalrymple said, shaking her head.

"This is why I make comments about being on Miss Morton's side," Cathy said.

"Besides, if the guests don't attend as planned, Miss Morton could simply use her Revenants to make 'refusal' impossible," Miss Wrathburn said, giving Cathy a pointed look.

"I will reply with an affirmative for my attendance," Mrs. Dalrymple said. "And you'll simply have to tag along."

"You don't think Miss Morton would notice if you showed up with an extra eight to ten people?" I asked.

"Well, no hostess would allow for invitations to be checked at the door," Mrs. Dalrymple said. "It simply isn't done."

Alicia said, "It's also not done, to send invitations by last-minute mirror message."

"You make a good point, dear," Mrs. Dalrymple replied with a frown.

"Miss Morton is going to be looking for us, certainly," I muttered, chewing on my lip.

Miss Wrathburn scoffed. "That's what spells are for."

"I suppose this is going to be a rather large order for my modiste," Mrs. Dalrymple said. She seemed to be sizing each of us up, trying to determine what measurements she should send to this absent dressmaker.

"Is that really a priority?" Cathy asked.

"Well, just because this could be the end of the magical world as we know it, doesn't mean we will meet it under-dressed," Mrs. Dalrymple sniffed, before sweeping out of the library.

I looked to Ivy. "Those social connections we made at school? It's time to take advantage of them."

"Do we have to put it in such a mercenary way?" Ivy asked, frowning.

"Well, not in the letters we write, no," I assured her.

"What about people like Callista?" Ivy asked.

"We write a letter to Miss Morton saying, 'Callista is our best friend, please don't hurt her or we will be so demoralized we won't be able to function?'" Alicia suggested.

"That is sinister," I told her. "Even for you."

"Fine, fine, we decide what to do about our not-quite-friends at a later date. What do we tell the people we trust?" Alicia asked.

"Jeanette was there, the night we first confronted Miss Morton," I reminded them. "We could use that. We just have to think of the right, vague wording."

While Ivy and Alicia nodded, Cathy leveled a look at all of us. "I'm not wearing a ballgown. I don't care what your grandmother's dressmaker sends."

~

MRS. DALRYMPLE FOUND me at luncheon the next day, poring over a list of girls from school I had contacted. Ivy was sitting in the parlor with Mrs. Winter again, watching over the silent woman as she stared into the fire. It had been difficult coming up with the right amorphous wording, which I'd had to copy, over and over again, as I scrawled it across my mirror to girls like Jeanette, Sofia Cortina, Madeline Sato, anyone from our study circle I thought we could trust. I'd discuss the weather, the recent spring interviews, wishing my friends luck with them, and then mention a common purpose at an upcoming social event, one that we would need to be prepared for, using all the tools at our disposal. I made veiled references to the number of owls at the country estate where I was staying, and how the tall windows in the library reminded me of our study circles at Miss Castwell's, studying the ancient magical families of England and their blades. And I reminisced about how often dance lessons on the lawn resulted in girls colliding with each other, arguing how the lawn "nearly became a battlefield." Then I signed it, *"With Affection, C."* C for Cassandra. I could only hope they would pick up the very unhelpful clues I had left to at least be prepared for some sort of fight.

Having attended Miss Castwell's and magical society events in general far longer than I had, Gavin, Ivy, and Alicia wrote to young people from families I didn't know, using much the same semi-coded language. We'd all received some confused, polite responses in return, and one note from a Madeline Sato's sister suggesting that Alicia stop using whatever addling substances she was dabbling with and come home to her mother – and to stop writing to her impressionable sister. Many of Gavin's missives were ignored entirely.

Mrs. Dalrymple sat elegantly in the dining chair, her expression serious. "I'm told that Mrs. Delgado-Winstone's kitchen staff has put in a large order for impswort, blade root, and dill. Impswort and blade root have virtually no value in the kitchen, but they are used often for medicinal purposes. And no one uses that much dill. It's a very divisive flavor."

"Good afternoon, Mrs. Dalrymple," I said, shaking my head at her single-mindedness.

"Oh, please, it's not as if you haven't devoted hours to scribbling your messages over the past day," she snorted.

"Need I ask how you have these details about Mrs. Delgado-Winstone's kitchen provisions?"

"Your mother is a housekeeper," she said. "Why do you think your mother spends so much time chatting with the servants from other households?"

"Companionship?" I suggested.

She rolled her eyes at me. "All servants spill their employers' secrets. From what Mrs. Winter tells me, your mother has always been adept at spilling few of hers, or at least, spilling only what Mrs. Winter wants spilled while extracting far more information from those around her. She's very adept when it comes to getting people to reveal more than they intend. I've always been impressed with tales of her cleverness."

My mouth dropped. My mother had served as Mrs. Winter's spy for all these years?

I would have to process that particular information at a later date. But the mention of my mother reminded me of my parents and how they'd dosed me with magical suppressants as a child, to try to keep me from being found out by the magical authorities.

"When I was still at Miss Castwell's, I did some private research into the suppressants my parents gave me as a child, for no other reason than to try to estimate the damage long-term use might have done to my health," I said.

"Very sensible," Mrs. Dalrymple commented.

"The recipe for suppressants almost always included impswort, blade root, and dill." I scrubbed my hand over my face.

She nodded. "So that would seem to confirm your suspicions

about Miss Morton's intentions to remove her guests' magic, by several means, if she plans to add those ingredients to the food."

"I'm going to have to write my friends all over again, telling them not to try the food," I sighed. "They're going to think I've gone mad… der."

"Just tell them that you've heard awful things about the hostess's cook, and that your cousin nearly died from a serving of bad clams from her table," she suggested.

A log crackled in the fireplace in the parlor. I wasn't even sure why we were burning a fire, other than it seemed to give Mrs. Winter something to stare at.

"She still hasn't spoken?"

"We don't know what to do," I told Mrs. Dalrymple. "I've never seen Mrs. Winter like this. She's always so resolute, unflappable. This is frightening."

"Her only child is in danger. I think I would be rather disappointed in her if she wasn't a bit disturbed," Mrs. Dalrymple commented.

"Stop talking about me as if I can't hear you," Mrs. Winter bit out, her voice sounding rusty from disuse.

Mrs. Dalrymple and I rose as Ivy served Mrs. Winter a cup of tea. She didn't drink it. It was like she had broken through the frozen surface that had held her down for the last few days, but was threatening to sink back into the more comfortable silence.

"Mrs. Winter, please, we need you right now. Miss Morton–"

"I'm tired of being needed," she shot back. "I'm tired of being the one who makes up for the risk *you* pose. I'm tired of risking my neck, my family's necks, for yours. Why didn't I simply turn you out onto the street that day you levitated a vase in my parlor?"

Hurt stung me right in the chest, but I understood. I had turned her entire life upside down when I'd conjured magic in her parlor. And I certainly understood the fatigue of dealing with one crisis after another for years upon years. I moved back, unable to justify what I wanted and needed from her, when she stood to lose so much more.

"Because you understood, even then, what was at stake," Ivy told her suddenly, raising her voice. Both Mrs. Dalrymple and I stepped back. "I wish we had time to worry about Owen. He's the only boy I can say I've ever truly cared for. But we just can't indulge ourselves. Because this is bigger than all of us. This is bigger than a mother's love of her son, no matter how deep. It's bigger than my love of a boy. It's bigger than my friends and my family. This is about *life* itself and making sure that it remains worth living. It's about being worthy of the magic we've been given and telling that rotten necromancer that she doesn't get to decide the course of our lives for us. You taught Sarah what it was to believe she had the right to decide that for herself. And frankly, this display is disappointing us all. Now get up, dust off your skirts and Raise. Your. Blade."

Mrs. Winter's eyes narrowed at Ivy, angry color rising to her cheeks. "Did you rehearse that speech in a mirror or was it extemporaneous?"

I feared that I might have to break up my first fistfight between my former employer and my best friend. But after a few tense moments of very intent staring, Mrs. Winter simply took a deep breath and hugged her. Ivy stiffened, but eventually leaned against Mrs. Winter and hugged her back. Alicia and I exchanged a look and relaxed slightly.

Ivy snorted, blinking to combat the hot tears of relief welling in her eyes. She patted Mrs. Winter's back. "It was improvised. Did it sound rehearsed?"

"Just the last bit," Mrs. Winter groaned, pushing to her feet. "I'm going to need a mirror and my blade."

Mrs. Dalrymple's eyes went wide as Ivy helped Mrs. Winter up the stairs. We stared at each other, and then at Ivy's retreating form.

"I'm sorry for everything I said about your friendship being trouble, young lady," Mrs. Dalrymple said quietly. "It is worth all the trouble, all the upheaval to see my granddaughter speak up that way. The fact that she spoke that way to Aneira Winter is only a tiny part of my enjoyment and pride."

"Her son is missing," I said gesturing towards Mrs. Winter.

Ignoring my protest, Mrs. Dalrymple turned me to face her and kissed my forehead. "As you have offered your friendship to my Ivy, I offer my friendship to you, Sarah Smith."

Mrs. Dalrymple left me, just as Gavin walked into the room. He flexed his cramped writing hand as he approached. "Did I hear shouting?"

"We had a bit of a breakthrough with Mrs. Winter," I said.

"Oh, good." Gavin gestured towards the sofa. I sat and he sat in a chair across from me.

"This plan of yours. Alicia has explained it to me," he said. "I don't like it. I don't think I have a better one. I just think it's risky. Robert and I have been concocting some defensive items, but I don't know how much use they're going to be."

"You are free to dislike it. But it's still going to happen, so you should probably adjust," I told him. "Though, if I could make alternative suggestions, it would be for you to recognize that I've put you and your sister in danger, and suggest that you take Alicia home and get as far away from me as possible."

"Not that again, Sarah," he sighed. "I've tried living without you and it's terribly boring. I much prefer being close, where I can mitigate the damage."

"I don't know if that's a nice thing to say," I told him. "But I get the feeling that it's not."

12

In the end, Cathy lost the battle in terms of wearing a ballgown. It was a pastel yellow gown, so she might appear to be a proper, gently raised Guardian daughter… but it did have skirt pockets, so frankly, I think she won the war.

The night of the ball approached and I didn't think I could get more nervous. We'd ordered the right clothing (with pockets). We'd secured as many allies as would believe our half-told hints. We'd spent many days in conference at the dining table, developing different strategies and battle plans – but gaining control of the Horn of Silence and turning it against Miss Morton seemed to be the wisest course of action. There was no known countermagic for items with that sort of power. Removing it from Miss Morton's possession was going to be our best bet.

So, ultimately, we were going to be fighting for control of an elaborate magical French horn, while in a crowded ballroom, possibly surrounded by the re-animated dead.

How lovely.

The Changeling children were to stay behind under the watchful eye of Mrs. Lumpkin. Yes, they might have survived our mad run from the Revenants at Hazelcliffe, but none of us had the heart or the will to put them in this kind of danger. They didn't accept our departure gracefully.

"We want to come with you," Meggie protested, tugging on the skirt of my pale pink gown embroidered with Boncalm family lilies. I thought it was a brilliant disguise as I'd never worn pink voluntarily in my life. "We like Owen, too. And the fancy lady. We want to help."

Lizzie was too fixated on Ivy's cobalt blue gown beaded with Cavill hammers to add her voice to the chorus. She whispered, "I just want my own gown."

"We know you're very brave and you could help us," I told Meggie. "But we'd really rather you stay safe. We'll be able to work better magic if we're not worried about you."

"This is stupid," Joseph told me.

"You're probably right," Alicia replied.

"I think he meant leaving the children behind, not our plan in its entirety," Ivy noted.

Alicia jerked her shoulders.

Meggie pouted, as did the other children. But when asked, they trooped up the stairs as they were told, to get ready for bed. It took another hour or so for us to dress and hide various magical weapons on our persons.

We stood in line, allowing Miss Lockwood to perform 'muddling charms,' on each of us. We would appear much the same, but her magic wouldn't allow people to look at us directly or remember seeing us. We would simply appear to be some anonymous person in the background of the party, unremarkable and unassuming. Miss Lockwood was particularly talented at this sort of magic, as she was descended from the Benisse line, a family that was known for it. The Benisses used this charm to hide at social events when they were attending with people to whom they weren't "publicly attached." It sounded a little scandalous, to be honest, so I didn't ask more questions.

To her credit, Mrs. Winter didn't tease Miss Lockwood about

it, as it was a source of tension between them. Tonight, we didn't need tension or personal agenda. We needed calm and focus. Mrs. Winter and Mrs. Dalrymple declined charms for the sake of what they called, "intimidation."

Gavin took my arm and led me to the gondola anchored outside the house. He and Robert looked quite grand in their waistcoats, though poor Robert tugged at his collar as if it was slowly strangling him. Alicia's lovely buttercup silk gown only distracted him slightly from this devious cloth conspiracy. The adults formed a sort of cortege of unofficial chaperones behind us, dressed in styles designed to devastate their rivals.

Mrs. Winter didn't carry herself with her usual cutting grace. She appeared to be too worried about Owen.

"Is it my imagination or is the boat, bigger than last time?" I asked, glancing around as Gavin handed me into the boat. There seemed to be at least another fifteen feet of deck space. And I didn't remember there being a storage bin at the aft end. It wasn't quite the size of the *Aventurine,* but it was certainly a more substantial craft.

"This is how I've spent my days," Gavin said, shrugging. "Nervously adding to the size of the gondola and making sure it flies more silently. I even added storage below deck for emergency supplies. I had to have something to keep my hands busy."

"It's wonderful," I told him.

Robert and Gavin got us off the ground in a few movements. Gavin was a far more considerate pilot than Alicia, rising from the ground with a swiftness that left no one tossing their lunch over the side of the hull.

I watched the Folly disappear from sight, thinking about how many of these homes I'd visited over the last year, how many families I'd made contact with – many of whom would be dancing at this disastrous ball tonight. I frowned.

"Half a penny for your thoughts," Cathy said, her hands stuck in the pockets of her violet skirts.

"Not even a full penny?" I asked. Cathy shook her head.

I sighed. "I realized just now, there's a flaw in our thinking. We're not just going to have Revenants to fight. There will be living magical people who will be trying to hurt us, to hurt people we love and we have to ask ourselves whether we're comfortable with hurting them in return."

"Yes," Cathy said, nodding sharply.

I blinked rapidly at her and she rolled her eyes.

"Do you think they're going to show us the same consideration?" she asked. "If Miss Morton points them at us and tells them we're a threat, do you think they'll hesitate because we're children? These are the same sort of people who were going to use us as cannon fodder to protect themselves. And they were perfectly fine with us being hurt if it meant saving their necks. You need to grow up."

"Cathy makes a good point," Miss Lockwood noted. "It's unlikely that you will receive any quarter."

"Shouldn't we try to be better than they are?" I asked as Miss Wrathburn disappeared below deck. I imagined she was searching for food among the emergency supplies Gavin mentioned. I'd been too nervous to eat all day and my stomach was starting to rumble. "Otherwise, what's the point?"

"We agreed to use non-lethal spells," Cathy sighed. "But we can't just lob candy floss at them."

It took hours of Gavin's skillful flying to get us to Starworth. It was the height of elegance, a vast sandstone edifice with three floors centered around a grand fountain, depicting the Winstone Pegasus. We were led briefly through the entryway with its high ceilings and walls practically encrusted with family portraits, to an open-sky ballroom behind the house. The black-and-silver checkerboard granite was legendary, setting a trend for outdoor ballrooms for seasons to come. A previous Mr. Winstone had paid Gavin's family handsomely to devise floating crayfire chandeliers to light the space from overhead. It would have been a breathtaking party, if I wasn't terrified.

Despite the fact that the entire evening was a social spider's web, meant to consume the magical powers of those present, Miss Morton certainly hadn't skimped on the flowers or the food. Great tables surrounding the dancefloor groaned with the weight of canapes and smoked salmon and pickled vegetables. There were no sweets, I noted, which would have made it impossible to hide the flavor of the dill. She'd designed the catering entire menu around hiding the herbs she needed to enable her magical theft.

Diabolical.

I longed to cling to Gavin's arm, completely unused to being in crowds after so many months of isolation in the country. But we'd agreed that the first thing Miss Morton would look for would be the girl attached to the McCray heir. He held himself apart from me, as if he'd just accidentally ended up a few feet away from me, but certainly didn't know me very well. It was desperately uncomfortable and I hated it.

Miss Lockwood's charm held, or at least, I assumed they did as no one shouted, *"There they are! The fugitive hellion schoolgirls who have gallivanted about the Continent unchaperoned! Seize them before they give our daughters dangerous ideas!"* At least, that's what I imagined them yelling in my head as we milled about.

However, the other guests certainly recognized Mrs. Winter and Mrs. Dalrymple. Some showed the usual social deference, bowing and curtsying as usual, while others eyed Mrs. Winter warily. Were those Miss Morton's allies, fully aware that Miss Morton held Owen somewhere? Or was it just the usual wariness that Mrs. Winter's sharp tongue inspired? Mrs. Dalrymple pulled Mrs. Winter away towards the buffet, so we might filter into the crowds unnoticed.

I scanned the room and recognized several faces from school – some friendly, some not. Jeanette was all the way across room. It would take me ages to pick my way through the dancing couples to talk to her. And frankly, the idea of moving away from Gavin was terrifying. What if I lost him? In the crowd? In the fight to come? We'd already lost Owen. I didn't know whether that state was permanent – and the light seemed to be fading from Ivy's face with every passing hour. Going through the same thing had been a frightening prospect in the abstract, but here we were, with disaster dangling over our heads and I found the very idea absolutely unacceptable. I would not allow Gavin to be harmed. Or Ivy. Or Alicia. Or anyone else I cared about. I just didn't know how I was going to accomplish that.

In the crowd, I saw Mr. Winter talking to his wife. To my surprise, he embraced her and let her bury her face against his shoulder for the briefest of moments. I didn't think I'd ever seen the two of them embrace in all my years of knowing them. From the look on Mr. Winter's face, she must have told him about Owen. I glanced back at Ivy, who was searching the crowd for her sweetheart, forlorn. I supposed I should find comfort in the fact that he wasn't here as a Revenant.

Yet.

No, I couldn't think that way.

Miss Wrathburn appeared to my left, offering me a glass of punch I was under strict orders not to drink. "I'm hearing some murmurings of some sort of 'spectacle' planned at midnight. I don't think it's going to be fireworks or a mock sea monster battle."

How had she managed to glean information from just a few minutes of eavesdropping? I looked at her and I suppose my expression gave away my thoughts because she replied. "You forget my education, my dear."

"Have we seen our hostess yet?" I asked.

Gavin shook his head. "That's not unusual. Mrs. Delgado-Winstone loves making an entrance long after the evening is in full swing. Or at least, she did."

I nodded, glancing at the oversized clock mounted into the

stone tower overhead. “Midnight? That’s in less than an hour.”

“Yes,” Miss Wrathburn said, “So if you plan to gather your friends, you should do so shortly.”

I nodded. Playing her part as a society matron, Miss Wrathburn made a show of introducing us and encouraged us to dance as she “so loved to see young people pair off.” I curtsied to Miss Wrathburn and let Gavin lead me onto the dancefloor. We only danced enough steps to get us across the room towards Jeanette. Miss Wrathburn disappeared into the crowd.

Over my shoulder, I spotted Callista Cavill, my only real enemy from school, smirking as she watched us. The very sight of her chilled my blood. If anyone was going to give us trouble, besides Miss Morton, it was Callista. And even though I knew the muddling charm was in place, being near her was unnerving.

The hateful blond snickered behind her fan, commenting to her favorite hanger-on, Millicent DeCater. “It seems poor Miss Reed was unable to hang on to her beau after all. Such a shame.”

I supposed stomping on Callista’s foot as we passed would probably give my identity away.

“Miss Drummond!” I called merrily in a tone much higher than my own natural voice. She frowned at me as I broke apart from Gavin. He hovered in the general vicinity as Jeanette glowered at his back.

“I happen to like the young lady who has an understanding with that boy,” Jeanette told me, her dark brows disappearing into the black fringe of her bangs. She was wearing the usual Drummond silver and it made her look like the powerful young lady that she was. I envied her, and I appreciated her loyalty, getting prickly over “someone else” dancing with Gavin. “And I don’t particularly appreciate you elbowing your way in during her absence.”

“Jeanette, it’s me,” I whispered.

She blinked at me, as if her eyes were ailing her. “Cassandra?” she whispered. “Why can’t I look at you directly?”

"It's a charm from Miss Lockwood," I whispered from behind my fan. "You're not supposed to be able to look at me. It's a little confusing, but effective."

"She's here?" Jeanette hissed, looking around frantically as if Miss Lockwood would jump out at any moment and assign Jeanette demerits.

"Yes," I said, smiling sweetly. "We're all here. Isn't it exciting?"

Jeanette blinked at me again, trying to interpret what I was saying.

"And I hear there is to be some sort of spectacle shortly, do you have any idea what it could be?" I asked.

"I've noticed that there seem to be guards posted at that gate nearest the garden," she murmured, nodding toward the far corner of the ballroom.

"Do you have other friends here who are also anticipating this highlight of the evening?" I asked.

She glanced around the room.

"I have a sudden need to visit the... necessary room," Jeanette said. "Should you like join me?"

"Delighted," I said, taking her arm. I stared at Gavin over my shoulder as we walked away. Jeanette coughed into her gloved hand as we crossed the room to a walled off area that hid the spacious ladies waiting room required when one threw such a large gathering.

"Your acquaintance, Jennifer, departed the school quite unexpectedly in the middle of the night a week ago," Jeanette murmured. "Two women showed up the next day, asking questions about her whereabouts."

I hummed, considering. Jenny disappearing in the middle of the night could mean that she was present somewhere in the crowd to do Miss Morton's bidding. But I hadn't seen her anywhere in the ballroom, and the fact that Miss Morton seemed to send a search team for her... maybe she managed to escape? I hoped that was true. I was still a bit angry with Jenny's betrayal, but I didn't want Jenny to be anchored to Miss Morton forever. I wanted her to find happiness somewhere.

As we walked, I noticed that more than a dozen girls filed into place behind us, casually making their way to the same room as if the need simultaneously struck them. Jeanette managed to make that happen, just by coughing. Miss Lockwood followed and removed the spells from Alicia, Ivy, and myself. There were at least twenty of us gathered, more friends than I remembered having at school, certainly. Dear Madeline was there, and Sofia, and Joan and all of our study circle friends. We tried not to make too much of a fuss as we hugged, knowing there could be people nearby listening. Miss Lockwood searched the room for outsiders and then cast a charm for privacy.

"What is this all about, Cassandra?" Joan demanded.

"That was the maddest note I've ever received," Madeline told us. "I'm sorry if my sister's response was rude."

I smiled at her, suddenly nervous. I announced in the steadiest voice I could manage. "We are not the same. My name is Sarah Smith and I was born a servant. I served as a maid in the Winters' house from the time I was a child. I only found out I have magic last year. I lied because I didn't trust you to take me as I am and I'm sorry for that."

I plowed on through because I couldn't bear the questions or the accusations. "Miss Morton, our former librarian, has been working to restore her house, Grimstelle, to its former glory, using her ability to manipulate the dead to occupy powerful people, including our hostess tonight."

I could barely be heard over the gasps as I continued. "She's planning on something awful. She wants to take magic from people she doesn't believe deserve it – namely, anyone who's not her. We believe she's planning some sort of ritual tonight to take magic from all your families. Ivy and Alicia and I have been trying to stop her, but we can't keep doing this on our own. We need your help."

"We understand if this is too much to ask," Alicia assured them. "And if it is, we would completely understand if you wanted to fake a headache and ask your families to take you home before her planned 'spectacle' at midnight. In fact, a thinned crowd might make things easier."

"But if you stay, you're going to have to fight," Ivy said. "And we'd like you to fight with us. We've learned that what Miss Morton is really afraid of is all of us, working together."

"When our magic is united in one purpose, it's much more effective," I added. "Think of how we learned together last year, how powerful the spells were. We need you to do that with us now, if you're willing. Listen to your magic and what it wants you to do, which spells it wants to cast. But ultimately, do what your conscience tells you is right."

While many of the faces in the room had gone pale and drawn, one by one, they nodded, drawing out their blades from their reticules. Jeanette took my hand. "We're with you... Sarah."

"You're not questioning any of this?" I asked.

"Oh, we have *dozens* of questions," Joan told us. "But it sounds like we don't have time for them now. We'll ask them later."

"Really?" I asked, laughing, despite the current situation.

"Well, we knew there had to be *something* different about you," Sofia told me. "We just didn't think broadly enough."

I laughed. "Thank you."

The next few minutes were spent furiously strategizing, with our side teaching the young ladies as many spells as we could think to share. That connection to Ivy and Alicia was expanding to include all our allies. I could feel all our magics nudging against each other, rubbing elbows like old friends. When we decided it was necessary to leave, Miss Lockwood put our muddling charms back in place and we prepared to leave the room in pairs.

I looked at the clock as I re-entered the ballroom. It was five minutes to midnight and Miss Morton's staff had crowded the guests into one end of the room, far from the exits. The curtain that covered the garden gate earlier was parted and a small platform stood in front of it, covered in a black cloth. If I looked closely enough, I could just make out a Grimstelle owl embroidered onto it in black thread.

The body of Mrs. Delgado-Winstone stood near the platform, resplendent in black and silver.

"My dearest guests," she intoned. "Thank you so much for joining me at Starworth for this grand occasion. As promised, I have something special to share with you this evening. A gift, if you will. A kindness."

She grinned and I could see Miss Morton in her eyes, her delight in a dramatic announcement. "I will kindly remove the magic you don't deserve, that you use selfishly. I will kindly remove the weight of controlling the world as you know it from your shoulders, because I will be determining the course of the magical world from now on."

Light titters rippled across the crowd, as if this whole thing was a joke to brighten the evening. When Miss Morton's false face didn't smile or laugh herself, the room grew quiet as a tomb – quiet enough that you could hear the sound of hundreds of shuffling feet across the grass just beyond the garden walls.

The guests instinctively moved away from the sound, to the center of the room. Miss Morton let out an eerie cackle as she whipped the cloth off her little platform, displaying the Horn of Silence. It was just as awful as I remembered, radiating an ominous power that made me hear screams in my head, even with so many people around. Next to the horn was a large mirror and several sinister looking items. Geodes and bones and mummified… bits. I supposed they were intended to boost whatever magic Miss Morton was about to wield.

Suddenly, a wave of the dead moved through the narrow garden gates just as dozens of Revenants poured through the house, into the opposite side of the ball room. We were surrounded. Miss Morton's army was comprised of the rich and poor alike. To my relief, I didn't recognize any of the faces, as I had in my nightmares. Owen wasn't among them, so I held out hope that he was somewhere in the house safe.

Well, as safe as one could be in a house full of zombies.

The adults in the room froze. They couldn't seem to process the sight of all those poor deceased people pouring into the ballroom. The smell of the grave was overwhelming. Around me, I could see my friends rolling their shoulders, gripping their blades, readying themselves for a fight.

Even those who had seemed at ease when Miss Morton began her announcement seemed shocked into silence now. So at the very least, they hadn't expected dead people and announcements of total governmental control. I almost felt sorry for them, but not quite.

As planned, Robert had already walked back out to the gondola and carried in two large bags filled with sharpened birch stakes before the arrival of the dead. He began handing them out like party favors, instructing each guest on their proper use. Most of them just stared at him like he was mad. Any time Miss Morton's staff tried to pull the weapons from his hands, Robert retorted with his fists. It was remarkably effective.

But Miss Morton didn't seem aware of these little "arguments," she was too busy reveling in the fear she was inspiring around the room.

"As you can see, I have amassed an army," she said, sweeping her arm towards the Revenants, who were standing in formation between us and Miss Morton. "And this is only the beginning. You will comply with my plans or die."

"And what are your plans?" one woman in Mountfort garb demanded.

"This is Miss Morton, former librarian of Miss Castwell's, using my friend as her disguise! She plans to use that Grimstelle artifact to take our magic away," Mrs. Winter yelled. Mr. Winter stood at her side, his blade drawn and a birch stake in the other. I felt the charms fade away and Alicia and Ivy were standing at my side, equally exposed. "Our young ladies have been fighting against her for the last few years and I'm ashamed that we've left this effort to them."

"What are you talking about, Aneira?" Mrs. McCray scoffed. "You know very well that 'our girls' are merely under the influence of your reprobate niece."

My shoulders slumped for just a moment. It was the end of the world and my sweetheart's mother *still* didn't like me.

"Will you really move against me when I have your son?" Miss Morton demanded, ignoring Mrs. McCray.

"It's for his sake that I do. I won't let him live in a world where you decide who has magic and who doesn't," Mrs. Winter told her. She turned to the other adults in the room. "Look around you! Your children are prepared to raise arms against her! Are you?"

It was as if the direct question had woken the other parents from their stupor. Quite a few people bolted, or at least, they tried to, but were stopped by the Revenants. Some stabbed at the Revenants with their birch sticks, but, unused to physical combat, those weapons were simply batted out of the way. Others were more successful. The shriek of dispatched Revenants filled the air.

Miss Morton seemed annoyed by this development and sent a violent orange spell towards a group of resisters by the main entrance. Another spell, lime green, intercepted Miss Morton's clearly harmful symbol. I turned to find the caster and spotted Callista, fully armed, having just thrown the spell in defense of our allies.

When I squawked in surprise, Callista shot me an arch look. "Oh, don't look so surprised. Just because I don't happen to like you doesn't mean I want society as we know it to collapse under the weight of an undead librarian."

With that, she grabbed a birch stake from the floor and went marching towards the Revenants, Millicent at her heels.

Ivy stared after her. "Callista is helping us, at peril to herself."

Alicia nodded. "The world *is* ending."

With that, the room exploded into chaos. A pack of proper Guardian mamas broke loose from the crowd, blades raised like a battalion, sending various spells toward Miss Morton. She rolled her eyes and batted them away with defensive shield spells. My Castwell's classmates began staking Revenants left and right, making their way towards me, Alicia, and Ivy. Gavin led a charge of Palmer boys, but they were repelled by a wave of Revenants.

Mrs. McCray was at the front of the mama pack, blade drawn and blood in her eyes. She sent a spiraling ochre spell at a large male Revenant who was getting close to Alicia.

"Mother!" Alicia squeaked.

"Raise your blade, young lady!" Mrs. McCray bellowed. "You fought hard enough to get the opportunity! You *will* do your family proud."

Brows drawn, Alicia began throwing magic alongside her mother. And it looked… right. When they stood side by side, casting, one could see the similarities in their form, the spells that they chose. It was the most in sync I'd ever seen mother and daughter.

But I would never tell Alicia that.

Ivy… was a dervish of elegantly executed rage. I didn't even see her move her hand. I only joined in. The other Castwell girls fell in behind her, Alicia included, and tried to copy Ivy's movements. After a few failed attempts, we eventually learned to anticipate her movements and guess which spells she was throwing. I'd never seen so many of us moving as one, and instead of making dozens of small symbols, we were making one large symbol.

With a yell, Owen burst through the garden gate, blade raised, the Changeling children at his back. Miss Wrathburn was among them, yelling encouragements as they ran, reminding them of the best defensive spells. Meggie was using her bubble to protect the lot of them, while her "team" threw a frightening array of magic towards Miss Morton.

"Owen!" I cried. Ivy ran across the ballroom at full tilt, throwing herself at him. He caught her, despite looking absolutely exhausted. It was testament to the turmoil surrounding us that no one noticed or commented on this completely improper, but perfectly romantic, behavior.

Gavin had fought through the mess of people to join our group. We cast, back-to-back, keeping the Revenants and Miss Morton's allies away from our distracted friends.

Mrs. Winter cried out, running to her son, who reluctantly broke away from Ivy to hug her as well. All his mother could say was, "*How?*"

Owen grinned cheekily. "The Changeling children. It seems they've figured out how to stow away on gondolas without being seen. Since they weren't going to be allowed to fight, they wanted to assist in my rescue."

"I found them below deck when we were already over the sea," Miss Wrathburn shouted as she cast spell after spell. "And since they were determined to behave recklessly, I decided it was best to channel their exuberance in the right direction."

My mouth agape, I turned on Meggie and Geoffrey, who were looking anywhere but my eyes.

"Well, it appears that you hardly need me," Owen marveled. "You're doing rather well."

"Don't mess with a bunch of girls in ballgowns. The corsetry make them crazy," Gavin said, with Alicia swatting at him.

Mrs. Winter closed her eyes, her bottom lip trembling with emotion. "Those children will have my support for the rest of their natural lives."

The next few minutes were a blur of bodies and spells and danger. I cast, hit a target, and moved, then repeated. I lost track of what I was doing, only feeling the magic moving around me like a current and responding. I was aware my friends were casting, but it was all I could do not to cast against them. I saw a weakness in Miss Morton's defenses and threw a concussive spell at her platform. She was thrown aside with a plume of smoke.

Ivy and Owen dashed towards the ruins of the platform. Miss Morton stood, her eyes blazing and threw a pitch-black, circular symbol at me, shattering any protective magic between us. I felt like I'd been punched in the chest and I went flying backwards. I could see Gavin's horrified face as I bulleted past him.

"Sarah!" he shouted, but it sounded like it was coming from underwater. My strange, distracted brain thought of how nice it was, to hear him call me by my real name.

Everything went dark.

When I came to, I was surrounded by smoke and screaming. I

sat up and found Gavin shouting my name again. I nodded but couldn't find the words to respond. He helped me to my feet. I saw Ivy and Owen running across the room, the horn tucked under Ivy's arm.

It was just as Lizzie had seen in her vision. And they were making very good time across the ballroom floor – right up until a rather heavyset corpse in blue satin breeches attempted to tackle Ivy. He missed, but caught Ivy's shoulder, making her stumble. The horn skittered across the floor tiles and back into Miss Morton's hands. Ivy yelled in frustration.

"Enough!" Miss Morton thundered, raising the horn. "Enough of this nonsense!"

Miss Morton crossed to me, seething with rage.

"Did you honestly think I wouldn't have thought of this?" she scoffed. "You forget that I have the Horn! I have the army! I have the numbers!"

"And you forget many things," I croaked, my brain not quite fully connected to the rest of my body. Gavin squeezed my arm gently and all the memories of the past few years came rushing back to me. Levitating the vase in the Winters' parlor. My first day at Miss Castwell's. My first fledgling moments of friendship with Ivy and Alicia. Meeting Gavin. Discovering Miss Morton's betrayal. Running from the mountain school with the children. Realizing I was more to Mrs. Winter than a pawn. Building relationships with the other Changelings. Growing into my power with Alicia and Ivy. Meeting Miss Lockwood as an equal. Recreating the Mother Book. Each of those pieces fell into place so we could get to this moment.

"We want it more than you do," I told her. "We want to keep our magic far more than you want to take it. You're one person, with some very misguided ideas, born of hurt. Now for the last time, stop this, Miss Morton. You were a friend to me once… in a way. I would give you one last chance to turn away from this path."

"And do what?" she cackled. "Wait for this body to fade with time? Become a specter? Haunt Miss Castwell's library? I don't need your pity or your paltry offers. I'm going to wipe you from the map, Sarah Smith, before I do the same to everyone you love. And I'll laugh while I do it."

"All right then." I looked back to my allies, my friends. Their expressions seemed to be one single face – determined resignation for what we were going to do. We held out our hands and took one single breath. All at once, we cast a single spell to call the Horn of Silence out of Miss Morton's hands. It jerked forward. She howled as it left her grasp and flew towards me. I caught it, just barely, and remembering that Madeline had studied music and dance for years. I tossed it to her.

"What are you *doing*?" she cried.

It didn't matter who played the horn, as long as it was played, while supported by the rest of us. Madeline was far more likely to make a legitimate musical sound than anyone else.

"Just play *something!*" I yelled. Shrugging, she took the horn to her lips and blew, a sharp bellowing note that just sounded *wrong*. I drew deep within my magic, reaching out towards Ivy and Alicia, towards our school friends, towards the Changelings, towards Gavin and Owen, and every person there I cared about – and thought one word. "*Reflect*."

The very magic that Miss Morton wanted to work on the people here, would be bounced back on her. The core magic she planned to take away would be stolen from her, just as the Horn of Silence did its work. All around the room, my compatriots made the same movements. A storm of magic brewed overhead while our streams of spellcasting blended together to make one large red symbol, a twisted spiral shape. Miss Morton watched with curiosity as the oversized spell flew towards her. It blasted through her like a strong wind, blowing Mrs. Delgado-Winstone's body back against the garden wall.

Across the room, I saw the rage and shock in Miss Morton's

eyes. She clearly didn't believe this outcome was possible, and yet, when she raised her hand to cast a reply, her arm dropped. Her blade clattered to the stone floor and her eyes rolled back into her head. Her body began to crumble into dust and her gown dropped to the floor, empty. Around the room, the remaining Revenants abruptly stopped moving and dropped to the ground as little piles of ash.

Time stopped.

The Castwell girls and Palmer boys in the room stopped moving and their parents dropped their stakes. People who hadn't quite chosen sides ran for the exits, as did some who had supported Miss Morton. Callista simply crossed her arms over her chest, and I thought perhaps she was waiting to be thanked. I half-panted, half-laughed in disbelief that it could possibly be over.

And suddenly, a man barked. "What the bloody hell just happened!"

I burst out laughing, clapping my hand over my mouth. The other girls laughed, too, hugging each other, dashing across the room to find their families. Ivy and Alicia and I collapsed against each other.

"Is it really over?" Ivy asked.

"I'm sure there will be some other evil we have to fight next week," Alicia sighed.

"Bite your tongue, Alicia," I told her sternly. I felt a tap on my shoulder. I turned to find Gavin standing there and for once, I was the one who threw myself at a boy. He caught me, lifting me from the ground as he hugged me tight.

"You did it," he murmured against my cheek.

"No, we did," I replied.

"If you're thinking about kissing this young lady in front of an entire room of people, you are not the young man I thought you were," Mrs. Winter announced. Gavin dropped me gently to my feet and we turned, our hands behind our backs. "Your mother is standing just over there, glaring at Sarah as if she could make her combust with her mind."

Gavin glanced across the room and blanched. He kissed my knuckles, quite properly, and said, "I'm going to go… mitigate the worst of the damage."

"Good idea," Mrs. Winter told him. She turned to me and took my hand. "So, that went rather well, I thought."

"Is there such a thing as 'going well' in this situation?" I asked.

"Well, it could have turned out much worse," she retorted.

"I am sorry about your friend," I told Mrs. Winter as we peered down at the pile of ashes Miss Morton had left behind.

"We will give her the grand memorial she deserves," Mrs. Winter said, smiling sadly.

Mr. Winter bowed to Miss Lockwood. "I think you should receive a letter of reinstatement for your position as headmistress very soon, if I have anything to do with it."

Miss Lockwood – Headmistress Lockwood, rather – looked very pleased. As Mrs. Winter *curtsied* to her, she was almost agog.

"Oh, don't make a to do about it, Dora," Mrs. Winter sighed.

Miss Lockwood blushed and returned the curtsy. It was as close to hugging as those two were going to get.

Alicia blew out a long breath, practically dropping onto a nearby bench, some of which had been chipped away by errant spells. "So what do we do now?"

"We could always return to Miss Castwell's," I suggested. "Finish our coursework?"

"I will offer you any amount of money if you don't return to the school," Miss Lockwood told me. "Consider the last few months practical exams. You've passed. Never darken the hallways of my school again. I will send you your diploma by post."

Ivy and Alicia snickered

"That goes for you two as well," Headmistress Lockwood told them.

They stopped snickering.

13

In the end, everything and nothing changed.

For a few weeks, the world was chaos. To be honest, I slept through quite a bit of it. Mrs. Winter took me to Raven's Rest, where I fell into bed without so much as a bath and slept for two days straight. Meanwhile, word of "The Skirmish at Starworth" spread. While quite a few Guild Guardians weren't pleased with those events – including the crushing revelation that magical talents weren't exclusive to the high-born classes – magic itself seemed quite content. Secrecy was abandoned and those who *could* practice magic, had it.

Suddenly, children from servant families all over England, all over the world, were exhibiting magical skills. Windows exploded with the force of temper tantrums. More than one housekeeper was transformed into a toad. Maids were levitating vases in parlors at an unprecedented rate.

A few families that had magic for generations suddenly lost it, as if it no longer wished to be misused. That was the real blow. Those families suddenly relocated to places like Australia and Iceland, unwilling to live in society as they once had, without the power they wielded. Callista's family held onto their magic, though I supposed after her help in the final fight, I couldn't begrudge her that.

Much.

The rich remained rich, but the poor had many more options than they had before. People who were content to remain servants stayed in service. But at the same time, the Senate voted, in emergency session, that all children with magic were free to pursue their education. We could test and join research guilds. Magical and non-magicals alike could travel freely, move to the New World if they wished it. We could pursue trades and relationships that interested us, rather than what was deemed best for us. There were no Guardians, no Snipes, only people. We had as much control of our lives as money and circumstance dictated, which was still a lot. But it was a step in the right direction.

I liked to think we influenced change for more than just ourselves. Society wives, no longer content to simply run society from behind the scenes, demanded that they be able to keep those activities running in the open. Mrs. Winter was right at the head of the pack, with Miss Wrathburn at her side. I was told it was a glorious and terrifying sight, to see her announce in Senate chambers that if their demands weren't met, the wives of the most powerful men in Lightbourne simply wouldn't participate in society any longer. Households would be left unmanaged. Research would be left undone. Businesses would be left unpromoted. Fortunes would be left to wane. It was a serious enough threat that various "ladies committees" were created by the Senate to help oversee education, social welfare, and other "gentler" aspects of government. Miss Wrathburn was the first department head appointed, running something called the "adjustment committee."

It was a start.

I spent more time at home, in the Warren. Alicia and Ivy were equally exhausted and eager to spend time at home with families they'd neglected lately. I missed seeing them every day. Phillip did his best to stay perched on my shoulder whenever possible, but it wasn't quite the same as seeing one's true sisters every day.

It was a strange transition, not working, but I was a servant no longer. Mrs. Winter had already hired replacements for Mary and myself. And honestly, I didn't know if I was fit for service any longer. I'd seen too much, done too much, to go back to scrubbing pots and carrying laundry from floor to floor.

And yet, I had nowhere to go every day. So I stayed home. I cleaned our own house from top to bottom, catching up on years of chores and repair projects that my parents hadn't had time for. I cleaned out Mary's room and boxed up her remaining belongings to ship to Boston, with a letter telling her of all my adventures. Mrs. Winter had found a placement for her there, where she earned a nice wage and wrote my parents at least once a month. And her employers found her accent to be sophisticated, so she was working for the lady of the house as her social secretary. In my letter, I told her that I wished her well, that I wanted her to find happiness. I sincerely hoped that with this new distance between us, we could somehow find a way to be friends, in a way we never had before.

Some part of me hoped that Jenny was also in America somewhere, safe and finding her happiness. She hadn't been seen since disappearing from Miss Castwell's. She deserved to find some peace. We all did.

Nevertheless, once the Warren house was organized, I had nothing to *do*. I broke up the monotony of wondering what to do with myself by visiting Mrs. Winter and my parents at Raven's Rest. I lived in a sort of limbo between the parlor and the kitchen, not a member of the family and not a servant, but somehow, the Winters never let me feel it. They welcomed me into the rooms I used to clean like a long-beloved friend. I supposed this was what happened when you fought for your life beside someone. The old boundaries sort of fell away.

Owen still didn't like Gavin, though. He made that very clear when I arrived at Raven's Rest, carrying a basket of biscuits I'd successfully baked myself. (Without unintentional flames!) Gavin was waiting in the parlor with a bunch of roses tied with a Castwell green ribbon. Owen was sitting on the settee across from him, arms crossed over his chest and glowering.

"Gavin, what a nice surprise," I said, crossing the room. I was wearing one of my nicer day dresses from home, but it was still a step down from the fashionable gowns I wore as Cassandra Reed. But still, he smiled and bowed to me, offering me his bouquet of roses. I saw as I stepped closer, that they weren't actual flowers, but blooms made of rolled up ribbon. And just like that first bouquet he'd given me, when I touched a fingertip to a buttery yellow blossom, it transformed into a butterfly made of silk ribbon, fluttering around the room with its fellow blooms until they rolled themselves into neat stacks on the sideboard.

"I thought you might have lost my first gift in your scampering about the countryside, saving the world," Gavin told me. Behind him, Owen rolled his eyes dramatically.

"I did. I'm sorry, but I still have this, though," I said, lifting my wrist and showing him the charm bracelet made of books. He grinned at me and kissed my knuckles.

Owen gagged audibly.

"Might I remind you that I've tolerated your courting one of my best friends with considerable restraint," I told him. "And I had plenty of time in the countryside to tell her *years'* worth of stories about you being horrible. You're being very unfair."

Owen straightened in his chair. "Good point."

He directed one last glare at Gavin. "I regard Sarah very much like a sister," he said, pointedly. "And I still think she can do better."

Gavin shrugged. "That's all right. I think Ivy Cowell is ten times the person you are.

Owen snorted. "So, we're in agreement, then."

Gavin laughed and extended a hand to Owen, who reluctantly shook it.

"If you two are quite finished with your posturing," Mrs. Winter intoned from the doorway. She stood there with a bemused expression on her face, shaking her head. Gavin and Owen snapped to attention, bowing to Mrs. Winter.

"Owen, if you can't do anything more productive than none-too-subtly insulting Mr. McCray, I suggest you go upstairs to your room."

Owen frowned. "And do what?"

"As you gave up your opportunity to take your guild interview in order to fight evil, perhaps you should find something to study for your second sitting," she said dryly.

"You make it sound as if I skipped an examination to go on holiday," Owen griped as he slouched towards the stairs. After he passed his mother, he turned and pointed his fingers at his eyes and then at Gavin.

Gavin didn't seem threatened by this gesture at all. And I thought it was rather sweet, honestly, in absence of a brother, that Owen should see himself as my protector.

"The sad thing is he thinks I did not see that," Mrs. Winter said, huffing out a breath as Owen closed his bedroom door. "As for you, Mr. McCray, I believe there are some people waiting for you two in the gardens."

I frowned at Mrs. Winter, but she merely brushed my hair back from my face as I passed. She kissed my cheek and gave me a wink. She was a softer person now, Mrs. Winter. It was as if her worst fears had come true and yet, she'd seen so much worse, that night in Starworth, that she knew to value what she had.

"I'll see the ribbons are boxed up for you to take home," she told me. "Well done, Mr. McCray."

Gavin looked quite pleased with himself as Mrs. Winter nodded towards the doors at the back of the house, leading to the garden. As we passed the kitchen, I expected to see my mother, cooking. But there was a stranger at the stove, a girl about my age. She waved cheerily as we passed by and I had the oddest, out-of-body sensation, like I was seeing someone else live the life I could have had. Of course, Mary was supposed to replace my mother as housekeeper, once Mum retired. But I could have been that girl, standing at the stove, though she looked much more content cooking than I ever did. Was she happy there? Did she want more, as I had? I supposed that now, she had much more choice in the matter, and that was worth something.

Gavin's gentle pulling took my mind off these questions as we exited the house into fragrant green. Father's pride and joy was the gardens, where he'd carefully arranged pools of pink roses, purple irises, and yellow lilies at the feet of various statues. It might have appeared wild and overgrown, but every bit was carefully planned to bloom in cycles, so Mrs. Winter might never be without flowers from spring to fall.

My parents were sitting, together, for the first time in my memory, not engaged with a meal or with some sort of work they were trying to finish before the day's end. My father was clear-eyed and my mother was *smiling* at him. It was *bizarre.*

I steeled myself as we approached the table. It wasn't that I was worried about my parents' behavior. It was Gavin's response that worried me. Even after all we'd been through, this was the moment that could ruin us. I couldn't respect someone who treated my parents rudely. They'd been through too much with me. If Gavin failed now… I didn't want to think about it.

"Mum, Papa, this is Gavin McCray. Gavin, these are my parents."

"Mr. and Mrs. Smith." Gavin gave his most charming smile and bowed his head to my mother. He extended his hand to my father, shaking it heartily. He didn't worry about the dirt under my father's nails or the dust that could rub against his own sleeves. Gavin simply greeted them as equal. No, better, he greeted them as two people he hoped to impress. "It's very nice to meet you. You've raised an amazing young lady."

"Well, Sarah almost raised herself," Papa mused. "So really, the blame lies at someone else's door."

"Oh, hush, you," Mum fussed at him. "Thank you, Mr. McCray."

"Please call me Gavin, ma'am."

Mum looked stricken. The occasional retort to Mrs. Winter aside, it would be a broach in social protocol for a servant to call a *McCray* by his first name. If Mrs. McCray heard it, she would likely drop in a dead faint. But at the same time, I could see she didn't want to deny Gavin the first request he made of her.

"We can work towards it," he told her.

She smiled at him, relaxed for the first time since we'd approached. "Thank you, I'd like that."

"So, Sarah tells us that you've built a boat that floats," Papa said, gesturing for Gavin to sit down. "Don't boats normally float? Otherwise, they would be called anchors."

Papa was teasing, of course. He'd seen the gondola for himself, but I supposed that it was a father's prerogative to give his daughter's suitor a little grief.

I listened as Gavin gave an explanation of how crayfire energy worked and how he hoped to apply it to transportation on a large scale. Mum served tea and I nibbled on biscuits while my parents examined my gentleman friend for flaws. I doubted they would find any, but it was still entertaining to watch.

Eventually, after an hour of interrogation, I mean, tea, Gavin was released by my parents and given permission to take a turn about the garden. I was sure that they were still watching, but it showed their approval, that they were willing to give us that much freedom.

"So, your parents," Gavin began, as we strolled among the roses.

"Yes?" My brows rose.

"They ask a lot of questions," he finished, making me laugh.

"And they will ask more," I told him. "I hope you're prepared for that."

"I don't think anyone could be, but I will try," he promised.

"I know that Mrs. Winter has been pushing for some sort of formal arrangement between us. And your mother is..."

"Less enthusiastic," he supplied.

"That's a nice way of putting it," I muttered. "But I don't think

I'm ready for any sort of official talk of my future. I don't know if I'll ever be ready to marry. I have a lot I need to accomplish."

He nodded. "I wouldn't expect anything less."

"But if you wanted to come to dinner some time with my parents, that might be nice. I would like to see you, very often, in fact. I just don't want to make any promises that can't be undone, right now."

"I think that could be arranged." He grinned at me and leaned over, kissing my lips lightly. He drew back after just a few seconds because anything else would be tantamount to a scandal.

I glanced toward the window, where suddenly the white lace curtains drew together, as if my parents weren't just watching. I laughed, rolling my eyes.

And suddenly, the thought struck me. Gavin McCray was paying suit to Sarah Smith. Publicly. What a strange new world we lived in.

~

AT ONE TIME, I would have been highly suspicious if Mrs. Winter had invited me to take a trip in her carriage to an undisclosed location. But this afternoon, it seemed quite natural for me to climb into the Winter carriage for an errand in town. I thought of a similar ride, on the morning she first took me to Miss Castwell's, and how nervous I had been. Once again, I had one foot in one world and one in another, but somehow, I wasn't as uneasy as I had been – desperately wishing to return to the childhood that had made me unhappy, but that I understood.

None of us could be absolutely one thing or another. We would all have to be something more now.

Out the window, I watched the Warren roll by. And though I knew it was my imagination, the skies seemed a little brighter, the air less gloomy. Children ran and played in the streets, just as they always had, and while I still couldn't join in with them, I hoped that they were happier than I had been.

The Winter carriage stopped in front of an old stately home, one that looked to be under renovation. Scaffolding clung to the Grecian façade, which appeared to be crumbling at the corners. But still, the building *felt* significant, like it was radiating an inner power. I was glad I wore the last of my gowns from Madame DuPont, a light blue day dress that made me look a few years older than my approaching sixteen. Whatever appointment I was walking into, it was important. And while I fancied myself not quite superficial, Mrs. Winter had taught me that one simply didn't walk into important meetings underdressed. It undermined one's confidence.

The signs of renovation only grew as we walked inside the house, which smelled of paint and plaster and all manner of *newness.* A pile of construction debris and dust was swept into a corner, just beside stacked furniture covered in canvas drop cloths. The one intact room was a parlor off to the right, recently painted a silvery grey that reminded me very much of Winter House. The furnishings were spare, a few navy and grey pinstriped sofas around a central table. There had obviously been a crest carved into the wall over the mantle, a harp with a pumpkin in the middle, a sigil I didn't recognize, which was no matter because it had been chipped away and placed at the side of a rather large marble fireplace. The space where it had been was plastered over and sanded smooth.

Cathy was there, along with Alicia, Ivy, and Jeanette. And while no one could really manage lounging in these dresses, they looked quite comfortable, reclining together on the sofas, drinking tea with Miss Wrathburn. Well, Cathy didn't look comfortable. She was watching everything warily, but the worried lines seemed to be fading from around her eyes. I supposed it was the presence of Miss Wrathburn that was keeping her calm. From what Mrs. Winter told me, Miss Wrathburn had taken charge of our Changeling children, providing them with a comfortable home at one of the Winters' properties while the Winters helped locate their families. Mrs. Lumpkin was mothering them all into submission. I missed her breakfasts terribly.

Mrs. McCray stood ramrod straight by a window, sipping her tea and giving me a long, hard look. I was not surprised.

The only one missing was Miss Lockwood, who was still mucking out the ruin that her replacement had made of Miss Castwell's. My former headmistress had written me several times, both blaming me for the mess we'd made of things and asking for my opinion on how to remake the school more comfortable for *all* students before it re-opened. She was far too busy for what appeared to be a tea party in a haunted house.

Miss Wrathburn set her tea aside and rose as I curtsied. Alicia and Ivy also rose, hugging me. Cathy merely sipped her tea, which prompted a sour face from her. Apparently, it wasn't to her taste.

"We've been waiting for ages," Alicia whispered. "Cathy is becoming quite cranky about it."

"I'm not cranky," Cathy muttered under her breath. "I'm *hungry*."

"I didn't know we were supposed to be meeting you," I whispered back as we sat down.

"It's all been very mysterious."

"I appreciate your attendance," Miss Wrathburn sniffed. "You must be wondering why I've invited you all here today."

"I'm afraid we do find ourselves at a loss," Ivy said carefully. "Are we going to be punished for our actions at Starworth? Is that why we've been summoned to an abandoned house?"

"Of course not. This is an old ruin belonging to one side of my family or the other," Mrs. Winter said. "The area's fallen out of fashion and no one's lived here in ages, so I've decided to donate it to a good cause."

"And with Mrs. Winter's generous donation, we are remaking

this house into the future home of the Janus Guild," Miss Wrathburn added. "And we would like to invite you to join."

"But we haven't qualified for a research guild," I reminded Mrs. Winter. "Technically, we haven't graduated."

"Our diplomas haven't arrived in the post yet," Alicia added.

"Well, I graduated, but the evil school administration didn't bother recording my results," Jeanette said glumly.

"Well, Miss Lockwood assures me that will all be remedied soon, once she unearths her office from her predecessor's quote 'avalanche of incompetence' unquote," Mrs. Winter informed us. "Cathy, too, has been granted an honorary degree, for 'exemplary demonstrated knowledge.'"

"That was rather nice of her," Alicia mused as Cathy's mouth dropped open in shock.

"And this isn't quite a research guild," Miss Wrathburn said. "Janus was the god of transitions. This organization is a sort of branch for the new government, one that will help us navigate the many adjustments we're facing. It's an adjustment committee, if you will. We need to find children who have magical talents their families might not recognize. We need to connect those children with magical schools that can provide them with direction and education. For that matter, we will need to establish magical schools in various parts of England to meet the growing demand. And while we're working on that, it wouldn't hurt to open *non*-magical schools for those who wish to study. Education should be offered to those who want it. And who knows what else will be required? This new world you've brought about is going to require a lot of changes on all of our parts."

"Since you had a part in setting the world on its ear, it's only fair that you help us find a new way to manage it," Mrs. Winter said crisply. "What better young ladies to help us organize than those who aligned all of the magical youth of the age at the Skirmish at Starworth?"

"You still can't bear to call it a battle, can you?" I asked.

"Proper young ladies do not *battle*," Mrs. Winter snipped at me lightly. "Not outside the drawing room, at least."

"Why does this *feel* like a punishment?" Alicia whispered.

"I prefer to think of it as a thoughtful penance," Miss Wrathburn said. "You will all be generously compensated and treated with the deference due to Senate appointees. Honestly, it's a high honor to be offered to girls, just out of school, however dubious that graduation might be."

"Me as well?" Cathy asked, setting aside her teacup.

"You did help the other ladies defend magical society, even when it wasn't to your benefit, did you not?" Miss Wrathburn asked. "You are being extended the same offer. Your young Mr. Robert received one as well, though he turned us down for a position at the National Library."

Alicia grinned to herself, even as her mother huffed out an exasperated breath.

"You will be an independent lady of means," Miss Wrathburn told her. "You'll be able to have a house of your own, your own money."

Cathy nodded. "I would have to think about it."

"Of course," Miss Wrathburn stated. "I should expect nothing less."

"It's strange that you mention a house of your own," Mrs. Winter noted. "It has been suggested by the Senate that all of you be allowed to establish your own House together. You can choose your own sigil, your own name, to symbolize your victory."

I glanced around at the other girls. None of them seemed terribly excited about this prospect. Mother Houses, Guilds, and the structures that used to keep us organized and separated. That was the old way.

Fortunately, Ivy read my mind just as easily as she always did.

"As much as we appreciate the sentiment, I don't think we would accept your very generous offer," she said. Beside her, Alicia nodded.

"I consider you all my family, in the ways that matter," I told them, taking their hands in mine. "But if we're going to succeed in this new way of life, we're going to have to be something more. We're going to have to build something new. Maybe it will work, or maybe it will become something even worse than what we had, but it will be ours."

"That's not terribly optimistic," Alicia said, snorting.

"Would you expect anything less?" I asked.

Alicia and Ivy shook their heads in unison.

"I think Sarah is right," Cathy said. "Instead of building on the old, we expand the new."

Alicia raised her hands dramatically, shielding her head. Miss Wrathburn and Mrs. Winter startled, drawing their blades.

"What is it?" Miss Wrathburn demanded.

"Cathy agreed with Sarah," Alicia gasped dramatically. "It's a sign of something horrible coming."

"You girls are going to turn me gray, I just know it," Miss Wrathburn grumbled into her teacup, though she looked quite amused.

The others began chatting about how to best speed the process of turning the old house into a workable space. Mrs. McCray, who had quietly lingered in the background, looking on with disapproval, approached my side. "Miss... Smith."

"Mrs. McCray," I replied. "Alicia seems to have recovered fully from our ordeal. In fact, she looks a little more energetic than I feel right now."

"It's true, you've brought out an unexpected strength in my daughter," Mrs. McCray told me. "But you should know, I still do not approve of you as a prospect for my son."

I smiled, without showing any teeth. "I can live with that."

Mrs. McCray's eyebrows rose. "You never have been content to let me bat you about, have you?"

"No, ma'am. But to be fair, I have had other things to occupy my time," I replied.

"I suppose you have," she snorted. "You handled yourself well, at Starworth, I will grant you that. And you protected my children, which I will not soon forget. But still–"

"You do not approve of me," I finished for her. "Yes, ma'am. But I suppose that's up to your children, to determine how they feel about that."

She gave me one last arch look and approached Mrs. Winter. Ivy and Alicia left Cathy chatting with Miss Wrathburn as they joined me on the sofa.

"Your mother still doesn't like me," I muttered to Alicia.

"Well, at least that hasn't changed," Alicia chirped cheerfully.

"Everything else has," Ivy sighed. "What do you think of this offer Miss Wrathburn has made?"

"I don't think we're going to get a better one, given our reputation for chaos and destruction," I mused.

"I think that's just Miss Lockwood, who thinks so," Alicia replied.

"Trust me, it's not," Mrs. Winter commented from across the room, making Alicia's lips pinch shut.

"You know we're going to take it," Ivy huffed. "It's too much of challenge not to take it on. This is what we wanted."

"Be careful what you wish for," I snickered.

"We are the living embodiment of that saying," Alicia said, laughing, lifting her teacup. Ivy and I raised our cups to meet hers with a clink, and a shower of gold sparks spilled from the rims.

"I'm still getting used to things like that," Ivy murmured.

"But we'll have fun while we do," Alicia added.

"It won't be boring," I agreed. "And we won't be alone."

I winked at my friends, and we drank together, each contemplating our new future.

THE BEGINNING

DISCUSSION QUESTIONS

1) Are Sarah, Ivy and Alicia doing a good job leading the other children during their time at Hazelcliffe Manor? What should they have done differently?

2) While Miss Lockwood may be trying to encourage her students, her advice to "snap out it" is not particularly helpful when the students are experiencing turmoil. Does she redeem herself later, showing them how to share their burdens and rely on each other? What do you wish the adults in your life would tell you when it feels like everything is chaos?

3) Sarah and her friends try and fail, then try and fail again, to bring back the Mother Book. Was this a good use of their time? What do you do when faced with a goal that seems impossible?

4) One of the themes of the series has been knowing when to trust and confide in adults. Was Sarah too wary of Miss Wrathburn when she arrived? Should Sarah have trusted Miss Wrathburn more easily?

5) Was Sarah wrong to be temporarily upset with Alicia and Ivy for hiding their (extremely helpful and effective) plans from her?

6) Did Sarah do the right thing, offering Mary partial forgiveness "for now?"

7) Why do you think Sarah is more forgiving toward Jenny, in the end, than toward her own sister?

8) Was Sarah foolish to offer Miss Morton one last chance to change her course during the final confrontation?

9) Did Sarah, Alicia and Ivy make the right choice, joining Miss Wrathburn in her new venture? If you had the same opportunity in this new magical world, what would you want to do?

ALSO BY MOLLY HARPER

The Sorcery and Society Series

Changeling

Fledgling

Calling

ACKNOWLEDGMENTS

Thank you so much to the patient readers who waited while I wrote this last installment. Thank you to Paul Allen for his support and encouragement. Thank you as always to my agent, Natanya Wheeler, for her refusal to let me quit. My gratitude to Brenda Rosen, author of *The Mythical Creatures Bible,* and Emma Sancartier, author of *Monsters You Should Know*. You provided inspiration for some of this book's strange creatures. And for my daughter, you were right, as always. It's kind of annoying, but I love you anyway.

ABOUT THE AUTHOR

Molly Harper is the author of more than thirty paranormal contemporary romance, women's fiction, and young adult titles, including the Half-Moon Hollow series, the Southern Eclectic series, the Sorcery and Society series, and the Audible Original Mystic Bayou series. Molly lives in Michigan with her family.

Be sure to check out https://www.misscastwells.com/ for more information on the Houses and fun fan goodies.

Where to find Molly
Website: https://www.mollyharper.com/
Twitter: @mollyharperauth

www.ingramcontent.com/pod-product-compliance
Lightning Source LLC
Chambersburg PA
CBHW071526120726
47907CB00013B/1082

9781641971942